Advance Praise for Seven Locks

"A tale both sensitive and clever . . . a remarkably persuasive story that gains power with each turned page. A poignant blend of the magical, mystical, and factual."
—Myra B. Young Armstead, author of *Freedom's Gardener*

"Vividly recreates life on a Hudson Valley farm in the years before the American Revolution . . . fascinating."
—Elizabeth Nunez, author of *Prospero's Daughter*

"A haunting depiction of physical and emotional survival, where truth is recognized too late."
—Charlotte Rogan, author of *The Lifeboat*

"Lives somewhere between landscape and memory, where regret becomes a prison, and a story told often enough becomes truth."
—Brunonia Barry, author of *The Lace Reader* and *The Map of True Places*

"The author gives spirited voices to the voiceless from the years just before the American Revolution."
—Regina O'Melveny, author of *The Book of Madness and Cures*

SEVEN LOCKS

SEVEN LOCKS

→ *A Novel* ←

CHRISTINE WADE

ATRIA PAPERBACK

New York   London   Toronto   Sydney   New Delhi

ATRIA PAPERBACK

A Division of Simon & Schuster, Inc.
1230 Avenue of the Americas
New York, NY 10020

First Atria Paperback edition January 2013

ATRIA PAPERBACK and colophon are trademarks of Simon & Schuster, Inc.

For information about special discounts for bulk purchases, please contact Simon & Schuster Special Sales at 1-866-506-1949 or business@simonandschuster.com.

The Simon & Schuster Speakers Bureau can bring authors to your live event. For more information or to book an event, contact the Simon & Schuster Speakers Bureau at 1-866-248-3049 or visit our website at www.simonspeakers.com.

Designed by Kyoko Watanabe

Manufactured in the United States of America

10 9 8 7 6 5 4 3 2 1

Library of Congress Cataloging-in-Publication Data

Wade, Christine.
    Seven Locks : a novel / Christine Wade. — 1st Atria Books paperback ed.
        p. cm.
1. Families—Fiction. 2. Farm life—Fiction. 3. Hudson River Valley—Fiction. 4. History 18th century—Fiction. 5. Catskill Mountains Region—Fiction. I. Title.
    PS3623.A336 S48 2013
    813'.6—dc22
                                                                            2012034987

ISBN 978-1-4516-7470-5
ISBN 978-1-4516-2787-9 (ebook)

CONTENTS

Part I

Part II

CONTENTS

De toekomst is een boek met zeven sloten.

"The future is a book with seven locks."

—Dutch proverb

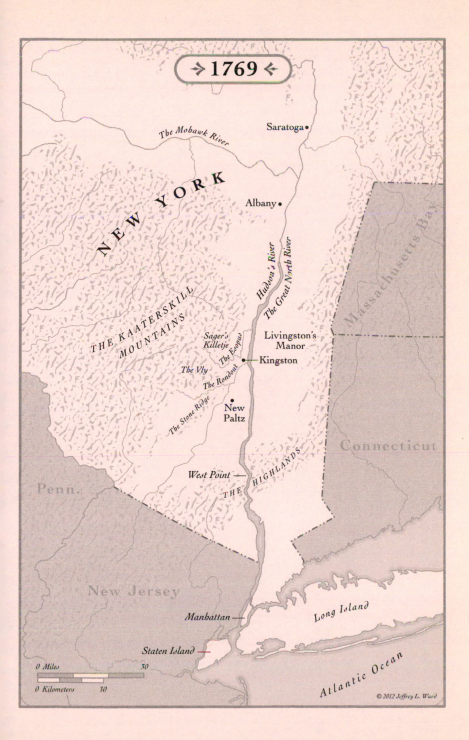

→ 1769 ←

The Mohawk River

Saratoga •

N E W   Y O R K

Albany •

Hudson's River

The Great North River

THE KAATERSKILL MOUNTAINS

Sager's Killetje

The Esopus

Livingston's Manor

The Vly

The Rondout

• Kingston

The Stone Ridge

New Paltz •

Massachusetts Bay

Connecticut

West Point —

THE HIGHLANDS

Penn.

New Jersey

Manhattan —

Long Island

Staten Island —

0 Miles   30

0 Kilometers   30

Atlantic Ocean

© 2012 Jeffrey L. Ward

PART I

✻

I know there are readers in the world, as well as many other good people in it, who are no readers at all,—who find themselves ill at ease, unless they are let into the whole secret from first to last, of everything which concerns you.

—LAURENCE STERNE,
Tristram Shandy, 1759

CHAPTER 1

Gone Missing

Hudson's River Valley,
Summer 1769

Als de maan vol is, schijnt zij overal.
"When the moon is full, it shines everywhere."

—**Dutch proverb**

THE LONGEST DAY of the year and a full moon. I read to the children for a long time. The boy's breathing quickly deepened, and his gaze subsided into the depth and darkness of his pupils, but the girl's eyes remained bright, and she continued to ask questions, not comprehending the story because of my own distraction. I could not answer her queries, as I was not listening to the words coming from my own mouth. My reading did not find the cadence in the tale, so absorbed was I within my internal heart. I had to backtrack in the text. Finally, I shut the book, kissed her again, snuffed the candle, and retreated from the bed, blowing her a kiss before I shut the door.

As I stepped toward my own enticing bed, the soles of my feet sucked up the coolness of the polished flooring, as if they were tasting something savory. The evening air too was honeyed, thick with summer. Lilies yawned around the house where I had planted bulbs in the autumn, and wafted their yellow dust, both spicy and sweet. My husband had scythed the grass in the yard of the house, which seemed a miracle in and of itself. The scent of maple pollen rode the wind toward the house from the woods, floating on the warm platform of the smell of the grass. Its golden dust settled on the sills of the windows.

I stood in the dark, drawing my breath up through the skin of my feet. Standing still with closed eyes, I could smell the salt of myself mingled with the odors of the night. I noticed the sensation of my ribs expanding and contracting, and I awakened to the rhythm of this. The breath rising and falling has its own sweetness if you attend to it. I pulled apart my thighs merely by shifting my stance, as the skin at their top was gently chafing. My breath ruffled the back of my throat.

Above the sound of my breathing in my ears, I could hear the high chirping of the tree frogs and the low burping of the bullfrogs, and knew exactly where he was. He lay on his back by the pond up the hill behind the house, watching the moon rise, swilling from a green glass bottle filled from a keg. The danger was that sleep would grab him and he would not awaken until the moon had crossed the sky, drawing the sun up in its wake. The back of his trousers and shirt would be soaked through by then. I inhaled deeply and, with my mind, called him to me. *Life*

*beckons you from your reverie. I am your wife. Rise up, Sir, and
come to me.*

I slid to the cupboard and removed my cap and then
my clothes. I took my brush and pulled it through my
hair. I smoothed my chapped hands with oil from a little
glass cruet. I drew the porcelain bowl from under the bed
and squatted. I patted myself dry. I donned my bed shift,
slipped between the cool linens, a wedding gift now stained
and worn but still quite a luxury. In the bed, I faced my
own peril. The work of this day released from my hands,
my neck, and my shoulders, but the work of the next day
was listed in my mind and wore me out. If I slept now, I
would be awakened by his snoring at dawn, and such a
sound would fill me to overflow with regret. Could I face
the particular dismay of yet another lonely night alongside
the labors of the day? Surely I could. I had long learned to
take refuge in discourse with my children, or even with
the cat or the farm animals. But the assault of a rising ire
could not be fended off in that moment when I first awoke
to the coarse and dry disappointment of the sound of his
rough breath rattling in the aftermath of too much juniper.
I willed myself to wait for the creak of the kitchen door
and the tread upon the step, no matter how long. I sat up
listening. Frogs, breath, tread.

When I got up, the cow was lowing. I went to milk. It was
late. The kitchen door, by far the portal most transgressed—
plumb from its lintel but worn at its saddle—stepped out

into a little fenced yard and flower garden. I grew the herbs there for season, for household, and for healing. Melissa, at the door for fragrance and good luck. Lavender, also for its sweet smell, easing of pain, and repelling of pests. Sage, to rub the skin of poultry and grouse. Dill, for pickling. Yarrow, to make an astringent for the skin. Cramp bark, for my monthlies. The wild rose bushes, for their sour hips. Marjoram, for sausages.

The house was in a clearing on a slope and encircled by sugar maples that had grown grand and stately since the pole saplings had been cut away. These were used to pen the pigs. The hardwoods beyond the maple sentinels were birch, sycamore, black cherry, sassafras, red oak, and hornbeam. The forest was not so thick with trees and vines that you could not find your way through it, but it was chock with stone as blue as water. The white foam of streams, which pushed the stones all together and then cut through or frothed over the boulders, always made it seem that the mountains were laughing at us. Ferns waved their verdance across the forest floor, and the sun spilt down through the canopy to touch the sway of their fronds.

The path through the garden led toward the fine Dutch beamed barn with its gambrel roof, wide planks, and wider doors. Its broad structure was built on the slope just below the house, and though as tall, we could look upon its fine roof from the upper windows.

The fence of the yard ended at the track, which was a sorry rutted thread that led to civilization. If we did not brave its puddles, we would see no one. The track led only one way: to us, so travelers did not pass by. My husband had picked the spot for its charm, seclusion, and its proximity to the mountain trails, and had discounted the prudence of living closer to our village. He was especially enamored of the knoll, as if it set us above our neighbors on the flatter plain below. The pond, surrounded by long-needled pine trees, gathered several streams together on the mossy rock shelf behind the house clearing. The water was clear and cold from the mountain runoff. Across from the track, we had a sheep pasture, bordered by stone farm walls wide enough to stop the sheep but not so very high. We grazed the cow in this meadow full of clover, butterweed, thistle, and vetch. Her milk was sweet enough.

One lone apple tree stood in our pasture like a beacon, silhouetted against the blue forests of the upslope at the edge of the fields. My husband and I had planted seven others in a circle we called our orchard on a rolling slope below the barn the first year we were here so that in spring the white blossoms would form a halo. One could feel blessed within such a circle. The deer would often come and help themselves to the low-hanging fruit of the laden branches. My husband would sometimes shoot a buck here for our stew pot, but, as often as not, let them eat, even as he complained when the cider barrels ran low.

Well into the morning, with the children fed a large breakfast and set to their tasks, I hear the footfall above the kitchen, and the pots hanging on the rafters gently sway. Then whistling, like a fife, that gladdens my heart. I had separated the coals on the hearth stone, for soon the day would be warm, but I now scraped them together and put up water in the heavy kettle. I have made flat cakes with

Indian meal on a pallet, and we still have maple syrup, March's harvest. I made a strong tea with the Dutch contraband (we did not drink English tea) in a pot, but when he came down, he went to the cider barrel and took a long draught. I could see I had mistaken the whistling for good humor. He was actually quite distracted and had a look on his face that let me know he would not speak to me. He did not touch or look at me either. Now what?

I asked him if he was well, which clearly annoyed him. He said he would go outside to smoke, which he did. And several hours later, after washing, grinding, chopping, boiling, frying, pouring, pressing, combing, sorting, folding, tending, singing, and answering questions, I called the children and him to dinner. He did not answer, so I went and looked to find him back against the hay, squinting at the sun, his hands clasped behind his head.

"Time for dinner, Sir." I turned my back to his face as haughtily as I could and flounced away as quickly as I had come.

I served soup first, made with early potatoes and all the new spring greens. Meat then, a spring lamb, devoured by all, grease dripping on cloth. I loved my table, a great slab of oak. The children's faces were alive above the dark wood of it, and their chatter spilled into the soup. He inquired of them and knew their world. I looked away from the food that stuck to his short, dark beard and dribbled on his shirt. He hunkered down at the table and over his pewter plate. I did not enjoy watching him eat the food I had prepared, with his elbows firmly planted on my table.

After cleaning up following the meal, I stalked out to

find him and asked him, "What do you plan for the rest of the day?" I could not subvert the insinuation of my question. "A hundred things need attending. Hundreds," I told him. A farm was like that. He thought for a moment before he replied with a curled lip, "As they always will."

"And what is your meaning, Husband? That you will leave them to me because there are too many tasks that require attention? If you do not stack wood, there will be a cold supper."

Not wishing to be beseeched by me, he fumbled to his pocket for the spall and tinder to light his pipe. Dutch men were always hiding in the crater of their pipes. "It is not so much that what you ask of me but that your tone implies that you are after me for more than stacking wood." His eyes were cast down to the bowl at the long end of the pipe handle, as he drew repeatedly, his suck on the tobacco a whisper between us. He glanced up but briefly before he turned away from me, as to remove the catch of the flame from any wind.

"Sir! Don't stride away! I have not done with our negotiation. What will you do today at the height of the summer? The blossoms and the berries, you hardly know to gather them. But where will sweetness come in winter? Surely you do not plan a forage in the glade from which you will return with nothing but the tale of your nap-cultivated dreams? What could that be worth? Our fields and livestock need cultivation, not your dreams!"

"You would be in my dreams if you would only enter them. Wife, I will do as I will, and your challenge is neither wanted nor womanly!"

"And how would I be a woman if I am but a drudge and you an idler?"

"Ah, you did not call me an idler last night. You cried out other noises, like an animal in the hay of her stall."

"That service does not put food on the table, you bed-presser! And you are not so skilled a pleasuremonger as you now claim."

I had insulted his manhood, and he now began to give me a mouthful of his own wind. "Termagent! Scold of a woman! Carp of a wife." I lashed back, and soon we were at familiar odds, our voices rising over the garden and venomous words spewing from our mouths.

"*Godverdomse Smeerlap!* Bastard, you! Illegitimate son of a snail!"

"And you, despot of a wife, you will not decide what work will be done and when."

I clenched my fists to my waist with my elbows behind me and inched my tormented face close to his. "Despot, am I?" I spat out. "If I shall not decide this, then who? A blunderheaded bedpresser? A wastrel?! He who gets up at noon and naps after dinner and nips through the night? *Ikke, ikke en de rest kan stikken.*" "Me, me, the rest can choke."

And then we follow each other around the yard, tensing out from our clothing and leaning into each other's faces, spittle on our lips and hatred in our speech. We circle, and cannot unlock. He calls me moronic, and I call him a cur, lower than the lowest pitiful, whimpering, wormy puppy. "*Hond!* Dog of a man! You cannot, will not, should not call me a scold for wanting the farmwork done and an orderly house! *Klootzakken!*"

His eyes widened at this, and his upper lip tremored with rage. He had not yet heard such vulgarity from me. I too was surprised that I could refer to a man's anatomy. Those round and tender parts, vulnerable at the base of the triumverate—the son and holy ghost beneath the ruling father. I enjoyed the shock on his face, for he seemed truly dumbfounded. This final word seemed to deflate him. I saw him now stubbornly turn away from me, and I knew what was next. Flight.

The long-legged and lanky dog, Wolf, never very far from my husband, had kept at the perimeter of the storm with his head down, his eyes wary, and his tail only wanting to wag as if it were he that was being scolded for digging in the garden or chewing a harness. The dog was like his master in so many ways—good-looking enough but giddy and vagrant. Now sensing that my husband might be making an excursion on which he surely would be invited, he made a wide berth around me in order to follow my husband into the barn. I swung my leg and kicked out toward him so that he broke into a trot, and the dust of my wrath swirled and glimmered in the sunlight before it settled again in the dirt.

My husband emerged silently from the cavern of the barn. I saw the old gun used for turkeys and doves at his side. His back was toward me, and he looked not in my direction—his jacket hiked at his waist and his shirt trailing beneath it, with the dog circling at his heels. The dog looked back with his yellow eyes only once, hesitating but for a moment. My husband tapped his thigh and the animal settled into a trot at his side. His breeches were torn and sagging over his flat quarters. He was a man of modest build—not tall, not stout—a pipe in his shirt pocket and the hat that shaded more than his eyes. I watched him walk away down the road, saying nothing to his children and nothing to me.

I did not want him to go, for I faced a long afternoon of lonely work. Lonely and wearisome. But neither could I call out to him, so thick was my dismay. I turned toward the demands of my labor and squeezed back the salt in the corners of my eyes so that I could see my many tasks more clearly. I never once thought back to the tenderness we had expressed in the night.

The shadows fell upon the day of my labor. I let the children catch fireflies that twinkled at the edge of the fields where the black trunks of the tall trees cast their darkness over the ferns. When the long light finally faded, and the softness of evening became the inevitable night, I sent the children to their slumber. When there was not another task or duty to perform and he still had not returned, I bolted the kitchen door from the inside. Let him sleep off his drunkenness in the barn, as he had dozens of times. I heated water that I had drawn and carried from the pond earlier and poured it into my widest and lowest barrel. I crumbled petals of wild roses and lavender stalks that I pulled down from the kitchen rafters. I stood naked in my kitchen with the smell of the herbs rising on the steam from the water and mixing with my own fishy smell. Then I washed it all away with ashes.

Judith Wakes in the Night

I wake in my bed, but I do not call for her. I can hear my brother breathing into his pillow. I go to the open window and look past the barn and garden where the moonlight falls into the sheep meadow. I fold my elbows on the sill. That is when I first hear it. Someone calling my name. *Choodhoo o hoo.* And then a hissing whisper. *I'm here,* I answer in my heart without speaking. I stand on my toes and turn my ear on the quiet, which is forever. *How do you know my name?* It comes again. *Choodhoo o hoo.* And then the hissing. It comes from below me. I think it might be my Papa at the kitchen door, coming in from his wanderings. Perhaps he will come now and tell me a story. Once more. *Choodhoo o hoo. Tsst. Tsst.* And then suddenly a flapping shape flies out from the walls of the house just below me, over the yard, and crosses the road of light that comes from the moon. It is not my Papa, but it knows my name.

Our farm was tucked up toward the mountains offset and above the river plain and a distance from the village. My husband liked to view the river from afar and often climbed the hillsides behind the farm to do so. He said there could be no finer landscape in all the Americas. And no wonder that our forefathers would have returned to such a spectacular territory, once it had been observed and reported. For were not the Dutch in their homeland limited to a flat, dreary landscape that disappeared at a distant horizon, with nothing of note between the good people and the vanishing point? Endless flattened fields laid out on a chess board—monotonous polders of colorless dirt stretching into ashen skies—and the sea held back only by stubbornness.

Our neighbor's pastures were spread like yellow butter amongst the slices and the rolls of the land of river silt below us. My husband said there was more blue stone than red earth in the foothills of these mountains, and that if we could eat rocks instead of potatoes, we would never be hungry. Yet the soil was rich enough, and our plantings thrived well enough. It was hard work. On that I would hand him no argument.

The kills run down the mountains through birch and hemlock, ash and maple. They stutter and roll, cutting through the rocky chasms and pressing boulders forward and away and finally flowing around them and falling off cliffs, in the white froth of brides' veils to reach the river plain. After the horse race of the scuttle and run down the rock faces, the kills widen and meander through our lush meadows and undulating pastures, and gather in our ponds. But these waters do not fool us that they will abide with us. No, they push on through the marshes and join the mighty ebb and flow of Hudson's River and leave us well behind on our well-watered farms.

I fetched the day's water. I had not found him in the barn when I went to milk. Another day elaborated itself with work, and by nightfall I was spent. As the dark of the evening descended at the end of the long day, my son called in the woods to the dog, but he did not come. My daughter would not go to the edge of the trees with her brother but stared anxiously after him, standing outside in her night-dress listening, a little waif in bare feet with the June glow bugs blinking about her. If the dog had come, I would have known, and so would they, that their father was nearby, perhaps lying on his back, elbows folded to cradle his head, and gazing at the summer moon. I called them inside and importuned them toward their beds. I insisted that the boy tell a story to his sister, for I was too tired to read one, but he did not wish to. "No story, then," I said. I coddled them not at all, for to do so would signal them that there was something amiss. I went to bed and slept soundly enough.

On the morning after the second night, fear welled in me, lodging in the lower belly and quelling any hunger I had for food. I kept extremely busy by making a large din-ner for the children with the new abundance of the gar-den food. I felt unsettled when I glanced at the woodpile. I expected him to walk in, and my resentments toward him were like a wall around my heart. He had ne'er been absent this long before. If he were to appear suddenly, I might be overcome by not only a vicious cant but also by an unbecoming—no, no, far beyond unbecoming—in fact, a dissolute violence. My eyes flickered to the road, the pasture gate. I checked the pond. But when he did not come, I began to doubt. Worse than fear, I began to feel the humiliation that all abandoned women feel. It was never only loss. The actual loss could be measured out in spoons: he would not replenish the woodpile, warm the bed, bring the game. I was uncertain, besides the wood and game, what his absence could mean. Would I miss him? I was fairly certain I could manage with my garden and my dairy. They were fruitful, and I produced enough for trade.

I was not afraid of hard work, or even loneliness, for surely I had been lonely enough, in spite of the occasional full-moon tryst in the marriage bed. Yet, while in the abundance of summer managing was not my worry, a seed of shame had sprouted in the earth of my feeling and was growing fast. It filled my throat and lingered just behind my eyes, where I knew it would be spotted if I managed to raise them to look into another's. I was short with the children and worked them hard. When I had enjoined them enough, I told them to leave me alone and sent them away to amuse themselves.

I must use the axe, as much as I hated to. Why must I? Because the time had come. I needed wood and would as soon sink its blade into my husband, were he to walk heedlessly into the yard. He would have forgotten the bile between us, and would hail me and ask cheerfully for supper. Such forgetfulness is a privilege, as are his midday dreams and jenever-soaked stories. So entitled is he in these boons that he wears them like his hat on his head. At the same time, he can hardly admit them for what they are—an escape from our world. An escape from me.

I could wait no longer. I was forsaken and ashamed, and I could no longer bear it. A black cloud had filled my brain. I knew that using a dull axe blade is dangerous, and the axe that was wedged in the splitting stump was certainly dull. The felling axe is a large tool for the cutting of upright and living trees. Its thin blade and long handle make it ideal for striking power. In order to perform its best, an axe needs to be properly cared for and sharpened, and its proportions must match the man. My shorter, lighter tool had been misplaced. I had looked but could find it nowhere. Now I must care for a tool that I could barely lift. And wield it with precision. Would the challenge to my spirit never end? Would ease ever, ever come?

I fetched a whetstone, water, and oil. There is no one way to sharpen a mistreated instrument, and all can be done in a short amount of time. I inspected the axe blade carefully and noticed it was badly chipped. Sharpening a dirty blade could cause an even greater damage, so I cleaned it completely, removing an oily grit. I then supported it on a block atop my oak table. I poured water over the whetstone and started with the medium-grain side against the blade, using long, smooth strokes at an angle and away from my body. I ran my finger along the edge and checked the grade, adjusting the stone accordingly. For every ten strokes away from the body, I stroked once to the other side.

It had not taken long. But it should not be me who sharpened the blade and pondered the dark days ahead. If I were to wait until my husband returned home, the kingdom would have already come. And because of this, we would all be angels in the firmament, and we would hover above him while he cowered below, unaware that the cloud that blocked his sun was the wings of his unprotected wife and children. Lost to him. His absence was senseless and wicked. And if he walked through the door at this moment, I would take the axe, dull or sharp, to the wood of his pate.

As this sinister thought bubbled in my addled mind, which had not sharpened regardless of my performance at my task, a shadow crossed my worktable, and I started. Looking up, I saw my son gazing at me with an expression of penetrating curiosity. "What, boy? What?" But if he had a question, he did not put it forth.

"Come, you will have to learn this now. And in your father's absence, I will have to teach you. Listen to me, your mother, that which you should learn from your father." He was reluctant, wary of my mood, which, while usually generous to him, had been foul. He tried to get away, but I ordered him remain with such a severity it made him pause.

Now that the blade was true, I moved to a smoother-grained whetting stone to encourage a very fine edge. I then showed the boy how to wipe the delicious extremity cautiously with an oiled rag. Suddenly I could see that my industry had caught his interest. Never mind that the axe was rather too heavy for either of us to lift, and that soon we would be needing wood, which would require an endless labor, more than either of us would ever want to perform. With a great effort, the boy raised the axe high over his head and landed the glinting blade in its stump. The handle had a perfect arc. He looked to me to see if I approved. And I suppose, in spite of everything, I did.

Our village, an hour's walk on a winding track, was not unlike any other along Hudson's River. The hamlet had come to be more than a hundred years ago as a settlement of trappers' huts amid the kills and falls that ran down from the mountains. Evidently a Dutchman, small in stature but large in reputation, and known only by the double diminutive of *klein sagertje,* or little sawyer, had once built a mill here, perhaps providing boards and beams to erect the grand estate houses across the river. So the place of our little bracket of a dozen houses was sometimes called the Sager's Killetje. Now, with its stone houses, it was steeped in its own traditions. We celebrated *Kerstydt, Nieuw Jaar, Paas*, and *Pinxter*. In the larger town of Kingston to the south lived carpenters, blacksmiths, masons, tailors, weavers, shoemakers, brick makers, sloep builders, sailmakers, and tanners. But in our little neck of the woods, almost all the families did a little of everything and took up what in the case of my husband is ironically called husbandry—that is, extracting from the land, and not without considerable effort, sustenance, and larder.

I did not wish to walk down to the village with my

shame-filled eyes. I forced myself, leaving the children alone at the farm. I decided to visit Nicholas Vedder purposefully and in the morning in order to avoid the tavern crowd, which gathered just prior to the afternoon meal. He was my choice over our parish dominie, who might serve me a sermon and, besides, who was here only on Sundays when his services were required—while a brewmaster did daily service in even a village as small as ours. I considered that the tavern keeper would have the ear of the men, while a churchman would have the ear of the women, and it was true that if you gained the women's sympathy, the men would follow. But I took my chances with the men because I thought the women's kindness might be out of reach. I did not want their pity, and I could not think how to approach them. I seemed to have had the double misfortune of not gaining the hearts and minds of other women, and the men had me pegged as the embodiment of all that they could suffer from their wives. By that I mean that the men could chastise me instead of the wife on whom they depended, and thereby a man could mark for her the boundary over which she must not cross.

Our village was one street with a dozen or more freestanding stone houses, lined up neat as a pin, and much alike in size and shape, with a stone church at one end and a crossroad, the King's Highway, at the other. Don't let the word *Highway* with the King's title before it fool you. The highway was a mud track much like the one that led to our farm, and not a penny of it was paid for by the King. The sloeps on the river, with their wide planks and high quarterdecks, were the most reliable means of transportation. The roads between towns were but rocky ditches, and cargoes were hardly ever transported along them. A well-made Dutch sloep had a high forward mast and lovely sheets, and could carry upward of a hundred tons upon her decks. And this is how our goods came to us—when the river wasn't iced over. In those winter months, we had no goods at all.

The tavern was at the turning from the village street north onto the highway. I kept my eyes low and hurried passed the houses. Much to my chagrin, Mr. Vedder was not yet up, and I found myself waiting on the bench beneath the grim portrait of George the Third. I had brought edging and worked my needle up close to my face so that while I nodded at any passersby, I quickly returned to my task, which kept them on the path of their morning's errands. Finally, when the sun was hot, I heard the tread on the stairs and the inn maid scurrying to bring the keeper his mead or cider, and his mild cough when she told him that I was waiting to speak to him. Still I waited, and when he finally emerged through the inn's door, he was tamping down his pipe. I was too tentative to express any annoyance by the wait, but he responded to the expected annoyance in me by being deliberately slow. After greeting me, he fumbled in his pocket for a flint to light it, as yet not ready to begin our conversation.

Eventually he asked about my family, and while I could not meet his eyes—for we were not exactly friends—I said outright that I had come to speak to him as to the whereabouts of my husband, which were unknown to me these past two days. Best to spill the flour on the table if one wants to bake a pie. He raised his eyebrows, gazing down his nose, drawing on the tobacco, and held the smoke in a bit. He was an ugly man with inflated pores in a sallow skin and patchy whiskers. But a man's appearance does not diminish his self-importance. If you asked me, he looked both brazen faced and sick.

Mr. Vedder had not seen my husband since the day before yesterday, when he indeed had stopped on the benches in the tavern yard. Drawing on his pipe, he reflected, "Yes, yesterday, come to think on it, his absence had been remarked. But this is not so unusual." The good Mr. Vedder ventured, seemingly without irony, that he had thought he might have spent the day working his farm. But I did not miss the tone of his speaking and what was not said.

Had my husband mentioned any pending journey? I asked the tavern keeper. I felt myself redden, as the question itself admitted the condition of my marriage. No, he had not.

I then told of how he had not returned to his bed two nights prior, after having set out in the afternoon through the woods alone with the dog. Mr. Vedder relit his pipe and then offered what little there was in assurance: "Your husband may have wandered too far in his search for game and, losing his way, ended in another village and stopped and visited awhile, and surely will arrive—footsore and primed with some new stories—sometime today. Water will come to the ditch."

I nodded at this point of view, giving the impression that I believed it and that I was consoled by him, even as the poverty of his assurance annoyed me. What kind of man could not find his way to his own farm? I knew not whether I was irked more by such a man or by Mr. Vedder, who spoke as if such occurrences were ordinary, thereby suggesting that my concerns were not. I asked if he would kindly notify the other villagers as they arrived to his benches about my situation, in case anyone might know of my husband's whereabouts. "If there were any news, would you kindly send someone out to my farm? Or tell my neighbors, who would surely come to me." Curtsying, I could not get away soon enough.

I walked quickly, with my head down. When I arrived home, I greeted my children, who had played in the glorious morning without an argument, I could tell, but began to test each other as soon as I arrived. I set them to separate labors and went into the cool darkness of my kitchen to make dinner. Faced to the hearth with my back to the doorway, I sensed a specter at the portal and turned suddenly, experiencing the peculiar admixture of relief and rage when I saw the dog saunter in and flop under the big oak table. I ran to the door and called, and then scuttled to the barn and looked everywhere with efficiency. In less than a minute, it became apparent by the cascade of fear and shame that quickly resettled in my throat that the dog had come alone.

Judith Learns a Song

I am nearly eight years old, and my father has gone into the forest. I cry at night because my mother cannot tell a story like my Papa, and my brother refuses to read to me. When I cannot have a story—an old story—I shake with my tears. The day after the evening when my father did not return to his bed, I make a house of mud and sticks with a little bed where he could sleep, and I put an acorn in it. I act out the stories of the forest critters over and over. At home in the forest, the chipmunks and squirrels always seem to find food and friends. Food and friends in the forest.

I live in a stone house. I have a rope bed. My mother feeds me dinner and makes me *pannekoeken* with jam. My brother teaches me this song when he finds me crying in the hen house.

> *Barney Bodkin broke his nose,*
> *Without feet we can't have toes;*
> *Crazy folks are always mad,*
> *Want of money makes us sad.*

It made me laugh.

My greatest and unspoken dread was to hear gossip that someone else was missing from our village. One of the young unmarried women, perhaps, or even a wife or, God forbid, a young mother. With most of my husband's afternoons and occasional evenings unaccounted for over the years, who knew with whom he had struck up, to meet in a stand of hemlocks, on a mossy knoll amongst the fiddleheads, near a cascade of rushing water that muffled the music of their singing, or even worse, their shared laughter. I knew he could be charming, and a picaresque world created with sweet talk and poetry was its own delicious contraband in a village where industry, modesty, moderation, and practicality were the agreed-upon currency. Philandering was not unheard of in our village but always seemed to happen elsewhere—in a French or German village, or among the British in the towns. And whether true or fantasy, such alliances flourished on the good wives' tongues. No word came of my husband, however, or, for that matter, that anyone else was missing.

On the morning after the third night of my husband's absence, I found myself preparing to return to the tavern, for I knew not where else to report. By this time, my children knew I was anxious and expressed their own worries with whiny behavior and disobedience. This vexed me terribly, and I was sharp with them. My son especially glared at me, and I could see his condemnation in a long, silent look. *You drove him.* He then wandered off, and the girl, sensing that she would be left alone by my departure, wailed and shrieked. When I still would not let her come with me, she struck me when I tried to comfort her, and I ended up turning my back to her as she threw herself upon the gate.

This time, when the innkeeper emerged from the door, I stood up quickly from the bench, catching the corner of the King's portrait, which swung from side to side. He kept his eyes on the motion of this rather than meeting the intention in my distraught gaze. "My husband has not returned and must be searched for. Can you gather the men with their dogs? My husband's dog has returned without him, and I have brought him with me. He should be set with the other dogs to find him." I had tied Wolf to the bench, and he looked up at the sound of his name, as his tail thumped elliptical loops in the dust.

I started to define the territory of the search, but Mr. Vedder must have found this an assault on his authority, as he promptly interrupted me. He who does not find himself important must not be doing a good job. Patronizingly, he consoled me. Yes, he would gather the men and boys and ask them to bring their dogs; yes, he knew the territory to be searched; yes, he would set the dog Wolf to tracking; yes, all would be done immediately, with concerted effort and community spirit. Farmers from the fields, craftsmen from their workshops! All would be interrupted, roused, organized, and charged to the task. He was feeling important now, a citizen. Teams would be hitched to ride out to the clove trails, setting searchers afar to comb the upper woods back and down toward the village. They would work a grid with their dogs as best they could. They would take lanterns to continue the search in the dark, which would come very late, as the solstice had just passed. Surely they would end up back at the tavern in throng, quenching their thirst with drafts of his ale.

As Mr. Vedder set to go about the town, I went to the most influential woman I could think of—the fat and imperious Dame Van der Bogart. We were such a small village that there was no Burgermeister, but a stout merchant with the grandest and widest stone house served as a village advisor and settled disputes, and I sought his even stouter wife. I walked with firm footsteps and Godspeed, lest I lose my courage, to a wide, two-chimneyed house just off the King's Highway. I approached the heavy oak door embedded with the ends of three green glass bottles like a ship's portholes to let light through the entryway. Mounting three broad stone steps, I reached above the glass to a comely brass door knocker in the shape of lion's head and, without hesitation, lifted the ring and rapped three brittle knocks.

The knocker sounded a sharp call that could not be mistaken in the quiet morning, and it soon became apparent that I had successfully summoned the mistress within by the sound of clogs on wide boards. The door swung, and the frame of it was completely filled by the girth of the great dame. Indeed, she was nearly as wide as she was tall, and I saw that I had interrupted her at baking. The hands she held high, framing her robust cheeks as red as apples, were pale with flour.

"Good day, Dame Van der Bogart. I am sorry to call you from your hearth, but Mr. Vedder suggested that I call upon you. I was hoping that you might—"

"Well, indeed you have. I have bread and pastries rising, and my oven is near primed to a perfect temper. Do you have *kaas*? Sausage? Pickles?" She peered eagerly toward the basket hooked to my arm and resting on my hip among the folds of my petticoat.

"Oh, but I come not to trade, Dame Van der Bogart. I—"

"Then why have you come?" She pulled her eyes from the basket and finally squinted directly into my face and paused. Since I was two heads taller than she, it was a long gaze across a considerable distance, and as the sun was behind me, and my face in shadow, I was not certain that she recognized me.

I retreated to the beginning and started round again. I could not falter now. "Dame Van der Bogart, not only do I regret that I have nothing to offer you in trade, I come to your door because I have experienced a recent misfortune. Or perhaps it is not I who have suffered a misfortune . . . and if God is willing, perhaps, if God is willing, misfortune has befallen no one. But three days since, my husband—"

"What, no cheese? Your cow is dry. I always trade for cheese. To cull curds and whey, I was not made for such a task. And my ovens are always too hot. I do not have the patience required. No, my talent is to sift, to combine, to mix up, to sweeten, to knead, and to watch dough rise to heaven. Master Van der Bogart gets me a barrel of sugar and the grains ground twice or even thrice at the mill—no expense is spared for good cake—and I make an art of it. My cakes are demanded at all of the weddings." She clapped her hands together, and flour billowed above her head, and between us, just before my face, in a cloud, and dusted through the sunshine that pierced the portal.

No longer modest in my approach, I plowed ahead, as if through wet snow. Somehow I had to wrest her attention from her appetite, from her hearth, and from the plans of her morning. "Dame Van der Bogart . . ." I lifted my voice a little, forcing it from my throat to will my woe forth. I cut through the snow and the thrice-milled flour and every other obstacle that one must cut through in order to be known by another, so that they will finally let go of clinging to their own immediate concerns.

"Dame Van der Bogart, I must tell you that my husband is missing. He has not come to home these three days. At sundown today, it will be four. He left with his gun and with his dog, and remains removed from our bower at the foot of the clove. His dog, ever by his side, returned without him. And now I am beseeching the help of my neighbors. Of you. Of you, the good Dame Van der Bogart, and of the generous Master Van der Bogart, for I am in need. Mr. Vedder is walking through the village to gather the craftsmen, and I thought, as you are so well respected, much more so than the innkeeper—so very well respected, especially amongst the good women—that I could bid you to engage them, so that they would allow their good husbands to come in from the fields and all their good endeavors to mount a search amongst the wood and waterfalls?

"For my lost husband," I added in case she did not remember where I had set out from. I was hoping she would not differentiate my husband and I from the goodness I had adorned on herself and all the citizens.

But could I be any more direct and abrupt?

I perceived her squint soften. Finally, she had placed me on my outlying farm and in partnership with my husband. Finally, she had awakened to my concern and called me by my name.

"Dame Van der Bogart," I implored, "please call upon your neighbors, arouse all the good village women . . . who are wives themselves and who could not do without their good husbands. Apologize for taking the men from their work, for I know that every day of summer is precious. Please beg their understanding, as I beg yours." I had seen how praise could be poured on the cogs of her wheels, and I continued to tip the jug. "You are well respected, you are a woman of stature, a woman of order, a woman of beneficence." Her eyes widened a bit, no longer pushed tight by her cheeks, as her face opened to my petition.

She was wiping her doughy hands on her apron now. She was turning this way and that, the breadth of her skirts whirling the flour that had powdered the floorboards.

"Of course. Of course. What could have happened?" She clucked. "Is it three days, you say?"

"Four, as of today, it is. And in three long nights, his shadow has not darkened our door."

"We shall find him, my child. Fear not. A man does not simply disappear, even in this wild land, and if ever he can be found, the good people of our stalwart settlement shall find him." And, as if I might not have heard: "The good people of our settlement will seek him, and he shall be found."

She puffed up and, unbelievably, grew rounder. I could

count on her awakening to her importance, as I had counted on Mr. Vedder awakening to his. I was not so naïve that I did not understand how a society worked. She swelled with the charge, if that were possible. When it dawned on her that she could take a role and enjoin the women of the village and tell them what ought to be done, what must be done, and when and how all would be done, she continued to enlarge. There would surely be gossip and, more importantly, good food.

As I backed away from her doorway, thanking her profusely, I heard her muttering that she would punch down her bread once more and cool her oven. The dough would rise again, to be baked later, and never mind the spent fuel.

As I turned again along the road, I asked myself why I experienced such distaste for her. Why did I feel a shame about what I had said and how I had said it? Why was I uncertain that her motivations were kind toward me? She had tsked, "You mustn't fret. He will be found." She was amicable enough and willing to set aside her baking. What exactly did I anticipate? And what was my desire? Am I as thankless and peevish a wife as my husband suspected? Or did I not feel that he, nor perhaps I, deserved attention and aid? My eyes fluttered with doubt as I contemplated my discomfort. What sort of woman am I? Or am I right to be wary of the professed sympathies of the good Dame Van der Bogart? Am I right in thinking that there are those who lick before they bite?

The early hours of the morning had turned to a heated midday. I did not yet know that the day would be a dreadful one that stretched into a long, dreadful night. My agitation faded behind my endeavors. I walked apace to my farm to fetch my children, and I could feel their relief in finally being included in what the village's call to action made clear as a flag run up a pole—and what they had known all along—that an event important and perhaps tragic had occurred at the center of their world. I packed as much bread and pickles, eggs, and my good cheese as I could carry, along with one of my husband's blouses, and then forced a march with them to the village. I went from house to house and knocked at every door and asked if someone could be spared to search. It was just the end of the dinner hour, and most were at table. I stood awkwardly, my children wide-eyed at my side. The villagers were not likely to refuse. And not one of them did.

Collection and readiness did not take long, as Mr. Vedder and Dame Van der Bogart had aroused some before me, and many were ambling to a gathering before the church. Mr. Vedder had long, belabored talks with several men about the best approach to cover the most territory. They drew maps in the dirt of the road with their boots and marked pathways and directions with sticks. Mr. Vedder then made a great show of setting Wolf to the task, asking for my husband's nightshirt, which he held to the dog's nose. I looked on impassively, with a good effort to hide my doubt and scorn. Wolf was indeed excited by the commotion and pranced about with the other dogs, but anyone could see what I knew for sure—that he was ill trained and hardly obedient. While he had a good nose and flushed game, he did so rather whimsically, just as his master had hunted.

Four brigades of four to six good men each—fathers, sons, and brothers—were organized for all the compass points. Dogs and a few farm horses. The women would pack food baskets and ride out in carts to meet the men and feed them as they returned. The search would intensify with both men and women in the late dusk at the circumference of the village. Teams set off—cogs in a wheel of order, where all knew their tasks, their capacities, and their duties. If there was a chink in such a circle, someone would step forth to fill it in.

The women continued their household tasks through the afternoon and evening, and had little to say to me. I ambled down one cow path or another with my children, passing the new site of the schoolhouse, which was being erected in honor of the recruitment of a new schoolmaster who would join the village in the fall. Although I had just only heard of such a plan, the structure was already framed and had a roof. The children called along the road and into the ravines for their father, but I could not muster a sound from my throat.

Hours later, when the day had faded, the baying of the dogs became audible as they charged down from the ridges and trails that had been climbed quietly in the afternoon sun. The women drove out the wagons that had been left hitched by the men in the yards. The waning moon was rising and cast long shadows through the hemlock and birch stands. The ferns were trampled underfoot, and if cover grew too thick, its tangle was entered and explored. And now the men came from the upper woods to the meadows in the flood plain, and dogs grew eager for home and moved the men faster over the fields, where they finally emerged on the road to drink the cider the women had brought and to eat bread and cheese.

Now the men fanned out again, and the women headed slowly back to the village on the roads, walking in front of the wagons and checking the ditches by lantern light. The women were fresh to the task, but the men were now squinting through the dusty sweat flowing over their brows, looking not so much for the man but trampling every glade to be able to say they had been thorough. The women hallooed out my husband's name as the men had over the mountain, and if some injury had befallen him that left him fettered and unable to move, he could have roused and found in himself to answer. But the sound of the voices calling again and again in the shadowed night echoed what I knew to be true—that I had called to him repeatedly but ever more feebly over the years from my own heart, with less and less a chance of an answer.

As the dawn came forth from the other side of the river, the men and women returned weary to their beds. Since our farm lay on the outskirts, I was dropped off at the gate, and after rousing the sleeping children from the bed of the wagon, we stumbled toward the house. When the village made communal effort, it was well used to success—many a sheep had been sheared and many a roof had been raised with an economy and efficiency expected by all. The women had few words for me then—little to say in the face of a practical failure. What could be done of this evening had been done, and it would take full sunlight to interpret the events of the night and devise a new plan.

Judith Wishes

The dogs come fast and barking in a pack through the pitch. I am frightened. With all their noise and froth, still they do not find my Papa. And nor do I. I call so loudly for him through the black trees, until my throat aches with the calling, but still he does not come. Where could he be? I weep then for my Papa. Who would tell me a story tonight? My brother sees my tears and puts his arm across my shoulder. If I call for my Papa just one more time, I am sure he will come, but I am so very, very tired. My brother helps me climb up to the wagon bed, and one of the good wives wraps me in a sleeping quilt. I lay back and look up into the many stars, and ask one—not the very first one, but all of them; every one of them—for the wish that my Papa would come home again.

I awake in my own bed, with the bright sun in shapes on the floor across the room. I listen for a snore, but the house is silent. I put my feet to the floor and run into the other room, and part the curtains of the box bed to see my Papa sleeping, but there lay my mother alone, and she does not open her eyes. Perhaps wishes come true only for patient girls who pay attention to the wink of the very first star when it is just born into the night sky, and not for greedy girls like me, who wait until the sky is filled with thousands and then wish on every one.

What were his possible fates? He could have drowned in Hudson's River, that great river of tides swinging from shore to shore, with its wide eddies and meanders carving through these hills, that was called after that British hero of Holland who had first anchored in these coves and brought the Dutch merchants to trade for beaver fur. Hudson's River was known by the Dutch as the North River, and that is what we called it to this day. For who would want to name such a grand waterway after a Brit who sold himself to a Dutch company? Probably for cheap, knowing the Dutch. Or because he had failed his own king? And who never did find China and who ended up set adrift in a shallop, among the icebergs, to perish by his very own crew.

I had never known my husband to walk east toward the water. However, how could I know what such a man would do? He could have suddenly had the mind to climb aboard a sloep and sail up or down river. Who knows? More likely that he had headed west toward the mountains, where he had often roamed. He liked a view of the river from above, on the overhangs to the wide alluvial plain. There is nothing like this Kaaterskill landscape, he would tell me with the astonishment of those who had lived on Holland's flats (although he never had), as square angled and dull as the eye could see. The rolling hills below and the blue forests above of stone and balsam that climbed toward the peaks were a spectacular sight. It was not only the land but also the way the light danced and tumbled between the river and the mountains.

Perhaps he had climbed a bit that day, lingered awhile in the glades, and then attempted to climb above them, finally standing upon a cliff above a dewy cascade. Then again, he could have lost himself among the maidenhairs and creepers and be living with wild people in the wild lands in a tight little clove between two mountains, where the water spills like laughter over the rocks and the mosses weep tears so that you don't have to.

My eyes were dry, but worry was not an unfamiliar smudge upon my brow; I had felt its blemish almost every day since my children had been born. Now it lurked there constantly and began to shape my body. Yet I had not given over to the idea that some harm had befallen him, and still clung to the notion that he had abandoned me for something as trivial as a game of wager and a draught of mead. Yes, it was possible that he could have fallen from a cliff or into the Vly. He could have been mauled by a bear. He could have shot himself while cleaning his musket. He could have been struck by men of the tribes. Drowned? Captured? Ill? Wounded? Lost? It's the devil that invents these questions, and no angel comes to answer them. I still find myself as much annoyed as saddened by whatever might have befallen him.

Sadness, however, filled me when I contemplated the faces of my children. The boy was silent; the girl, disconsolate. I set them to separate tasks to keep them from bickering. The boy would not tolerate my instruction. He thrust his tools at the dirt at the slightest vexation and stormed away. His sister watched him and cried out to him to return. Once she started weeping, she could not stop and beat her fists against her sides. I held her to me, but she found no comfort, and her brother would not be called back but lingered beyond the borders of the yard, sulking.

"Where is Papa?" she wailed, and her sobs pulled at me. My apron became damp with her tears, as she locked my legs with her arms and threw her hot body against me. When you are the mother of such a sweet child, you gather yourself. So I rallied my voice of assurance, "Ah, *meidje*, weep not. We can never know the future. Our life is like a book, a book that is locked. We have to find the key, or we cannot know what is on the next page. And we don't know the end of the story until each page has been turned and the story has ended. But we can tell ourselves our hope and hope that it is true—that your father is safe and longing to make his way back to us. Your father may be lost, but he will return to you, one way or another." It was the best I could do.

Now it became clear by their increasing distress that the children would bear the brunt of the loss—and, in their innocence, no possible responsibility. I was enraged in their defense. And I could not be so certain that I would be free of an accounting, which added to my shame. This simmering ire protected me from any concern for him. Deep inside me, I knew, was a kernel of love for him that was etched over and smoothed again, like a stone in a river, by the failure of our partnering. I was not used to disclosing such a sentiment, even to myself.

How was I to fondly remember the man who commonly, when he took the last log from the kitchen wood crib to add to the fire to warm his feet of an evening, would not think to fill it? So when I awoke to make the morning meal, first I must clean his cup, then remove his stockings from the floor before the hearth, then start the fire fresh because the coals had not been preserved, fill the wood crib myself, and then turn to my own work.

My son would often bring our farm tools from the distant field or yard or animal pen mud encrusted, rusted. Then someone must use cooking fat to clean them and scrape them down. I would set my children to this, for I needed those tools as tasks demanded, and a day could be wasted in the hunt for them or in their cleaning. Sometimes when I planned a task, I would hide the tools required, so I could find them again. When I thought to do this, I became aware of how rarely my husband actually asked for them.

And speaking of rusty tools, after my son was born, my husband did not want me in bed so very often. (The midwife said that women more commonly had another complaint.) Always he chose sleep, or warned of waking the baby, or came to bed quite drunk, or complained of how I spoke to him, or what I asked of him, or of what I did not speak. He was tired. He needed rest.

It was not that he never did what was asked. It's that asking became a habit of mine that he despised. Once ired, he shut himself off, behind a bolted door, or hid himself by some other means, or stormed off to smoke. After years, I discerned a pattern: I saw he provoked me so he could be alone. I would hear the door clatter, his boots on the step, and then watch him from the kitchen window walk to the pond, bottle and pipe in hand.

Judith Churns Butter

Mother says Papa has gone to the woods and cannot yet come back to us. And we are not to think about the future but to tell our own true story. The future is a book we have not yet read. Once we find the key, we can turn the pages. And it will be soon enough. We can end the story as we like, and I will end it with my Papa returned. And then *he* will tell *me* a story at bedtime.

If it says bad things in the book, I will throw away the key and never read it again. I do not want to churn this butter. *Dun wanna.* My arms ache, and my brother doesn't have to have a turn. He is bigger than me and should do it himself.

I am trying to remember a song that Mother taught me, but I can't find the tune or the words, and she says she doesn't remember which one I mean. The cat jumps upon the urn. I am stroking her, my face close to hers, when Mother comes to the back door and scolds me. "But Mama, my arms are tired, so, so tired, I can no longer lift them." She calls my brother, who runs in, and she sets him to it. He makes a face at me, and perhaps I will pay later. But for now, I pause at the door and flounce both my hair and skirts back. "Come," she says. I skip ahead to the garden gate. "Weed with me." When I sit down in the plant rows, the words and tune come to me, and I am so happy I sing aloud.

In a green, green, green, green, turnip, turnip land
There were two little hares, sitting very smart.

And the one was blowing his flute, flute, flute,
And the other one was drumming.

Then came along a hunter, hunter man,
And he has shot the first one.
And the other, who I'm thinking of,
The other one died of sorrow.

For the next few days, the men still gathered in the afternoons and elaborated additional excursions. An afternoon was spent by the most diligent along the firm ground surrounding the clogged marshes east of the village toward the river. Another group walked the river's banks to the south on late afternoons and early evenings. And yet another headed north. Of those they encountered, they asked. No lone man fitting my husband's description had been noticed anywhere. Some stayed on to fish and brought back fine breakfast fare and extra for salting but saw no bloated body floating pale in the coves and inlets, nor washed up on the pebbled beaches. Gradually routines in the village returned to as they were. No one came to my farm to announce an end to such endeavors, and I simply stopped inquiring. No need to embarrass anyone. They had given what they could and failed.

And amongst the good people . . . who knew if my husband were even missed? Did anyone notice his absence? Mr. Vedder perhaps lacked one steady patron of stout and jenever, but surely any newcomer or a farmer's son come of age could take my husband's place on the tavern's benches. My husband had been liked well enough by the men in the village. They were called to task often enough by their own wives to sympathize with him without too much scrutiny. Clear lines had always been drawn, and everyone knew that women's expectations of an ordered world were beyond how men's hands could shape it.

They had already stopped calling on him to raise buildings, for he was too often not to be found, and the trouble of finding him was hardly offset by the roughness of the masonry and carpentry he contributed. I can't say that he could count these men as friends, exactly. The men were defined by their work, and my husband's ideas about work were distinctive and peculiar. The common notion that work was a way to identify yourself, to get closer to God, or to come together with your neighbor (or, for God's sake, with your wife) was beyond him.

Nor did he find work a channel to organize the chaos of the mind's fire and the heart's water. He would spend the better part of each morning organizing his mind's fire and his heart's water by lying in the sun, and if a chore or economy called to him, he would weigh each piece of work by its advantages and efforts with great elaboration before he determined to set to the task. The gains were made to seem of little consequence, even of no use, and the efforts were made to seem enormous and overbearing—so much so that a man's body would be worn through by them. Not only that, it was perceived that there would be more work to be done at the conclusion of each and any task. Work well done would but lead to more work, until the end of a man's life came upon him, abruptly, before he could take stock.

There is some truth in his view. Even I could see it. A man's labors must be balanced by life's pleasures and the world's beauty.

In a week or so, women sent their husbands or sons with cuts of venison, or a rabbit, or a grouse, for the women were nothing if not dutiful. And a good roast was said to cure all ills. I dreaded these deliveries and often hid silently in the cottage rather than receive them in hand. Truth be told, I had more game during the aftermath of my husband's strange evanescence than when he was bringing it to table. I observed with diligence who brought what and made sure to write a note of thanks to the woman behind the delivery. I often slid the note under the kitchen door or onto a window sill on a Sunday, when I knew the entire family would be at church, even as I regretted the expense of paper and ink.

Several weeks went by, and these offerings faded, as communal attention moved on to a stillborn baby, or a man's hand slammed by his own pickaxe as he broke stone in his fields, or a barn burned by a lantern carelessly spilled. The shift in heed I considered a blessing.

I could not avoid all village banter, for certain. Commerce was necessary for survival. I had to market my cheeses, eggs, sausages, and wool. The market is where rumors unfolded and stories with underpinnings were told and retold. Women came together, as women do, to braid their tales. And these braided tales formed ropes for hauling secrets out of wells, for tethering all that is valuable to home. And, of course, for hanging.

When I approached such gatherings, I came upon abrupt silences followed sometimes by cold formalities.

No matter. I came to ply my wares and exact my business. I readily turned back toward the Blauwberg. With my back to them and my footsteps on the road, I could hear their mirth but not make out their words, as the sounds of their commonweal wafted after me. What was so amusing about a bad marriage? Why did a scold engender scorn and comedy, and a lazy man tolerance and pity? Choosing a husband is often the only decision a woman can make to affect her fortune, and certainly the one with the most consequence. Perhaps they had chosen better than I—or were more skilled in enticing a husband to their biddings without injuring his pride.

At least no word came from the other villages that any young women were missing. Or no word that anyone dared say to me. In every encounter with my neighbors, however, no matter how ordinary and pleasant, I saw in their eyes a judgment: *You drove him . . . You drove him.* And in mine, I took that they saw my shame: *He's left me, he's left me.* And in all those summer days, he did not reappear.

Nothing rose in my mind or was occasioned by others to contradict my thinking, and I had very little to say to anyone. The children played, the livestock and garden thrived with my care. I swept the boards of my kitchen floor with vigor. At night, when the children were put to bed and I was too exhausted to perform any task, I would be drawn to his flask of jenever as he had been every evening, and the hot fire of the white liquor and the bittersweet of juniper would raise a heated but pleasant flush upon my breast, throat, and cheeks. I could hear his voice then, even as his face had become a shadow: "Drink without sorrow, your head won't hurt 'til the morrow." It was not too many evenings before I had emptied his stores and licked the last oily drops from my fingers.

My father's grandfather Friso Dinkelager had served Peter Stuyvesant in the Dutch colony of New Amsterdam as a ledger keeper and accountant, and then when the governor fell, moved to Staten Island to finish out his days. When the Dutch turned over their colony to the British, life had gone on much as before. Landowners kept their land, and worship of any Christian sect was not suppressed. Indeed, conditions of tolerance surpassed what existed in England. And ordinary citizens could arrive from the Old World as humble carpenters and become owners of massive tracts of land and influential men in the new colonial government, even as they retained their Dutch names and customs. Settling the colonies had, however, proved too daunting for many, and many had sailed back to their homelands. Now that the government was decidedly English, fewer and fewer Dutch came. The villages were insular. Our domain was fortunate, however, in that it did not suffer from Indian attacks the way the Dutch farmers did farther north and west, on the Mohawk River.

My grandfather, being the youngest of his brothers and sisters, had been adventurous enough to travel up the North River to New Paltz. And then west to the Stone Ridge, where he built four houses in the Dutch style in a village that was, in those days, Dutch in every respect. It was a little too far west for the times, but, without trouble from Indians, nothing much happened there at all. My grandfather died when my father was young, and he, by working ceaselessly, managed to build an import and export firm using the old family's business connections, which supported him and his mother quite well. From his uncle he inherited a shipyard in the Highlands where sloeps were manufactured in the Dutch style with long tillers of local hardwoods. And it was there that he had boats skillfully made with false bottoms and high decks, so that he could smuggle goods and avoid paying taxes to a British king.

My father imported everything from cloth, to tea, to beer and brandy. He was known for an assortment of tiles. He was the sole local supplier of cast-iron triveted ovens with well-fitting lids with a coal lip, for which the Dutch were famous, and that came in several sizes. They baked more evenly and lighter than any known method, without coating the loaves or cakes with coals and ash. They were much in demand and sold short. My father shrewdly held some back, watching the prices rise, knowing that every household must have one or three. And indeed, there were traders that bought them by the dozen, though they were not easy to transport because of their bulk and weight.

My father did not marry young, and when he was older could not find himself a young wife. Although he had money, young women were scarce, and certainly few were inclined to live in a tiny, unprotected village. Through his shipping connections, he asked that a wife be sent to him from Amsterdam, and so she was, but she died on the hazardous voyage across the sea. As it was, there was a woman of a good age aboard the same ship who was asked to bring him the news, as she was on her way to her sisters in Wiltwyck. And so he found my mother, Margriet, a Dutch widow almost his age. She proved fertile, though, and immediately I came to be. I think my brother was unexpected eight years hence, and from the moment he was born generally favored over his sister.

My mother viewed the Netherlands and its capital as a civilization, hardly comparable to this village on the fringes of a wilderness. She went on often and at great length about her wish to return to Amsterdam, her wish to die there. It was clear she did not consider these shores her home. Her sisters had abruptly returned not long after she arrived, forsaking her now that she was bound to a New World husband. My mother did not complain with my father present. However, what with the Stone Ridge being quite far off the river where most business occurred, he was hardly ever so. She had plenty of opportunity to complain to me, and I became the audience for her discontent. Although she did not want of goods, she often despaired of the quality found here and spoke much of the limited choices available. My father never seemed able to get her the right thing, and the food at our dinner table was flavored with disappointment.

Through her peevish musings, I learned of a wider world; an entire continent of flourishing societies beyond our ken. I begged her to tell me of Old World cities and their riches. Life in the Netherlands when she grew up there had been pleasant enough. Dutch ships had encircled the world in the previous hundred years and had traded for fine goods and novelties on every continent.

She described the tall, fine houses with crowstepped gables and common walls built around the canal ring in the great city, not just for rich merchants but for any common citizen. Amsterdam was the prosperous center of European banking and the heart of the world's diamond trade, thanks to its tolerance of Jews, who flocked there and brought their gems with them in velvet purses. The city had grown rich on its commerce and the interest on loans to the rulers of Britain and France for the finance of their wars. The abundance of its great economy had benefited the many who built canal house after canal house with gabled façades, elegant stairways, imposing parlors, and long corridors lined with tapestries and paintings. Such houses were often five stories high, and the views from their upper floor windows were a marvel across the vast and carefully planned city intersected by the glimmer of waterways shining like the chains of a metallurgist—elegantly forged to lace neck after neck of beautiful women.

My mother would stand a tinderbox on end and my father's snuff box next to it on the table, and surround it with her garnet necklace to show me the design of a great city encircled by the grand canals. She called it a *bootjesketting*—a chain of little boats—and while I saw the deep-wine-colored gems of the necklace representing the dark green waters of the canals, I knew that she had conjured the sparkle of her former life as a young beauty and that she was lost within it. The dullness of our pastimes and the roughness of this colonial town could not compare.

I knew my mother found herself at loose ends, especially after her sisters were no longer in the next town to augment her society. I had no inkling about what had drawn her over the oceans—for she hardly seemed an adventurer. Her compunctions seemed to mount over the years into a cold resignation. And the chill of them spilled into her relations with me, as it was not clear at all that her many threats to return to Europe included plans to take me with her. She seemed to think she had alighted temporarily and could sail off as if in a dream—that we belonged here with our feet in the sod of the New World, but she did not.

A child accepts what she is born to, and only when it is too late for her own good does she speculate and understand how the decisions of her parents' lives were made. I was not an overly curious child, was given what I was given, knew what I knew, accepted what she told me. I did not ponder until much later that she had somehow fallen in her former life probably because of her first husband's death. He had not left her secure. And not being well connected to his or her own family, she found herself adrift. A woman without a husband or a father is a woman at risk, even in Holland, where wives and daughters could inherit and own property. It was then that she had booked passage and come to the New World, probably because her life had fallen down around her, and there was no reward to widowhood. I was most likely the product of a pragmatic Dutch forbearance rather than a fortuitous passion born on the winds of adventure. My parents' marriage was opaque to me, and I thought not too much about it. I only knew that I wished for something different and was sure, as every young dreamer always is, that I would have it.

Today I absolutely resolve to have a better attitude, to be a better mother to my children, to do my duty as God would want. I cannot spend the whole day in a bitter cloud. I must enjoy my work and find a cause for thanks in each hour of the day.

In all the farms I had come to know, the husband and wife must have a partnership, or all was lost. My husband said that a marriage was not shared work but something else. Certainly confidence and intimacy do not—indeed, cannot—exist apart from duty and consequence, I countered. He lectured me in lofty terms, with a harsh voice that seemed not his, saying that he valued another view of partnership and that I must barter with him to have my way. And what a bargain! We could not come to terms. He would mutter, "O cursed marriage! That we can call these delicate creatures ours and not their appetites." But who was delicate? Me? So often accused of indelicacy, if convenient? Was he not delicate, he who was so wounded by the questions I put to him? "Will you mow?" "Where is the wood that assures our warmth?" "Can you mend my barrel?" And to what did he refer in my appetites? Did he know the hunger of my soul? And the food that could satisfy it? I think he did not know all that he claimed, and his rough excitement indicated fear and not certainty.

I cannot, especially now, be captive to the times when

anger would sit on my chest like a boar rooting in the dirt of my heart. I remember how I would not necessarily know the beast was there, but then it would charge out from underneath my collar, and I would experience a blackening of the mind that could be expelled only by a torrent through my mouth. I detested him then. Waves of rage would well up, and I would go and find him to discharge all my bitter words. He did not seem to want success for our farm. He treated his dog better than me. He spoke to Wolf with kinder words and more consistently. He gave him morsels from the plate. But sometimes cant did not suffice, and I found my rage move from my mouth to my fingers, which I would point close to his nose. Eventually my fingers would curl into a fist, and I would pound upon his chest.

He would shove me hard away from him and disappear. More and more he made it clear that he wished to be left alone, unapproached and unaddressed. And that was the single message of all his actions. I would search him out, for his silence was a violence too. And we would go at it. The children heard the bile between us, and the great shame of destroying their innocence enveloped my heart.

No sooner had I had an outburst than he would pick up his gun, whistle for the dog, search one of his hiding places for the jenever, and be off. Without a word. If I ran after him—my heart pounding in my chest, my bonnet fallen back, and my hair in my face, voice raised—through the gate, he would shake his fist at me, and the dog would cower. He would return who knows when. Undoubtedly at night and surreptitiously, perhaps sleeping in the barn under the horse blanket or even on the kitchen table, which was long enough to lay out flat. If the latter, I would bang the milk pail with a purpose in the morning, the spite ringing out and signaling the cow to begin lowing. When I reentered from the barn with the milk sloshing in the pail, he would have crawled up to my bed of linens, which were steaming with my body's warmth, generated alone all through the night. I resented his advantage. He stole the profit of my body—my boots and bonnet, so to speak—wherever he could. I would carry on banging pots and shouting loudly and cheerfully to the children, fooling no one.

What is the use of such remembrances? My days cannot be shrouded in them. And as for him? Perhaps a certain man feels shame in being beckoned and called by a woman. Perhaps it is put forth by certain men as a man's shame. But it is not practical and need not be so. *Nou breekt mijn klomp.* "That breaks my shoe," as well as my heart.

CHAPTER 2

A Path Well Known

Autumn 1769

Heb je geen paard, gebruik dan een ezel.
"If you don't have a horse, use a donkey."

—Dutch proverb

WHILE STRUGGLING TO accept that my husband would not return and trying to invent what I could possibly tell my children, I noted that not only my husband had gone missing. When the summer moons rose over the river and shed their thick moon dust on the fertile fields of my farm, I had bled but a spot at midsummer, and in August not at all. I thought it was the hard work of harvest. By now I could feel the heaviness and weight in my womb and knew that any day soon I would bleed out in a cascade like the Kaaterskill Falls. But then I did not.

Before I had time to digest the shame of his absence—to fully comprehend my predicament—and write a letter to my family in the Stone Ridge, a missive came to me. *Spreek van de duivel en je trapt hem op zijn start.* "Speak of the devil, and you'll trip on his tail." We were still harvesting, and my son had gone to town to sell eggs and butter, sausage, and an excess of early squash and some beets. He handed it to me in the kitchen, and the children stood at attention, as letters were not common in this household. I shooed them out of the kitchen, but they hung close by. My daughter stopped to finger the Melissa that grew in abundance by the door, attending to it with great interest and crushing the leaves for the stimulating fragrance. I imagined that they thought it might be news of their father. I knew it was not. Portents of my husband would not come this way. But some news was contained in this letter, and it must be opened. I looked at the script and carefully broke the wax at the fold. "Dearest Sister . . . My deepest Regrets in inform-ing You . . ." I had never received a letter from my brother before, and, oddly, it was in English.

My father had dropped into his soup, and the servant who had left supper for him had found him there in the eve-ning when she came to turn down his sheets, slumped with pieces of carrot stuck to his nose, with his spoon on his knee breeches in a wet chair. My brother had been called from the port where he conducted the family business, and he wrote these details to me. Well, not the carrot and the wet breeches. I filled that in for myself, out of a picture in my own mind—knowing what was most likely to be in the soup and knowing full well the spigot in a man's breeches.

Dulled to the tragedy, I could not find the sense in it. My hand at my collar, I shook my head to awaken. The first thought that came to me was that at least I would not have to tell him about my own misfortune, although perhaps he had heard of it by now. Perhaps he heard of it and for this cause fell into his soup. No, this certainly could not be so. I am not the center of the world. I felt a certain relief from worry. In fact, a vast relief. However, this did not seem right. Yet it was difficult news. I knew not what to think. Now I am no longer a child. Only a mother of children and a wife, embittered and abandoned. And to be sure, no longer even a wife. Stranger still, the letter informed me the funeral had already been conducted, and I could visit my father's memorial stone in the yard of the Dutch church. Engraved upon it were the words

Here lies deposited the remains of

Cornelius Dinkelager

He was beloved by his acquaintances
for his many amiable virtues. He
is lamented by those who in him
have lost an example of meekness
and unaffected piety. The righteous
are taken from the evil to come.

"Meekness and unaffected piety"? Did I know this man? Who would have chosen such miserable words to be etched in stone and remembered by? My father, sadly, was not a man to envision joy in a world without him. I do not recall that he was particularly righteous, but perhaps he had a different idea of himself and an interior discourse that I knew nothing about. People do. I knew I had threads in my own mind that I would never reveal to anyone.

In any case, I feared my father's judgment, which seemed everlasting, a force enduring the course of a life and reaching northward to these mountains. He had not liked my husband, nor approved of his choice to move north, farther into the wilderness to the little rocky farm at the foot of the Blauwberg. He had objected to my husband's selling off some of the fine stuff of my dowry to build the farmhouse and buy animals. He had maintained a coldness that increased upon my mother's death. He had not once visited, although he had both boats and wagons at his disposal. His Dutch was so arcane that even I had trouble interpreting his two brief and formal letters, occasioned on the birth of each of my children. And now the chill between us would ne'er warm.

I had ventured to see him with the children when my mother was alive, making the long day's journey on the muddy roads by a coach whose fares we could ill afford. When she died, I had attended her funeral, of course, and then quickly returned for the spring lambing. At her burial, I stood in the March wind, wearing her own black gown pinned up to fit me, a stiff collar around my neck and a heavy bonnet on my head. I wore the clothes of a matron but felt like a child. My husband had refused to come and had used the lambing as his excuse. I stood alone, and my children cowered behind me. The dominie was from the big town, and I did not know him. Nor had he known my mother. He spoke in platitudes and without affect. My father frowned at the children and consorted only with his colleagues.

At the house, smoke and the smell of juniper filled the parlor. I had instructed the servants about the food, and they had completely ignored me. I had sat on an uncomfortable chair and made talk with my mother's one friend. Visitors came in and out the entire day, and I heard my father regretting the expense and instructing the cook to hold back the platters of food. I was overcome by slumber as much as sorrow and crawled after my children to bed as soon as the dark descended.

The following morning, my father had handed me her tea set and instructed the servants to pack it carefully. He told me to sort through her clothing and take what I wished to remake as my own. I asked for her brooch, but he told me it had been buried with her, along with her wedding ring, although I don't remember seeing it pinned to her gown. He gave me her Bible and mending kit, and a garnet necklace with matched earrings. All this was transacted after the funeral with the pragmatism of shop trading. I do not remember my brother, eight years my junior but by then a young man, being about. As brother and sister, we had found little to say to each other.

My father's business of carrying untaxed goods in sloops with false bottoms up the North River on the tides and winds had its advantage. He ordered a box of Dutch tea (which was illegal) and tulip bulbs packed in a crate for me, along with two very fine cast ovens and other useful kitchen items. He was more than generous. But I did not have the chance to repeat my thanks to him, and little did I know that we had conducted the last-ever transaction between parent and progeny. For when the wagon stopped to pick up our bounty and return us to the Blauwberg, my father could not be found, and we bid farewell to his clerk.

Sick as a dog, I retched beside the kitchen door. All dry heaves. My daughter raised a wary and curious eye from her play. She was decorating mud cakes with mint leaves, and I told her not to worry about a bellyache—that I was stricken because my father had died. I saw the shadow on her face as she speculated on the fate of her own father but knew not that I could have altered what I said to her, given that my father had died with certainty—and the truth about such things must be told.

I drew the *pannekoeken* from the pallet and chewed it slowly. I spread hers with butter and jam and observed with contentment as the dark berries stained her mouth, cheeks, nose tip, apron, and hands. I sent her to gather chamomile flowers. With what sweetness she handed me feverfew, folded with tenderness in her apron and delivered with sticky hands. I had not the heart to send her back for the other plant, although by now she should know to discern them. I chewed a leaf. I thanked her and wrapped my arms around her. *Mijn schat.* "My treasure."

She asked me what happened to people when they died. I explained that her grandfather was old and his heart had grown tired; that his body had been laid out in the church, put in a box, and buried in the churchyard with a stone next to his wife, her grandmother, whom she probably did not remember. To authenticate this, I said we could visit. She asked what happened in the box. And I told her we would all come to ashes and bone. Again I watched the shadows on her face as she conjured a box full of bones.

"Does his flesh fall off his bones? What happens to the blood? When I cut my flesh, there is blood. Will the blood dry up?"

She examined the skin of her palms. "Will his clothes still fit him?" She clasped her apron. "How does his spirit get out of the box and up to heaven? Heaven is so very far above us." Then growing ever more perplexed, she added: "Who will live in Grandfather's house now? Who will answer the door when someone rings the bell? Will Grandfather's house be full of bones?"

These questions I could not answer. The boy hung back, pretending not to listen. As I struggled to thread meanings together for my daughter in between waves of bending and retching, I realized without a doubt that I knew a certain thing in particular. I knew that my courage, if I had any, was called upon now. I knew that I had but little time. I can't say I knew the future of my family or my heart's happiness. But the future is a book with seven locks. Had I not said this before? In that very moment, when the truth of life's mystery was demanded of me by my daughter, clarity came forth from confusion, as a key turns in a lock. The breeze on my cheek as I wrapped my arms around my daughter, with my son standing just to the side, swept away the clouds behind my eyes, and I could see the articulated detail of the steep and unknown path I must find in my heart to take. I knew I had to put a sturdy plan in order and do so with the utmost expediency.

Judith Reads in English

Mama vomits in the morning. Not every morning. But I can hear her by the kitchen door below the window to my room. I think she is sick because my father has gone away. I do not know where he is or why he has gone, but it seems to have made her sick. She will not tell me and says only that she sometimes gets *malaise*, like me. That is a French word for bellyache. The cow gets it sometimes too. And then you can hear her lowing. This happens if you don't milk her on time.

Sometimes my mother hasn't done it by the time I get up, so she sends me out to the barn. I do not like to go in before the light of the morning. I am also afraid that cow will kick. Once I squeeze by her haunch, I sit on a milk stool with my back against the stall and my forehead pressed up underneath her ribs. But I am not such a strong milkmaid, and I have to pull hard. I don't think the cow likes me. She turns her head and rolls her eyes up. Mama says I should thank the cow after I milk her, and I do. I am grateful for the milk, as we don't have much meat. I spill some from the pail into the barn aisle because I am hurrying to get away from those sharp hooves. I tell my mother that was all the cow would give.

All in all, I am glad when the chores are done and it is time to go to school. My brother and I walk along the track an hour to the schoolhouse. When I walk along the track, I look between the trees. Just perhaps I will see my father. I don't tell my brother that I am looking for him. He would call me foolish.

The schoolhouse is new and shiny. I have my own place on a bench and a trough on the bench in front of me for a porte-crayon and extra leads. Hornbooks with the alphabet and numbers on them hang on the wall. The master holds them up, and we recite them and copy them, and then he hides their face, and we must write them from memory. A reading primer is called *A Little Pretty Pocket-Book*, and the master let me hold it. I can read almost as well as my brother. I am learning to write. We read and write in English and Dutch. The schoolmaster says it is not easy to find Dutch books. The Bible is in Dutch. He praises me for my reading, and I fly through every book. I love to practice script with a quill, although I spilled ink on my apron, and Mother became angry. I think he is a kind man, and I am glad to have such a teacher. He thinks I am cleverer than the other children, although he does not say this to me or to them.

At dinnertime the youngest are dismissed, and we walk back. I am tired then, and hungry. I look down at my shoes instead of between the trees. Sometimes I take a nap after dinner. Once I woke up and found my mother sleeping next to me, which was strange, because she usually does not sleep after dinner, and I don't remember her lying down beside me. I cannot wait until I can stay longer at school.

I knew where to find him, but choosing the right time and circumstance would require some thought. I was sleepy all the time and sometimes woke sweating from a nap that I didn't remember lying down for. After a full day's work, in the midafternoon, I wrapped up *pannekoeken*, my sheep's milk cheese, some slat meat, and pickles. I carried a bottle of cider in a sling. Regretfully, I went to my dowry *kast* and rummaged within. I put two fine apples in my apron pocket and walked into the village. As I rounded the bend onto the main road, I scanned both sides, the bench outside the inn, under each of the trees. I did not wish to ask for him. In fact, I could not.

I walked behind the inn, and there he was, a pack beside him, on his back and snoring. I sat on the garden wall, listening, but with my back to him. If anyone came, it would look like I awaited my children, not that I sought business with him. Eventually he stirred and coughed, then sat up and spit. He glanced at me and then looked hard. I waited for him to acknowledge my presence. He reset his black felt hat and tipped it toward me.

"Good day, Sir. Do you know who I am?" He squinted at me. I believed he did.

"I have brought you dinner. In thanks for your help in searching for my husband at the midsummer." He looked relieved and eagerly opened the napkin. I fished for one of the apples and held it forth. The trapper's hands were filthy, and he smelled, but his eyes were intelligent and suspicious.

He walked to a water pump set in stone at the inn door and drank for a long time. I waited while he ate.

"I have another errand for you, and it will have its own reward. I wish to enter an agreement with you, but I must ask for your confidence and your complete discretion. I know that you are a man of skill and honor." In fact, he had a reputation for skill and knowledge of the country outside the villages, but I knew nothing of his honor.

I could see, or I could hope, that I had intrigued him. His Dutch was accented but serviceable and much better than the little bit of French I could muster. Did he know the Indian village? How to find it at this time of year? I determined that he knew the place. He did not ask me why I wanted to go. He would depart for the season shortly. "*Ouay, ouay, ouay*. Within a few days." Was this place along his route? Will he take me there? A two-day journey over known trails?

"Well, a day and a half if you can walk apace."

I told him I could give him a gold chain with garnets. "And earrings to match." These were the legacy of my mother. "Such things are not made here and come from the old country; they are highly valued. With the right buyer, you could become a rich man. Surely an insurance policy against a poor trading season."

"You overstate your case, Madame. It is perhaps difficult to find such a buyer and could take quite awhile. Jewels only trade to the most elite of patrons, and such patrons are not easy to approach, especially for someone like me." I met his gaze and then looked beyond him. I pulled from my pocket two earrings and poured them onto his dirty palm. The necklace matched, with the fine goldsmithing of Amsterdam jewelers.

"I will reward you further but only for your absolute discretion. After you depart the village for the season, and only if I have heard not a word. I must be sure that the flagons in the tavern, which you soon will be able to well afford, will not loosen your tongue. And you must trade in a village far from here or in a town where the buyer need not know the source. Or trade to the French; a fine French lady would covet such a piece. But if I hear one word, I will skewer your reputation in this village and you will not find yourself trading here. And, believe me, my daughter will hear what is said at the school, and my farm is not so outside the village that I do not hear news," I assured him, although I was not entirely certain that I would either have his reputation within my power or hear all or any of what was said in the village.

"Fair enough. *D'accord.* Madame, I am a gentleman trapper." He grinned, and his teeth flashed beneath a dark beard. "My word is good, and I give a fair trade." Did he mock me? Or was he a man laughing genuinely at himself?

And then I begged him. "I implore you, Monsieur Jacques-François, to keep these travel plans between us. If such plans were disclosed in the village, I fear it would produce many suspicions and increase my hardship. I am not favored by the women of this village, nor most probably by the men, and I have few friends."

Stating my vulnerability expanded it, but such a risk must be taken in hopes of gaining his sympathy and his counsel. "*Ouay*, I take your meaning. The women have no use for me either, except when they want the goods that I bring, but the silence also has her price. Speaking is silver, but a still tongue is worth more than salt."

He squinted right at me, boldly. He was a trader, after all. He said he found the village women stingier and shrewder bargainers than even the Dutch men, who loosened with jenever and laughter. "But the women are most serious when trading and grow even more astringent if you entice them with drink, though there were times when they took it in their tea. Nevertheless, they remain tight in all aspects, their fingers wrapped tightly around their goods." I perused him carefully to see if there were salacious meaning in his words, but he gave all indication of sincerity. In any case, these last remarks I took to mean that I had been much too generous with him. Necessity never makes a good bargain.

We agreed on the date of departure. I asked him to fetch me three mornings hence at the farm. I then went into the inn and inquired of the maid on which day the coach came this week to the towns in the South. I chatted for a moment and revealed that I had plans for business with my brother who lived southwest of the big town at the Stone Ridge, which were not my plans at all.

I had walked the children to town the day before. The schoolmaster had nervously agreed to let them stay at the schoolhouse in exchange for chores done by the children, and gammon, eggs, and milk from my farm. I asked him to see to it that they were fed for up to a fortnight. He took his dinner with a family nearby, and I arranged for them to take dinner there too and to clean up after the meal. I knew my absence would be remarked, as I knew the schoolchildren would talk to their parents, so I told the boy and the girl that I must travel to their uncle at the Stone Ridge to see about my inheritance. They begged to go with me. I told them it was too expensive. The girl had cried and clung to my skirts for two days, and the boy had fallen silent.

We rose in the dark and coaxed the cow along the road with us. The boy had to walk behind with a switch. We tethered the cow at the schoolhouse. They could milk her there, and she should be safe enough betwixt the houses. My children could treat the other children and perhaps sell a jar or two. The boy would have to come back to the farm to feed the chickens and let them roam and to see to the dog, who would watch the sheep. I told him we depended entirely on him, and I saluted him for his bravery. The girl draped upon me and wailed. I unclenched her hand from my petticoat, set it firmly in her brother's, and left them before other children arrived. With children, example is better than canon, so I resolutely showed no outer sign of distress, although my eyes were stuck to the sack of corn I would take to the miller for grist.

My day was full of worry. I turned journey cakes with the newly ground Indian grist, *pearlash*, and eggs, and filled two ovens, topping them with coals from the fire, although there were days when I felt that dough made with corn and not wheat was a paste of despair. And this was such a day. I boiled vegetables, wrapped slat meat from the kitchen rafters, and fetched a round cheese and *hoofdkaas* from the spring box. Perhaps dining on the boiled brains of a pig would make me think more clearly. I buried my jewelry and money in the backyard, marked it with a stone, and hid a box of books and gowns in the attic of the barn. I secreted my extra oven underneath some barn floorboards. I went through all the cupboards, seeking items that I could spare, and turned each one in my mind. Each weighed with the history of my little life, and some with the value of usefulness. I also considered their weight upon the scale, as I would have to carry all. I nibbled on the food I cooked. My stomach did not plague me, and I ate throughout the day.

In the dark, I arose and pulled on my son's last-year boots, for his feet had grown larger than mine, and my oldest Brunswick undress. I braided my hair and hid it under a cap. I slid my hand mirror into a pocket of my underskirt. Drinking a second cup of strong tea with the last of yesterday's milk, I found myself fully prepared and waiting on the stone stoop with a neat carrying bundle, and my eyes upon the road by which he would come. Waiting made me angry and nervous. Surely I was God's fool to trust this man. I hoped only that he had cheated me in the price but not in the goods. *Wie boter op zijn hoofd heeft, moet uit de zon blijven.* "Those with butter on the head should stay out of the sun."

He showed up shortly after the sun rose and asked if I were well ready. I replied, "As I will ever be." We walked all day through the forest away from the village, first north up the river and then west up the mountain and down through another clove. We did not speak, and I simply followed him. I had brought red cloth strips and once off the road I marked the trail, as I would have to find my way home. He laughed at my tricks, but I ignored him. I also used my mind and made notes in a little book of paper. I carried food. The iron pot I ported was heavy, and my back soon ached. When we stopped to rest, he ate the boiled eggs and bread I offered. He looked at me directly but said nothing.

When it was too dark to walk, we stopped at a stream. He quickly gathered wood and built a fire and told me he would soon be back and disappeared. I unpacked, fetched water, and put it on to boil. After a good hour, he returned with two squirrels. I don't know how he could have got them. He pegged them on the ground and skinned them and tossed their bits into the pot. I was glad to have already drawn water off the pot for a cup of tea. I tossed the last tea leaves from the bowl. I added cooked potatoes, a carrot, chopped cabbage, and wild leek from my bag. He brought some leaves from out of his jacket and pulled them off their stems. He chewed one. "Bitter in the mouth makes the heart healthy," he grinned. Suddenly there was soup.

Eating, he asked me if I expected the Indians to find my husband. So focused on my dilemma that I had not even thought of this, I managed to nod over my surprise in an effort to disguise it. "Do you think they could?"

"If your husband has gone wild, they may know of it, and they might know if he has died somewhere. Or if he lives somewhere. These people know many, many things, much more than any ever admit."

"He could be anywhere. Would they tell me if they know?"

"Well, they might or might not, and there is little to discern if they have or have not revealed what they know, and so there you are. Or will be soon enough."

"Have you brought gifts?" he then asked. "For the sachem? The headman?"

I had not thought of this either. My thinking was more about the women, and I had not imagined I would be received by a chief. "Will this iron pot do?" He said it ought. It was the most valuable item I had brought. It was imported from Amsterdam, where the best were made, with smooth surfaces and a well-fitted lid with a rim for coals. After my mother died, I had become somewhat rich in pots. I drew out all the items I had packed from the kitchen and toolshed. I held back the hand mirror, not certain I could give it up. I had a pair of pliers, two bowls, two spoons, forks and knives, some glass beads, two blankets, some rough cloth. He handled everything but did not ask for anything. He said I must start with the sachem—that everything would follow from that or would not follow, as was his habit of speaking. And that I should let events unfold in their own time. It would not be a quick and forthright transaction. "Their style is different from the European style. You will not recognize it. You must present everything as a gift and not ask for anything. Hold a few items back."

I had not thought how to present myself, but now it was forming in my mind. I would ask them about my husband, and the other matter would hide behind that.

"Can you translate for me?"

"Well, some. You cannot get directly to your questions in the way that you are thinking. It will take time. Getting

70

to the village would be not just the half of it; certainly not the whole of it—lucky if the half."

As the fire died down, the part of the evening I was most afraid of was coming. I did not want him to touch me and feared he would. I knew that I had another sort of resource to barter, but the risks of such negotiation would be extremely high. At the same time, by this peculiar endeavor together, I felt partnered and less alone for the first time in my summer days and perhaps for the first time in many years. I lay the blankets on the ground and set the bundle for my head. I felt him watching me when I took off my cap, so I retreated from the fire ring to comb out my hair, as my braid had loosened. And when I came to lie down, he was already asleep.

For breakfast I offered him journey cake with *hoofdkaas* and watched him look at it carefully.

"It's made from a pig's head."

"I know it. We call it *tête fromagée* or sometimes souse."

With the cheese and cider, he offered his admiration. "Amsterdam food is quite good. It's why I always stop at the Dutch villages. There is only one thing worse than the British politics, and that's the food."

We took up again anticipation of our destination.

"Who are these people?"

"They are a great tribe who live along the river between the Kaaterskill and the large lakes to the north. They are intelligent and canny and know everything to live. They are diplomats and honor their word, much more than any give them credit for, especially the British. The Dutch have had friendly relations since the *Half Moon* sailed up here, however, and could not have survived without their aid. Many of them speak Dutch, especially the sachems. Up by the lakes, they have learned to speak my language in an old style. Their people like to talk even more than the French and have astounding oral traditions. They come together at times in conferences on the eastern side of the river—between the river and the mountains on that side— by the thousands and have recitations that go on for days. All politics and agreements, treaties, trades, and such are recounted for all to know and remember. I attended one, and it was truly more astounding than anything in Europe. They have lost much land on this side of the river in disputes with the Mohawk tribe.

"Your little territory by the Sager's Kill is *le terrain d'aucun homme*: 'the no-man's-land,' the border land between the Esopus tribes and these people. However, they are allied and friendly with the Esopus, so your village has not been caught in disputes, as the villages along the Mohawk River have. To be caught between two enemies is a great danger—there can be such viciousness between the tribes. Their cruelty is never understated."

This short treatise by the French trader was more than I had ever heard about how our village was set in a landscape, in a region, among peoples, unrelated to its distance from the larger European-settled towns or from Europe itself. I looked again to him to see if he would say more.

Jacques-François could see he had my attention, and he paused before adding, his eyes flickering, "This I heard from a Dutchman, and not from the people themselves, so it could be a Dutchman's tale. You know how they are and how they are likely to enliven and exaggerate. The North River people believe their world was created when a pregnant woman fell into a place all of water, and a great tortoise took her on his back. She scooped and paddled her hands in the water until it gathered up the earth, which finally became higher than the water, except in the plain of the river, which she scooped all in one direction, so that it flowed toward the sea."

I wondered as he told this tale if he knew my secret after all, and as I now had little doubt as to his cunning intelligence, I wondered if he was letting me know that he would not use his intuitions to harm me.

We walked along a stream, and canoes came toward us. Jacques-François called out to them with strange sounds and waved his arms around. They were silent and disappeared again, but when we walked into the village an hour later, we were expected, and people came to greet us. I sat while chattering groups came to look at me, and the children rolled on the ground to look up my petticoat and pull at the tops of my boots. Women touched my hair. Jacques-François told me to stay put, or not, until he returned. His habit of speech was to give an order and immediately propose its contradiction, so it seemed like although you had a choice, you would be likely to follow his initial command. I would not move. I pulled my skirts in tight and leaned against the bundle of my goods. I did everything I could to not fall asleep, including pinching my belly as hard as I could. I chewed on a journey cake, as I was starving, and offered bits to the children, who ran away.

Jacques-François returned and guided me toward an open shelter where a roof was set up upon a configuration of poles. Men in a variety of states of undress and of near nakedness sat on piles of blankets set on the ground. The chief seemed to be sitting on the biggest pile and to be wearing the most ornamental clothing. All of this I gathered with a furtive gaze, for I was too shy to look directly at anything or anyone. Jacques-François told me to sit quietly; that he would tell me what to do. "Unless you think you can figure it out yourself," he added, which he clearly did not consider a good option. The men talked for a while, and some of it was in French, but it was a French I could not understand. Eventually he told me to extract my iron oven from my bundle and a blanket, which I did. He set the oven in front of the chief, and lifted its lid, returned its lid, and set its clasps, ran his finger around the cupped rim, then lifted it by its handle and turned it over to show its three legs. It was an example of fine Dutch design and craft, but I wondered if they appreciated it, as they did nothing but frown. Their language came out of their mouths in fierce bursts of sound. Then he unfolded the blanket, which was large and thick, with deep colors—a very fine blanket—and laid it out before the sachem, who fingered its edge.

Jacques-François continued talking, and I believe he said that these were small gifts and that I was a small woman from a small village and that my small husband had disappeared. He gesticulated toward me and came over to me, framing my face with his hands. We sat for a while, and I was not sure what was happening. He then asked me to get out the spoons and beads, which I did. And these he presented with much ceremony, talking all the time. Some translation went on, for it seemed that two men could understand Jacques-François's dialect better than I could. I was doing my best to stay awake. I did not hear any talk about my husband, and for the rest of the long afternoon, I was completely ignored. I stifled my yawns.

Eventually the chief stood up and wandered out, taking both the oven and the blanket, along with the spoons and the beads. And we were left with the men, who were talking amongst themselves. When the sun dipped behind the trees, the men called to some women, who brought us alien and awful food on a wooden trough, which I took in my hands. I was ravenously hungry and ate without curiosity. I then tried to wander off, but the women and children followed me about, and I had no privacy. I did not quite know what to do with myself, so I tightened my thighs against a growing discomfort and waited for darkness. We were brought by one of the French speakers to a fire circle and shown to lay out our blankets on piles of brush. As soon as I lay my head on my bundle, I shut out the strangeness of the day by covering my face with my apron. In spite of—or perhaps because of—my nervous apprehension of my circumstance, I soon fell away to oblivion.

I awoke when a small hand drew my apron down below my nose, and I looked up into a pair of dark, curious, and smiling eyes set in a rounded face framed by shagging locks. She was probably six, and daring, as her less courageous counterparts set themselves apart and giggled outside the sleeping circle. I sat up in fear but told myself that she was my Judith, come to arouse me from my dreams. She looked not at all like Judith. Her straight hair had a mineral sheen so rich and stark that the angled rays of the early sun reflected brightly off the slick sheet of its surface. I thought that if I gazed hard enough, I would find myself mirrored in it. Her teeth were pearly and even and glimmering in her brown face, a chiaroscuro not ever found in Europeans. I pondered how such dark features could be so luminous.

She stood in front of me grinning like a bulldog, and as I was now sitting, we were face to face. She reached out slowly with both hands and ran them over my ears, drawing her softly cupped fingers forward over my jaw and cheeks. Then she let her hands drop to the sides of her little leather shift. This was such a soft and reassuring gesture, executed with such aplomb, that I was not alarmed by her touch. On the contrary, in the morning sun, I found myself near enchanted.

I stood up then, but did not know what to do. She, however, took my hand and led me toward the woods. She turned and called out to the other children, shouting out to them insistently and gesturing to them I knew not what. We stepped into the shrubbery and walked a path. She trotted in front of me and then halted. She pushed me off the path and pressed her back to a tree and squatted. The stream of her urine ran out beneath her. I walked around the tree and squatted too. The release of my aching bladder made tears come to my eyes. I think I understood then that I had come under the aegis of a little ambassador, who represented a very pragmatic people.

Back at the fire circle, after eating an odd breakfast of a cornmeal glob served on a piece of bark that my little friend had brought me and which I scooped to my mouth with my fingers, I conveyed to Jacques-François that I was ill and needed to see a woman who knew medicine. He showed no surprise at this and displayed no curiosity. Still, he attended to the problem. He said that he thought the doctors were men who were very strange and practiced a very magical medicine. They wore masks. I insisted that it was not this kind of doctor I needed but a woman who knows about woman's ordinary things. He did not know about the women; had never heard about or thought to ask about their ways and customs. He did surmise that the women held a certain sway and enjoyed a certain status, as the men came to live in the houses of the mothers of their wives, and the elder women chose the chiefs. His speculation I took as proof to my point. I insisted that there must be women healers, women who helped in childbirth. I do not exactly know how I knew this to be true, except that it must be true. Were they not a people upon this earth? He spoke to one of his friends, who took me across the village, which was quite large, comprised of over a hundred long dwellings. I did not ask Jacques-François to go with me, and I think he was glad to be left out of it. My little ambassador trailed behind us without a word.

As soon as I stepped through the door of the dimly lit, smoke-filled hut, I began to gag and retch. I put my hand over my mouth, but once I had started, I was completely compelled, and soon my hands had caught the contents of my stomach. Considering what I had eaten, it was not pretty. Tears were running down my face. I said I was sorry. Someone brought a handful of leaves. I had dribbled on my tucker. I knew they all knew. I held my hands out and started to cry and hiccough. They stared at me, and I was much afraid at their strangeness. They exchanged some words, and then one of them left. We all sat down on piles of skins, and I was given the root of a plant and shown how I should suck on it. I did as I was told, as the root had a sweet but peppery tang, like what we used for ginger beer and the feaguing of horses, shoving a bit between their haunches to make their tails come alive.

Soon the woman returned, and she brought a young man with her. He talked with them for a while and then much to my surprise turned to me and spoke directly to me. It took me a moment to decant the unexpected cadence on my ear.

"You speak Dutch!"

I had heard that they do, but somehow it still seemed strange among so strange a people.

"Yes, I can speak. As a boy, I lived with a Dutch farmer by the Mohawk River for two years." He looked so little like a Dutchman that I could hardly fathom what he was saying, although he spoke quite well. He did not say things that a Dutchman would say, and he did not ask the same sort of questions.

He asked me why I had come. I told him my husband had disappeared in the forest. He asked me where I lived.

I told him between the southernmost Blue Mountain and the North River. He said that he knew that many were known to disappear in those narrow valleys, among the stones and waterfalls. "It is a land between nations where the mountains butt up against the Great River and spirits rule. I have climbed the escarpments there for medicine, and from them you can gather the mountain berries and see well into the past, and if you eat medicine plants and stay through the night until the dawn rises on the river, you can also see the future."

"Was it wise to live in such a place?" he asked me. Had I seen a large bird—he did not know the name—that day or night? "Did you hear this sound on the night your husband disappeared?" He clicked in the recesses of his throat and snorted through his nose. I had seen no owl.

"Or any bird of prey?"

"I can't remember. No, I did not."

He said something to the women and then turned again to me. "We can probably not help you find your husband."

"Why do you ask me these questions?"

"If you saw an owl, your husband is most likely dead. If not, he might have headed south."

I turned my face away so they would not see my eyes roll back in my head. This was not the counsel I sought. I would better listen to the whispers and tales of the women in my own village. For they had interpretations of the direction a pig's tail curled or how tea leaves spun in the cup. I hoped I could hide my annoyance.

He turned to leave. "Wait. Wait. Wait." I looked at my hands. "I came for medicine." He spoke to the women.

"I have two children. I must take care of them. I need medicine."

"Medicine for what?" It was not clear whether they really understood me. Language was not the only barrier. We were talking about things which I knew they knew about—they were women after all. And yet I certainly did not know exactly what I thought and felt about my plans, even as my purpose was firmly set. I did not know how plainly I could speak. Would they bring me medicine for what I dared to intend, or would they bring me leaves that would help me keep my food down? I yawned with anxiety. My frustration and desperation were mounting. Had I come all this way to be misapprehended? I finally looked directly at the young man and stated it plainly. I did not need medicine to quell my nausea but something stronger, to change my fate.

I could see comprehension roll over his face. He said but a few words to the women, and they answered back.

"They will help you," he told me in Dutch. "They will bring you medicine, but they must go get it. It will take two days. And medicine must be given with ceremony, or it will not be effective." I had no idea what he meant, but I nodded with gratitude and called on myself to be patient.

The next days were dreamlike, and I was unafraid. These women had taken it upon themselves to service me, although I had no idea why. They brought me strange tea made from plants soaked in water, and strange food, and I slept amongst them without qualms. Jacques-François came to bid adieu, for he was off to the north country to trade amongst the French and would travel with his friends from this village. He asked me to assure him that I could make it home by myself, and I hid my trepidation from him. I wanted to appear noble in a way I had never quite imagined before. I was already so far beyond the boundaries of what I had conceived of as womanhood. I asked him to make sure that my mother's jewels came into the hands of a woman who deserved them.

"What sort of woman deserves them?" he asked. Without hesitating, I answered, "One who has made an unfortunate marriage." I quickly regretted adding that such a woman should be easy to find. He said he would do what he could.

So the women returned, and I conveyed to them that I could tarry no longer. I must walk for two days and return to my children. They wrapped up plants in packets of folded birch bark. There were six packets in all. They called for the Dutch-speaking boy and slowly went over the instruction for each of the six days. I rummaged in my bundle and gave each one of them a gift. A spoon, a handkerchief, a bit of lace, some ribbons, my cup and bowl, my apron. I then reached underneath my petticoat for my shift pocket and pulled out my little hand mirror. This made the greatest impression and was passed from hand to hand with laughter and much chatter. I became happy that I gave it up, even as I cherished it. I felt light in spite of the heaviness in my belly. In the evening, they sang songs and waved a smoking stick about me and laid their hands upon my head and breasts and belly. All was so strange that I did not mind and found myself at peace. On my last night with them, I slept hard and fast without dreaming.

They walked with me for the entire morning and half the afternoon. Then at a fork, they halted and gestured where I was to go but turned away themselves. I quickly could no longer see them but heard their strange calls to me, which I interpreted as best wishes and farewells. I wanted a call from my heart to erupt wildly in my throat, claiming the forest as my own, but I only waved to them without even a murmur on my lips. I was a silent deer among yipping foxes.

I walked in the quietude until dark and was curiously unafraid. My load was so much lighter than when I came. At times I knew the path and at others I just followed step after step. I found the bits of cloth tied by a young woman to find her way home, as in a children's tale. That woman seemed like a child to me, as if I had known her long ago.

Night came and with it, fear, for who does not fear darkness when alone? During the days of my journey, I had not let my mind touch on this night—although from the outset, it had been part of my plan—lest I be overcome by the terror of it. Now a night alone in the forest did not seem so completely onerous. Somehow what had daunted me at the journey's start, beyond being able to think about it, now seemed like an appropriate interlude; a transition from a strange dream back to the familiar life with my hens and pigs. I saw that in my daily life alone at the bowery, I was most anxious in the anticipation of small things that hardly mattered. When it came to childbirth or sleeping in the woods alone, I mustered myself. I resolved to remember this steadily and anon.

Darkness can be a comfort as well, like a soft cloth wrapped around you. I did not make a fire and removed myself well off the trail. I found a hemlock stand with a depth of needles and moss to settle upon and lay down with my head upon my bundle, which now contained my six packets of plant trade. I heard the low, repeating hoot of an owl not too far from where I had lain. It called me to sleep. And I wondered if that Dutch-speaking Indian boy had been right about owls. Does an owl's presence portend death? To hear an owl . . . is that enough? Or must you see with your own narrow eyes the blinking of their wide windows of sight, the tips of their feathers, the hooked and burnished beak, or the branch-clutching talons to know that death will come? You hardly ever see owls. They, like death, are a bird of stealth, but you know they perch in the trees with a great patience, watching with their uncanny vision, like death, for their prey. Now I remembered that Judith had told me about the angel's wings that had swooped from the side of the house the night her father disappeared, and I, not wanting to conjure phantoms, had told her she must have seen an owl. Portents. Portents.

But of what? Ah, owl or no, death will come to us all. But whose now? Has my husband faded into the air? Sifted to dust? Melted to a puddle? Rotted in the peat? Petrified to stone? In any case, I cannot bring forth life in his name. Does the owl call for my infant? I cannot do what transforms a mere woman to a mother, no matter that I am called to the sacred task of it. I cannot do what a mother must—labor viciously to open her body, howl at the sky, and then shift to tenderness, and clutch the newborn to her warmth, and name the infant, and suckle it to life. I could not.

I awake with the early filtered light that splays upon a large shelf of orange and yellow fungi above my head. I know these to be delicious because my husband had sometimes brought them to me from the woods. They are unmistakable and thereby safe to eat. Here I will collect them myself. I carefully break them off and wrap them in a small food cloth and am suddenly homesick for my hearth and my children.

I pull on my boots, eager and hurried. I chew on a stale journey cake as I walk. Within two hours, my heavy legs draw me from the high ground down, down toward the river plain. The trail straightens, the forest becomes less enclosed, the view through the trees promises to open out, pierced by daggers of light from the canopy to the ground. Hemlocks give way to familiar oaks and sycamore, the yellow birches and the white ones that serve as sentinels on the trail.

I stumble to a rocky escarpment and suck my breath in. There in the distance is my farm. I can see the roof of the house and the barn and a gleam and sparkle that must be the pond. The grass has not yet frosted to brown, and the clearings of our little world spin out in a green circle of sweetness. The leaves are not yet blown from the trees at the edge of the rounded clearings, so my little bower is ringed in gold, a glowing halo of comfort and assurance, even if it would not last longer than the next autumn wind.

From this purchase, I can look beyond the farm and see

the glimmer of the great North River—Hudson's River—silver in the distance, as it coils through these perfect hills southward to the world beyond. When I see the river from afar, I know I am not alone in the world. I believe it is why my husband always climbed high. From above, the sight of the valleys and the ample spill of the river toward the sea is a comfort. The broadened horizon reminds me of all the teeming lives who bravely farm these lands. All the kills from all the mountains filter through bowers such as ours, through the fields of other families on both the western and eastern shores to form this vast and lovely waterway as it curves in a colossal serpentine swath through the rolling valley. The very sight of it catches hard in my throat.

Finally, with my toes stinging at my steep and speedy downhill stumble, I step upon a gentler trail that leads me to my pastures. The melancholy end-of-the-day shadows flow from the wooded mountain and follow against the back of my jacket and cap, but before me the sun plays its afternoon pipes. As I step down the last rock shelf, I see a rabbit in a clearing, and it stops still before me, unable to run, unable to hide, and I stop too. Just to look at it. I am close to home now. Alert but frozen. A moment passes when I echo its stillness, and so, sensing I will not or cannot harm it, it begins to nibble on the blades.

I arrive at the farmhouse after dark, kick off my boots in the kitchen, and feel my way in the blue-black night to the top of the stairs. I can hear the heaving of my own breath when I pause and lean against the portal to the room. My breath comes short and rushes into my ears, flushing the quiet of the night. I shrug my clothing into a heap upon the floorboards, and my sheets, my bed, my pillows call me into them. I would die here, at least to this day. Blessed oblivion descends to me from the stars through the window to my aching legs and heart.

I was condensed by sleep in the center of the bed, but the silence in the house gradually enlarged the morning. I unwound. A shaft of the sun on the pillow of my own bed pointed right at me and to the tasks at hand. I gazed about my familiar things, and their familiarity staggered me with incongruence. All was changed forever. Downstairs the dimmed kitchen was cold and smelled of ashes. I unwrapped the roots, leaves, and berries and laid them upon the table in piles. The flint weighed on my wrists as I struck over and over for a spark. I mixed flat bread for the oven, and the flour stuck to my reddened hands. In the iron kettle, the water came slowly to a boil. My patience settled heavy below my belly, in my thighs and feet. Hunger gnawed me, but I deliberately turned the mind away. The leaves curled and broke in my hands as I chose a bowl for them. This seemed important, and I reached for my finest white bowl. Pouring the hot water over the plants, wisps of my fate drifted to darken the water. I mixed the first order of leaves; they floated on the surface in a mesmerizing pattern.

I decanted into a jug and headed with the warm flat bread and a cup to the woods. I walked behind the pond and climbed a rock shelf above the farm. There I lay out a deer hide and blanket, and in the autumn sun slept with ease. I awakened in the afternoon and gazed upwards. And now awake, I resumed waiting—waiting as women have waited for all time.

From my supine position, my face caressed by the star moss, I watched my son come to the farm in the afternoon and perform what was asked of him. He let the chickens run and fed them. He spent time in the coop collecting eggs. I watched the boy—still my boy but on the cusp of something else—from a distance. With a great love and sorrow, I watched him work. Soon he was chasing the chickens again to their coop. He did not linger.

Each evening, a half hour after watching my son pull the bar across the barn door, I walked back to the house and made a fire for tea. I could assume the house was mine again and my presence remained unknown to anyone.

On the third night, after two days of drinking the bitter tea, I awoke in pain, with the sheets stuck to my legs. I reached beneath the bed and squatted as dark clots dropped onto white porcelain. Rocking back and forth on the soles of my feet, I called out. But to whom? I did not know who could help me now. Not one benefactor came to mind. I thought of the ewes in the pasture. They knew what this was about more than I did, and I finally understood the peculiar admixture of fear and acceptance in their lowing.

In that early dawn of cramping and bleeding and vomiting, I thought perhaps I would die alone on the floor of the loft next to my marriage bed. The thought of my children alone in the world was my torment. I lived every sorrow of lost love and companionship and possibility a thousand times. I repented my every sin and sins I had never known were mine. My regrets were black smoke upon the lime-washed walls.

But I did not die.

I could not move for most of the morning. Eventually I found it in me to draw the sheets from the bed, and shove them beneath it with the chamber pot, which was full of a bloody mass.

I pulled myself up and staggered to my kitchen. All had come to pass as the women had foretold, and I sensed the worst was gone by. I made tea from the plants set aside for the aftermath. I followed every instruction and drank the bitterness gratefully. I walked with slow deliberation out to the pond and lay down on the mossy rock shelf. There I hiked my petticoat from behind and spread it like a wheel around me. I bled through the star moss into the earth. But the flood had tapered, and in a numb stupor I watched the sun crawl through its stations across the sky.

Hours later, when the sun hung low into the trees but its stripes still struck across the meadow, I arose and made my way. I was shaking with cold and longing for my bed. My legs itched with dried blood and the imprint of pebbles, twigs, and bits of moss that my heels had dug up with my writhing.

Surely the boy would have come and gone by then. I could drink my tea and recover in my quilts. I stumbled from tree to tree, wrapping my arms around the rough bark of their trunks and standing with them a moment as they imbued me with fortitude. I made my way. I made my way. Until finally I found myself near the garden. The size and shape and color of the pumpkins on the vine offered a comfort that I noted.

I must have left the door open or the boy had forgotten to latch it in the afternoon. I swung it wide and, stepping on the threshold, nearly jumped through my skin. For there he was sitting in the shadows at the table with the dog at his feet.

He said, "Greetings, Mother," and asked if I were ill. I must have looked wan and small to him. And I said, "Somewhat," but added that it was not serious and that I would soon be fine. He had given me such a start that I was slow to speak. But what a fortification to see my child! Finally, I told him how glad I was to see him and what a fine job he had done with the animals. What a brave boy he was. A true and dutiful son. Praise children, and they shall prosper. Even the dog wagged his tail, as if I were glad as well to see him and as if praising my son had stroked his own back.

He asked me how and when I came there, and I told him I did not come by coach but that a wagon had traveled through the night and shuttled me on its way from Esopus to Schenectady. I was so tired from my journey that I had fallen asleep at the pond. I had planned to come for them on the morrow. I watched his face to see if my lies were discernible, but I could tell that he was still of an age when his mother interpreted his world. Soon enough it would not be so. He came to embrace me, and in that embrace I knew him to be taller than when I departed.

I asked him would he mind fetching his sister and our cow, for although they would have to return after dark, I could no longer wait to see her. The boy eagerly set to the road and called that he would be back within two hours. I watched him trudge, his boots loose, his pantaloons too short, the image of his father in body, the dog by his side. I called out to him to give repeated thanks to the schoolmaster, but he did not turn around at the gate and let it bang behind him. I turned upon my hearth.

What do peas look like after they've been cooked for half a day? If you know not, then you have never seen *snert*, an ugly-looking but surprisingly tasty pea soup perfect for a fall evening when there might be frost. I set the dried peas up in the pot and went to collect eggs. Crawling on my knees, I looked my hens directly in their red eyes and greeted them as if for the first time, knowing that we held our safety and our bounty in common.

Judith Steps on an Egg

Mama will not tell us about her visit with her brother. She says nothing about it. When I ask, she does not answer and only orders up more chores for me to take on. So I stop asking but still I have little time to read and learn my spelling. She seems to think I should be able to practice my spelling while I churn butter or spin or knead dough or wash dishes. These tasks are often too hard for me. I forget to pay attention, and she becomes angry. Once I poured out a bucket of water she needed for laundry, and she sent me to the stream for more. That yoke is too heavy for me. My brother usually fetches water. She has been very strict and cross since she returned, and I wonder what worries her so. Did she not have a good visit with her brother? Then why did she go and leave us at the schoolhouse?

I liked sleeping at the schoolhouse. I was frightened and lonely at first, but we were given candles, and my brother let me stay up to read all the books. I tell my mother to be proud that I had not cried at the schoolhouse. She looks at me and said she is, but my brother tells her that I am lying; that I had too cried. "You did too," he said. He ruins everything. Now winter is coming, and the school will close. The schoolmaster is going to Boston. I will miss the other children.

It is true that sometimes I wake up in the night crying. What happened to my father? Why does he not come? How will he survive the cold, white winter in the woods? Of course, he is certainly taken in by another family and has found another little girl to tell his stories to. He would be pleased and astonished that I can read my own stories. Though I like to think of him taken in, I do not like to think about that other little girl.

Mother had an accident. I saw the bedsheets brown with blood. She must have cut herself with the axe, but I do not see a wound anywhere. Not on her whole body. I look and look. And I lift her skirts from behind and crawl underneath them. But although her legs are tall and white and she smells funny, there is no blood. She swats me out.

I am the smallest child and sometimes hide in the chicken coop, but only when my brother has changed the hay. Once I stepped on an egg so hard it broke, and I could see the yellow baby chick's eye and little feet.

CHAPTER 3

Stuff of Dreams

Winter 1770

Soort zoekt soort.

"Kin can be found amongst kin."

—Dutch proverb

WINTER MAKES THE whole world smell different. The leaves were off the trees, and the colors were gone even from the ground. It had snowed on the mountains, which made them blend toward the sky. The ferns had shriveled and rusted. I could smell the season and its portents in the air on the few times when I walked to the village. As the weather turned cold, the village seemed even less friendly. I spent most of the fall harvesting, putting up food, and calculating the woodpile. I traded less and stored more.

Sinterklaas rode his white horse, and the coal-faced *Zwarte Piet* distributed his gifts among the children. I had little to contribute, and subterfuge was impossible. I thought it best to hold on to my mother's gowns. No one knew I had them. I knitted wool stockings, made a whole set of new candles, and decorated *koekjes* with sugar and nuts. The children made crowns and decorated them with juniper berries and pinecones.

The boy knew that *Sinterklaas* was the new schoolmaster and recognized the neighbor's horse, but he was silent among the believing children. How soon they grow up! The girl was still entirely fooled, even as the schoolmaster in his pointed hat and white robes spoke directly to her and called her by name. My son and my daughter had stopped asking about their father. And no one in the village said a word about him to me.

When *Kerstydt* came, I took them to church. We were not warmly received, although the Damen, in their dark wool jackets and starched bonnets and collars, pressed a gift basket to me. I did not want their pity, but I grasped their offering with my fingers and forced my smile and *danken* awkwardly across my face. I had been avoiding the church on Sundays, which did not curry any favor among my neighbors and did not make me feel particularly welcome at Christmastime.

My husband had always laughed at churchgoing and was never in the habit. He often said that neighbors were nice, provided you don't see too much of them. I guess this was excepting those he saw often enough at the tavern. In the early years, I steadfastly left him on Sunday mornings and occupied my pew. Eventually I thought that my presence brought even more attention to his absence. I could not answer questions asked of me with any conviction.

Yes, my husband stayed home to mend the plow, for we were so pressed to plant as soon as possible, given what the weather had been. In fact, our plow was rusted and left in the mud of our cornfield. My husband stayed home tending to a pregnant ewe, I ventured. My husband, hearing this particular invention as a reason for his absence, laughed hard, bending over in delight, his short fingers pressing into fists. "It is pregnant *you* that I would tend to," he said and grabbed me about my waist. His whiskers tickled at my neck.

How could I have married such a man? I had been drawn to him because he was not so typically Dutch, in the saturnine and stingy manner of my father and his colleagues, with their pantaloons and waistcoats, black-brimmed hats, and a corresponding sternness. He was irreverent to almost everything that I knew and had been raised to think important. When I expressed fear that our neighbors would ostracize us for not attending church, he was quick to remind me of the Remonstrance of Flushing, a protest made by our ancestors in New Amsterdam in defiance of Peter Stuyvesant's order to evict the Quakers. Their demand to perpetuate religious tolerance in the New World as it had been practiced in the Netherlands was satisfied. Which is more than you can say for what happened in New England. Just as I began to take my husbund's discourse seriously, he interjected, "I will remonstrate you to Flushing . . . or romance you to blushing!" I did not miss his intent, and by then the blood had risen to my cheeks.

Why had these impertinences been so attractive to me? Indeed, at first I had been a bit repulsed, but then he related a story I could not resist. He told me that the moment he had seen me in my father's establishment, he had known that I would be his wife and set about to make it so. There was something about my face, my look, my carriage that told him I was more than this village, this shoppe, this family could ever know, and it was he that could reveal it to me. Sensing my fading resistance he told this story often. And erelong I was wooed and won.

He had found work and was staying at the inn that I walked by every morning and evening. Soon he was waiting for me on the porch and walking with me until just before the turn to my parents' house. On these strolls we learned more of each other. He had read considerably and told wonderful stories of the wider world. He romanticized the land and wanted to go to the west. He wrote poems which he spoke aloud to me and knew the words of other poets by heart. I am not sure I understood them but had never met such a man. He thought the native people were marvelous and not quite so dangerous. That *of course* they had sensibly allied with the French, as the British required a thrashing. He thought slavery onerous—the idea that people could be owned—and, like a Quaker, would have none of it. He told stories of the North River, which he had sailed a few times. He never spoke of his family, except of a young uncle who had at one time taken him downriver when he was but a lad to the great port city once called New Amsterdam and now called New York.

He had a wondrous laugh, and soon I found myself fishing for it. I believed by his attentions that I had become witty. "What a snake tongue emerges from those pretty lips," he said to me, and great admiration was in his eyes. Soon we spent our walks making fun of the townspeople. I would catch his eye in church and could not hold back the delight of my heart, which I am sure showed on my face.

He managed to get his employer, a tradesman like my father, to introduce him at my father's business. It was not long after that he sought the advice of the dominie, who then spoke to my father. He came to our parlor, and I paced upstairs and heard nothing but my father's cough as my fate was decided. My mother came to me and said in so many words she had hoped for better—we Dutch, we're so plainspoken. But if I wished it, it would be so.

I wished it. There was nothing in me that hesitated. I thought her ignorant for supposing there might be some-one better. *"Wat baten een kaars en bril als de uil niet ziet en wil,"* she muttered. "What's the use of candle and glasses if the owl doesn't want to see?" By which I think she meant that she thought the same of me.

The dowry was to be negotiated. My husband-to-be asked his employer to negotiate for him. I heard my parents arguing at night, my mother taking my father's stinginess to task. She made up for it by giving me fine things—a tea set, linens, blankets, gowns, cutlery, dishes, kitchen sets, and a spoon rack for luck. I had stopped walking to my father's business and spent all my time at the house with my mother, who doted on me. During the month of our engagement, I did not see him except in church and missed him so. My parents never invited him to dinner.

We had a solemn ceremony and a formal dinner at

the inn with my father's business associates. Some gifts from them sweetened our future. My mother had altered her wedding gown, adding lace to the hem for my height. He had borrowed a jacket and a fine embroidered waist-coat, and all that was telling were his shoes. When it was over, we went upstairs to a fine room with a fireplace that seemed luxurious to me. He gave me brandy and told me stories; made such mockery of the dinner guests that we laughed and laughed. My only nervous apprehension was that someone might hear the sound of our laughter and the short, sharp cries of my pleasure that I could not suppress.

It was not that I did not know there was a certain danger in not showing myself at services, but I soon followed my husband. That's what women do. And I look back on my willingness with envy and longing for a time when that could be so. He told me that the churchwomen clucked like chickens, and the men frowned and coughed in judg-ment and then slept. My husband proudly stayed home to sleep, preferring feathers to a hard pew. He quoted, "'Tis warm weather when one's in bed!" And what sort of poet would say such a thing? "A fine one," he said. "A very fine one."

In his mind, both our cherished children were conceived on Sunday mornings. My husband called it God's work, and in those days, I was inclined to see it so. Not attending services left me entirely naïve of village news and depen-dent on my husband's tavern reports, but it saved me from the requirements of the village women and a certain work I was too young to see the value of as an investment for my future.

Once I was pregnant, I was utterly in my own world. I felt blessed and quiet within. I went to see the midwife, who promised to come to me. I believed her, and in her presence I was strangely unafraid. She became my friend and a source of news and learning of an entirely different kind. She taught me much about plants and flowers, and my garden grew rich with herbs that I preserved in my husband's jenever by siphoning small amounts off his jug whenever he went to refill it.

During the births of both my children, she came quickly and stayed long, making sure that the boy was tended and fed while the girl came forth, that there was a huge kettle of soup for me, and that cups were ladled and brought upstairs so I did not catch a chill. She was the one who took the afterbirth to the garden and buried it and then told me what to plant there in the spring.

Three years after my daughter was born, the midwife left the village. She had been the only unmarried woman. It was before the schoolmaster came. She was about ten years older than myself, and although old for marrying, she had found a husband. She then had moved downriver to the port town, where she had a daughter of her own. She sent me a few letters, but finally, after a year or two, did not answer my last inquiry as to her welfare and fortunes. In any case, after that I had no need of a midwife and paid little attention to how the other women in our village fared and who attended to them.

I fried up some *oliebollen* to celebrate the New Year. It had been bitter cold both on the river plain and in the tight little valleys closer to the mountains. It had snowed and snowed. But the sun shone on New Year's Day, and I encouraged the children: *"Schijnt de zon op nieuwjaar, geeft het een goed appeljaar"*: "When the sun shines on New Year's Day, it will be a good apple year." It snowed again, day after day. I waited for abatement, burning rapidly through our wood. I sent a letter to my brother and told him that when the snow would let me travel, I would come to him, for I had matters of personal import to discuss with him. I did not receive a reply for longer than a month. He had taken a new English wife. The children and I stayed in the kitchen, spinning, baking bread, making cheese from the little milk from the cow, basket making. We all went out to tend the animals together. We took turns reading. We sang songs.

Elsje fiederelsje, *put your little clogs by the fire.*
Mother makes pancakes, but the flour is so dear.
Tingelinge, *pancake, flour with raisins.*
Tingelinge, *pancake, come see us here.*

We ate potatoes, *kohl*, and chestnuts. On sunny afternoons, we strapped runners to our clogs and tied padding to our bottoms. We scraped the snow from the ice on the pond. We scuttled across, falling often, and our laughter burst from our mouths in clouds. When darkness fell, we all crawled into my marriage bed and piled the quilting high.

The snows of winter eventually melt off the track, and then patches of earth begin to show in the yard. The landscape darkens along with the bright skies and becomes more sinister as the white of the fields begin to disintegrate. The sweet meander of the maple sap from its prison of winter wood has been followed swiftly by days of torrents and freezing nights. It begins to rain and then rains a cold, hard rain for days and days. The yard is a pond of mud, and every time I step from my doorway, I return with my clogs soaked and my skirts stiff with ice and sludge. I cannot keep an apron clean.

The children are sick, and I am afraid. The boy had gone down first, and soon after, the little one woke in the night. They are hot in their beds, with sticky heads and stippled faces, a glaze to their eyes. Fortunately, in the summer, I had put up elder flower in jenever and now wrench the stopper from the bottle's neck. I drop the clear liquid into a cup and pour some boiling water from the kettle over it. The oil from the jenever curls on top. When it cools, I bring it to them, make them sit up, and feed it by spoons into their mouths. The fever subsides a bit, and they sleep.

I am beside myself because I had sent the boy in a downpour to borrow a trap from Mr. Stroop, the ironsmith. I need the trap because a weasel has eaten the rooster, and I know the hens are next. I had found the feet and the comb and a wad of wet feathers floating in a puddle. I kept the hens in the barn and made a game of having the children find holes to be stuffed. I put the dog in the barn at night but knew he was no match for a weasel with hens on his mind. A weasel would study until he found his way. So I had sent for the trap. I hated to ask because I hated to owe. I could not offer butter or eggs because the cow had no milk and the chickens laid nary an egg. The boy had gone reluctantly, but I had insisted. He returned pickled to his skin with the heavy iron leghold trap in a soggy grain bag. And now I had my trap and a boy who was burning in his bed.

The hay is almost gone, so I had not laid out new for the cow, and she stood sullen in her stall. The stench of the piss-soaked hay mixed with damp boards and feathers is more than I can stand, and I retch. I lit a lantern in the barn, but I can hardly see by its lame sputter. I set the dog from the house across the pasture to bring the sheep in, and, of course, he had launched with tail raised and a quick start but almost immediately checked himself at the yard gate, already sopping, and turned to look at me. I shout, "Go on, then!" but my call is sucked across the wind and does not ring out. Despite my enjoinments, he turns and slinks past me into the reaches of the barn, his tail now low and tucked under. I know I must go myself.

Crestfallen that I have no help whatsoever, I pull my shawl up over my head and step out into what had become, as the evening fell, pellets of ice crashing through the sky and bouncing off the stiffness of the freezing stubble in the grazed meadow. My face stings with them as I trudge through the pasture brush to where the sheep are taking shelter under the birches. Circling wide of them and coming through the trees to drive them out with a switch, I run behind them waving my arms and shout, *"Donder op! Donder op!"* Pelted and stung and now weighted with the ice stuck on my clothing, I run at them. My ewes are clever or stupid as sheep could be in an ice storm, or, for that matter, at any time, and the one persistently circles my charge. I finally whack her on the nose, and she stops cold, so to speak, and bleats high, not now knowing how to turn and avoid me. I thrust the point of my switch at her rump, and she heads across the pasture, and the others trot behind. I run and stumble to keep up.

Once at the gate, they stop, afraid as it swings toward them on the wind and out again on its hinges and so confuses them. I have to thrash the one behind, but she bunches up against her mother in the lead. I clutch my shawl at my throat and implore them, "Go now. Please . . . The barn will be better than the birches. I promise you. I will find you some dry hay." I doubt my words are true, but I need to hear them, even as they are swallowed in the gale. A small miracle it is that the sheep move forward across the track between the pasture and the yard.

Now through the gate, I close it and hope they will stay together and at least move in the direction of the barn without going behind it, where they would be lost. I run around them, giving a wide berth, and come upon the barn doors, where I heave the bar that releases the doors outward. There are iron hooks to hold them back, but I cannot fasten them and just hope they will not swing too wildly and startle the sheep as they approach. I circle back behind the ewes, which are standing nose to nose like a trivet. I urge them forward and thank God when they turn and trot single file into the barn. Behind them I step out again to fetch one door and swing it closed. I prop a stone left there for the purpose of preventing it from swinging out. I slip on the slick hay and mud and turn to fetch the other door and draw it inward. I cannot stop to fasten them, so set another stone as prop.

The barn is cavernous—a long center aisle split through it, with pens at each side. It is a fine Dutch barn, at one time my pride. Now I see it is overbuilt for its uses. For where is the industry to fill it? To contain the sheep, I must now get three of them into the pig's pen, where there is not enough room to swing a cat. They will stay warm side to side. In any case, it will have to do, as it is the most secure place for them together. We had taken the pig to town in the fall and traded a loin for slaughter so as to eat bacon and ham through the winter. The pen stands vacant enough and away from the cow, who is now wild with agitation, rolling her eyes back in her head and kicking out at nothing behind her and pulling against her tether. I press myself narrow against the pens and sidestep by the sheep in the aisle so that I can slide the door open on its rail. Then I place over-turned buckets as obstacles in the aisle so the sheep have no choice but to turn into the pen. I cling again to the rail and sidestep along the aisle so that I am once more behind the sheep. And then, spreading my arms wide, with my hands grasping the ends of my shawl like some huge bird of prey, I herd them down the aisle.

The last ewe brushes by the hook where the lantern hangs and crashes it to the floor behind her. She leaps forward, more frightened of her past than of her future. The flame flares but does not gain purchase in the aisle's puddles and wet hay—the one good fortune of the rain being that no barn fire could satisfy its hunger in such a deluge. The light sputters and dies, but I can see that the lead ewe has turned at the buckets in through the opening of the pen, and before they can reverse in the small space and emerge, I pull the door closed on its rail and slide the hook in its eye.

Now I stand panting in the dark. I say some soothing words to the ewes, and they turn their heads so they can stare at me with blinking sideways yellow eyes. The wet of their wool is fragrant. I call out to the cow, and she ceases her thrashing. I turn into the aisle, which is dark and slick, and take some cautious steps toward the door. I can only hope that the hens are safe in their coop. I feel along the floor with my feet for the fallen lantern, although I have no box or spall to light it. As I bend to pick it up, my soles fly out from under me, and I end flat on the mud-wet floor, the soak of my skirts bunched in a hard wad beneath me and my face forced down into the grit and filth.

My courage has come to its own natural end. The splatter has knocked my wind beyond me and curtails any of my remnant pride. I squint against the mud splashed into my eyes and begin to heave and tear. I cannot raise my head but turn my cheek to the side in the grit and stalk grist. I shake with cold and sobs and do not lift my head. Behind the sound of the wind's howl and the pellets' drive against the boards of the barn, I hear the call of my name.

Startled, I hold back the snuffle of my tears and listen. It comes again. I look up and along the aisle in the damp and dark but can see naught. As my eyes elevate to the gap between the seam of the barn doors where one door is farther behind the other, I make out the shape of a person. I try to raise my head by pressing on my arms, but my hands slide forward in the cold slime. I apply an effort of mind to place the voice. And as I concentrate my effort, I find I need no mind to recognize that timbre after all. All I need is to suspend my doubt. The voice is one I know in my bones. It is the voice of my husband.

And there he stands.

Time slides from its mandrel into the mire, and embeds itself in the elements of earth and water, where it sticks and does not move forward. I succumb to the halt of its march. The noise of the thrash of the storm seems distant and muted. My throat thickens with ache, and I cannot pull any words up from my feet to make my mouth answer. My chin touches the floor as my astonished eyes pierce the dark to the doorway where my belief is on trial. But there he stands—and his voice had called my name. What did I see? Was that tenderness in his gaze? *Husband, where have you been? Did you forsake me?* I call from my heart without sound. *Are you now home?* And though the tenor of my voice is withheld, he seems to have heard me and says, "Lambkin, my ewe, I could not forsake thee . . . I am but lost. Never you mind. This is how it should be. This is how it is. You will fare and prosper and all will be well." *But have you come home?* "You can see me with your own eyes. I am here and will be with you always."

Suddenly I cannot hold my head up. I am flooded. My splayed body swells as if all the infinite sadness of the lonely winter has gathered and distilled in it. The wet has been drawn out of mountain stone, and all runs to my ditch. Now I can surrender into the swell and all that is my stored grief would rise to pour from my eyes. I would be light again. I lift my glistening face with a longing and ardor I had not previously known that I harbored.

And find him gone.

I do not move, locked rigid in my earnest listening, and urge the animal of my body along the aisle toward the shadows where moments ago he had stood. But I cannot move. Now only the huge sinister portals of the barn clamor together with nothing to separate them. Hail. Wind. Dark.

I awoke in my daughter's bed, aching everywhere. Swallowing gave me great pain, and even the dull light in the room hurt my eyes. I put my hand to my forehead and found that it burned. The girl snored beside me. Still, I knew that I had slept too long and that I must rise and make tea for my children.

The chimney opening had dripped out the fire coals, and I had to set a spall to tinder that I kept in a box. I pulled my shawl around me and stood shoeless. It took me a long time, and I swayed before the hearth. I set some water on the hook and sat and stared at it.

My remembrance of the previous night was a puzzlement. My thoughts would not gather and mesh. I had charged through the door to find the boy standing in his stockings in the entry, his bed quilt wrapped around him and ice dripping from his hair. We stood wide eyed, facing each other.

"Did you come out to the barn, you foolish boy?" But he told me he had only leaned out the door, calling me.

I asked again urgently, "Did you come to the barn?" He said, "No, Mother," and looked as if he were about to weep at my harshness. I looked at his stockings, and they were not mud soaked as they would have been if he had made his way across the yard to the barn.

"I called and called for you. I was frightened. You were gone such a long time." He stared at me, and I must have looked like a banshee, with my hair loose but frozen in clicking strands and the front of my clothes and hands and face dark with the color of the earth. I softened to his distress.

"Come, boy. Get back to bed. You should not be up. You are fevered." I put my arm around him and steered him to the room with the beds. But he turned and gripped my waist with desperation, with his head against my pounding heart. I rubbed his wet head. "'Tis all right now." I pressed him backward.

My girl sat up and looked at me with horror on her face. She shrieked with fright and huddled in her coverlet. I said, "It's me. Your mother. I fell bringing the sheep in from the storm. It's only mud. We are all safe now." She heard my voice and fell back whimpering. The boy crawled in his bed and turned away so that I would not see that he was weeping too.

I left them and went to put water to warm and strip the heavy burden of my clothes in front of the hearth in exchange for a nightgown. When the water was tepid, I poured some to a washing bowl and dipped a cloth to wipe my cheeks. My hair was caked and stiff about my face. When the water came to boil, I drew down the dried chamomile and threshed it in the teapot. The fragrance soothed me as I let it steep, the steam rising to my nose. I had no honey left, and how I longed for that little taste of sweetness. I took the pot and three cups to the children's room. The girl had fallen back in her fever. I stroked her hair off her face, and her eyes fluttered. The boy said simply, "I am glad you are home."

Two days later, the storm broke, and I awoke in the eerie quiet of a dry, windless morning, listening for any sound. I could not get up but lay there, ears cocked. Finally, I clambered from my bed and pulled on a jacket over my nightshift and made tea for the children. The heat of my fever had abated with the storm. The boy's had cooled the previous day, and he had tended the fire and made tea and brought it to me in my bed. I could see the worry in his eyes, and I smiled at him and told him I was getting well— even as I could barely sit up to drink and hardly believed I would ever feel any better. Today, though, my head was clear, and I coughed without pain and blew green phlegm into rags. The little one was yet weak, but her face was no longer blotched with fire either.

I knew the animals were starving and drinking dirty water, as they had not been well tended or given any feed but the hay in their stalls. But they had ceased their lowing, because we had been too frail to answer. The hens too would last not much longer, not killed by the weasel but by my neglect. The dog also had not eaten and must be weak at his knees. I pulled on my work clothes and stepped out into the morning and went to tend to my chores. With trepidation, I opened the doors of the barn, not letting myself hope for any good news.

Standing with the warmth of sunlight on my back, staring into the bleak of the barn, the animals clamoring again with excitement and need, my eyes were drawn like a winched rope to a row of pegs on the far wall. I scurried forward down the aisle where not long ago I had splayed totally defeated as a being. I put my fists into my eyes and turned them in the sockets, to rub away my disbelief. Then I had to reach out to touch it—first perceived as a gaping wound against the vertical boards but then fluidly mapping into something so familiar that I gasped. Hanging on its peg was my husband's black felt hat.

In short days, I set the farm to order. I released the chickens so they could poke about for worms and soak the sun into their feathers. The sheep were returned to pasture and tied to loggerheads so they could not wander into the low pastureland where Noah could still sail his ark. They would end with hoof fungus, to be sure, if they did. I pulled at the cow's udder, although she was too thin for milk. I turned her out as well, as I had no remaining winter feed.

I baked an Indian bread that the boy ate, but I could not chew its heavy coarseness and spit it into my hand. Instead I boiled cabbage and potatoes in a thin broth and spooned it into my daughter's mouth. While we slept, the weasel penetrated the fortress of the barn and slaughtered all but one. I had not heard even a squawk in the night and so was startled by the carnage.

"All my pretty ones? Did you say all? What, all? Oh hell kite! All? What, all my pretty chickens, and their dam, at one fell swoop?" I was talking aloud and to whom? I quoted the tragedy of kings but could summon no irony. "My beauties," I moaned. "My girls," I whispered, "how I will miss you." And I could feel a bitterness enter all my organs that I had ne'er to this day previously known.

One lonely, bewildered witness remained clucking after her lost sisters. She would not descend from the height of the barn beam that had saved her and from which she must have had a bird's-eye view of the massacre. She had not yet reached heaven with her sisters, but she knew that hell had flared its flames not far below her. She would not come down.

The one lone hen remained on the broad beam for days. Did she know that when she finally descended, as she must, it would be me and not the weasel who would slit her neck? I could not keep her if she would not lay, and surely the bloodbath would put her off laying. I would forfeit her beauty to feed my children, no doubt.

I located the clutch trap that had begun to rust in its damp sack and took it out to behind the barn. I oiled the springs. I saw how the iron teeth of the clutch would snap on the leg of the animal. I tucked my skirts up into my apron band and carefully stood on each rim and stuck a thick stick and then a log in its jaws until the undersides flattened to the ground. I backed away cautiously with my legs wide. Our house mousetrap had produced a mouse to set for bait, and I dropped it carefully in the center so that the weasel would have to crawl across the trigger for it. I tied the dog up in the barn so he would not become three legged. I warned the boy to the spot.

I could not keep my mind from the set trap. The revenge of my hens occupied every turn and corner of my mind. With effort, I pushed my thoughts to other things— my work, my children's blessed recovery—but I was as soon drawn to the might of iron teeth that would crush and maim as I had bid them. I was impatient because I was frightened. My aviary was devastated, and now I must borrow for chicks as well as a piglet. My dependence put me in a dour frame of mind. The world had become unfriendly, or perhaps always had been. It was one misfortune to lose a husband but quite another to lose every chicken. Now, that is true calamity.

The forces of nature had threatened to burn up my children with fever at the same time as sending a deluge to drown them, and now the fates conspired to starve us. Was it the forces of nature that had abducted my husband? I could not fathom, for in my mind he had abandoned us. In the light of the mornings and the heat of my labors, the sentiments that the icy deluge had brought to my heart were desiccated—dry as bone.

Now that sunshine brightened the days, I settled that I had heard my son calling me as he leaned into the storm from the kitchen door. Hearing such a sound distorted on the wind, I had simply conjured an image of my husband in the portal of the barn out of desperate need to imagine that I had once been cared for. His hat? It had been hanging on its peg all along, for who had the wherewithal when working on the demands of the barn to notice its ornaments? Surely he had owned two and left this one behind to haunt me. Now that I knew that the ghost of my husband had come back to mock me in my tenderness toward him, a vengeance swelled in my joints, and my brain rallied from the lull of its fever to dwell on the trapping of my enemy.

I rounded the corner of the barn and immediately locked gaze with the suffering animal. The eyes did not ask why but were full of rage. The animal was more than twice as big as a weasel. I had not expected such a size. Nor such a look. I think they called this one a fisher. They were known to clean out coops and murder beyond their appetites. I stood still.

I too had rage in my heart that had quelled any curiosity as to the nature of my suffering, and this was not likely to help me. Now what? I must calculate. I could see that the trap was too heavy for the fisher to move much, but I had to know how much it could move. "How dare you thwart my industry and slaughter my innocents? My poor, defenseless, silly girls, who layed for me so well!" I stepped forward, and it lunged but covered no ground and reared back and screamed a low, growling scream. I saw that it could make a circle. The beast could pivot with its torment at the center. I looked to see how the leg was engaged in the trap, and it was clutched well above the paw, which had swelled to a round black ball.

As I examined the animal's dilemma and my own, my son came around the corner behind me. I warned him away. He stopped and did not move, and there we were—mother, son, and trapped animal.

"What are you going to do?"

"I don't know. But we must kill it. It is harmed. I have harmed it." He looked to me with curiosity and something else on his face. The fisher let out a renewed growl, mean and low. "Go get an empty grain barrel." My thoughts were flat and incomplete. I thought at first if I could get it in a barrel and a lid clamped, I might throw it in the pond, where it would fill up with water and sink.

I did not move, and the fisher turned and gnawed at his wounded quarter, leering back at me from time to time. The boy came, and I held the top rim of the barrel in front of me and walked it toward the animal, which went wild with gnashing.

"What are you going to do?"

The truth was that I knew but little about what to do. I had no answer for the son who looked to me. I was weak minded from my days of fever and lacked ingenuity, strength, and intent, all of which were sorely needed to vanquish such an enemy. A life's pulse is not so easy to extinguish. Blood vibrates and swirls, especially in a creature as wild as this one. The heart wants to beat and labors faithfully on, the lungs take in air, will grasp for it. Though wounded and doomed, the animal was still vibrantly alive with the rage of betrayal and the urge of survival. I knew that rage and urge. Sensibility lingers behind the eyes, muscles release and contract, the viscera do their internal work relentlessly until well after the mortal injury; until well after the violence of the intent has been observed. I could not help but see myself in this creature. And how I despised it.

I told the boy to go ask Mr. Hommelbeens to come and bring his musket. I sent him off firmly and went to the barn to get the hoe and the wood hatchet. Then I walked with determination and dread back to my captive. I backed the animal to the wall of the barn, and it twisted its supple body. It was quiet now. I put a barrel upright so that it had little room to maneuver. I turned the axe on its side and raised it up over myself. I could see my shadow on the barn boards. With all the might of my muster, I swung it down aiming for the head, but I smashed its back. It did not scream but looked at me from where it had fallen on its side, and those eyes locked to mine without judgment but with wonder. Did I see pity there? For surely I was most pitiful when I raised my arms again and smashed its head with the thick side of the axe.

I stood there, my legs shaking. I willed their stability. Sensing a constriction, a rent both in my throat and in the fabric of living, I gulped for air and took it in with a shudder. In the silence before the sun-bleached boards of the barn reaching for the sky, I heard a hiccough that I could not fathom. Then behind me it came again, and I twisted to know the creature from which the gasp sounded. My arms were pulled forward by the axe resting on the earth at my feet. I saw my son, who had stepped back around the corner of the barn. He had not gone for the musket as he was told but turned back along the track and come quietly around the corner of the noble structure of our barn to witness what his mother might be capable of—her own peculiar violence. His face was stricken now with disbelief and horror, his gaze riveted to the blood and brains on my apron that drained and dulled his eyes.

Judith Provokes Her Brother

The schoolmaster has returned! And with him come new books, I will wager! Winter is ending, and even if ice tears glisten on the branch tips at dawn, they are melted by the time my brother and I take to the track. An icy drop falls on the back of your neck, but the sun shines bright enough that you can feel it heat your skin. My mother had taught me verses of a great English poet! I cannot wait to tell the schoolmaster what I memorized over the winter and recite it all for him. I beg my brother to bring me and my mother to let us go because I was not allowed alone on the track. We must find out when school will start. I am not willing to miss even one day. The winter has been long and lonely, with nary a visit anywhere. I am tired of my days of chores and eager for new books and to meet other children.

We walk for an hour, and I am happy. The schoolhouse is shuttered still, but we approach and knock. No one answers. "Mr. Van Bummel!" I call out. "It is Judith. Are you returned?" The March wind whips behind me and causes my brother to pound again on the portal. Perhaps because we had stayed in the schoolroom in the fall, we are familiar enough to try the door, which is unlocked. So we enter. I am gladdened and excited to see the coals red in the hearth. It is true! The schoolmaster has returned and will surely show up to greet us.

I see a stack of books and pamphlets on the table and run to the front of the room to look at them more closely.

I pick up a folded paper and push it flat on the table. Across the front, I read the date and the title: *Boston Gazette and Country Journal*, March 12, 1770. I have never seen a newspaper before and do not know the word *Gazette*. I think it might be French. I puzzle over the big, black, curly letters across the top. Then the words "The Boston Massacre." I do not know the word *Massacre*, either, but I have heard it before. I think it is a very bad thing. Something concerning Indians.

I implore my brother to read the newspaper. And he seems curious enough to try. He leans over the table, spreading his elbows and pressing me to the side. "Tell me what it says," I beg him. He ignores me as long as he can, by fixing on the page. "Read it, read it," I beg him again. He starts out slowly:

"The town of Boston affords a recent and mel-an-choly de-mon-stration of the de-structive con-se-quences of quartering troops among citizens in a time of peace," he continues, moving forward hesitantly, "under a pretence of supporting the laws and aiding civil"—until he stumbles on the word *authority*. He starts again.

"Every considerate and un-pre-ju-diced."

"What does that mean?" I ask.

"No idea."

"But Brother, you must know."

"Well, I don't."

"You should study more," I scold him. "Then you would know."

It is true I am mocking him, as he is certainly a poor student. He is a boy and should do better. I am only just now eight, and I can read faster than he and interpret the text. He stops reading and turns his attention to the strap on his boot. "No, don't stop. Read it. Read it." I do not leave him be and buzz him like a bee. I whine. He begins again, this time whispering the words out loud, and I cannot help but laugh when he does not know the word *apprehension* and trips over it. I can see the red climb upon his face. He finally looks up from the newspaper on the table and turns his face to mine. He stares at me, and I look right back at him. Our gazes lock until he says the horrible words that I am not expecting and that make me wince.

"I am clever enough to know this, Little Sister," he says coldly. "Your father is dead, and your mother has hidden his body in the barn."

I catch my breath and cannot take another. I can feel my eyes sting with the disbelief of his words.

"What is your meaning, you wicked boy? My Papa is your papa too! And he is not dead! And my mother would not harm him. She is our mother!" In my confusion, I think that my mother could explain everything, but she is not here. "She would tell us the truth!"

Then he says more bad words. Worse and worse. He looks at the ceiling. "I am not born from her loins, but you, you little wench, you are her image. They found me under thorny branches in a glade. I am not his son! Nor hers! I come from another world. And I shall return to it. I will leave you alone with her, Bower Girl, and she will work you to the bone."

I squeeze my eyes so I cannot see him, but this makes his words echo in the room. I back away from the table into the aisle between the benches and start sobbing then, and the long, drawn hiccoughs hurt my chest. I look at him with shock and wonder. I can no longer stand on my legs and fall first to my knees and then forward to my belly upon the schoolhouse floor, my face to the crook of a wet sleeve. I cover my ears to hear him no more, but he is quiet again and lets me sob. Finally, all the air of weeping and wailing is finished. But, although I sigh and wait, he does not take back the words. Suddenly I remember the smell under my mother's petticoat. And I too am quiet. Does my brother know something that I do not?

Before a picture can form in my mind of what my brother might be getting at, in the very next moment, the schoolmaster stomps on the step and stands in the opened doorway and asks, "Judith, what are you doing on the floor?"

So discouraged was I by the bleakness of the prolonged winter that I knew I must garner some help. Now in early spring, before the farmwork would prevent me, I planned a visit to my brother. Since when I had ventured north to the native village, I had told my children and everyone that I had gone south to visit my brother, I now had to devise a curtain for the journey I had made in the fall. Oh, how true it is that one lie engenders others and can set you on the devil's path. I told my daughter the plausible story that the autumn visit with my brother had not been successful and left an unsettled feeling for my brother and me, so she was not, under any circumstances, to mention my previous visit or to refer to it in any way. This spring visit would be a new start in our family relations, and Judith could help make it so. Lies about my autumn journey, which had been to another place entirely, rolled easily enough off my tongue, and the injunction from referring to it might seem normal enough. Judith, at the age of eight, was already verbally astute and loyal to a fault, so I had every reason to believe she would collude in suppressing a topic that her mother wished to avoid. And God forgive me for exploiting the good in her.

Finally, in early March we trudged on the muddy track to the village and asked about a wagon going south. No one knew how this should happen. But ten days after the excursion, some Hans, a Palatine, who spoke German and hardly any Dutch or English, came to pick us up. We managed with Dutch. We packed quickly and closed up the house. I left the boy behind to care for the animals. We stopped to drop him at the neighbors. Could he sleep at their house and work for his dinner? He did not wish to show me his fear and abandonment, but I saw it. There was naught to do. I clutched the girl and waved bravely to him. He looked away. "We'll be back soon!" I called, but my voice broke in the wind, and the little one, not fooled, wept against my apron.

But for my dream of a journey to fetch magical herbs, I had never been anywhere, except along this road. I had grown up in view of both the southern yellow cliffs and the Blue Mountains to the north, but stayed in the Stone Ridge, never far from the town. The Stone Ridge was high ground, near to the quarries for the stone houses, just west of the Huguenot town of New Paltz and a good ways from the river where all the transfer of commodities—taxed or contraband—occurred.

My father's occupations, sloop building and trading, were a day's long ride from our village. He often took my brother south on the river to the great port of New York for his importing business, but he never took me. My mother was asked to stay home and manage her house and garden with me by her side. When I married, my husband left immediately for the Rondout, the port of the town, and it was there, not a week after my wedding, that he traded my dowry for farm tools and a contract to build a house. At the time, I did not mind, thinking there would be money for new gowns, tablecloths, pewter, and even porcelain and books in my future. I was surely in the hands of an admirer who would take care of me, money would come from the farm, and I was capable and cheerful myself. In two months' time, just after Easter, he returned for me, and I traveled by wagon through the big town near the state-house and church, all Dutch built and now under British governance, but still essentially Dutch.

We had traveled north along the great North River and circumvented the Vly, a large swampland, and passed by a sawmill and through a village of charming but rustic houses to the foot of the Blue Mountain. Our house was a little apart from the village, and my husband praised its location as the very finest. The house was built and thatched but did not yet have windows and doors, nor was it finished inside. He promised me a tile roof. There was a bed where we happily spent the week until there was no longer any food. These memories floated up to me on the dust from the track and distracted me, while my daughter peppered the wagoneer with questions about everything. He was kind and engaged with her, so I was left to my dreaming of old dreams.

After the day's long ride, we came after dark to the door, which my brother opened, and his new wife stood behind him in the entrance hall. My eyes went imme-diately to her tucker, which I saw was pinned with my mother's brooch. I had thought that brooch buried with my mother, but I guess my father had been mistaken. We were brought into the parlor and sat in the high-back chairs until my daughter nearly fell over with fatigue. Then we were taken to a familiar room, and we slept in the rope bed of my childhood.

I should have come before Christmas. The end of winter is a stingy time. My brother and I did not really know each other. He and his wife were lodged comfortably in my father's house. I had no gifts to bring, although it seemed to me that they wanted for nothing. Because of my father's business, they had many new things, even in these times of want, and because they lived on in my parents' house, they had all the old things too. It was odd to hear English spoken, but that is what they spoke together, and in such a pattern that I could not understand. And their little looks and smiles I also found uninterpretable.

"Brother, I wish to speak to you. My husband did not return after a hunting trip this past summer. However, his dog returned. The villagers searched. He may have fallen from a cliff, or sunk into the Vly, or suffered some other misfortune."

"I am so sorry, dear Sister," he said in Dutch with a veil over his eyes. I waited, not wishing to overstate my case but fearful that it was not well understood. Now the cow was out of the barn. I waited to see who would milk her.

My brother left me alone with his wife. We could hardly converse because she spoke no Dutch, and I could bring forth only a little English. It was odd to have the servants prepare the food, as I spent so much time at it on the farm, and I knew not what to do with my hands. I set about to visit my mother's friends. One had died, one had widowed and moved to her sister's in another town, but yet another invited me in for tea and hung hard upon my arm with her bad breath and all the gossip. My brother's marriage was a topic. His young wife was not beloved; she refused to attend the Dutch church. She passed by on the street without greeting. Her friends came in carriages and stayed at the town inn.

I thought that her unpopularity in the village should give me common ground with my brother's wife, but we did not find it. She told me she often went to Fort Orange, which is where she had met my brother. My brother had lodging in a fine house, and there she saw her friends and had connections through her family. She said she would invite me, as she was sure that they would spend Easter there, and I could buy new clothes, as she knew a fine dressmaker and milliner. My daughter's face brightened with delight but darkened again when she caught the bewildered look on mine. I had worn my best gown and jacket and knew not that they were wanting. It became apparent that my brother's wife could not or would not put her attention to my predicament.

After dinner, I requested a private audience with my brother. Did my father leave a will?

"No, he had not."

Men made wills knowing they would die.

"Our father was not so old."

"I believed," I blushed and coughed, "that we should inherit equally."

"Sister, Sister, this is simply not so. Under Dutch custom and law, it would be so, but we are now and have been for many years under British law, and women do not inherit and must live through their husbands. No court will grant you. I wish you no hardship, but our good father provided you with a dowry, and your husband did with it what he willed. Your farm is still productive; your husband may return. I can provide you with surplus from our business, but times are hard, and the features of our economy are ever changing and challenge my acumen constantly. We need the house here to start a family and to provide security if ever importation shuts down completely. The Stamp Act was withdrawn, but the British King will keep to his purpose of exacting wealth from his colonies in any way that it can.

"Besides, it was I who ran the business for these years and sheltered our parents in a changing world. You knew nothing of their troubles and did not return to care for them. Our father stubbornly made decisions in the old way and did business only with Dutch companies. We lost much wealth, and I have mortgaged our houses. I am endeavoring to reestablish the business on terra firma. But to tell you the truth, for reasons I hardly expect you to understand, I spend an enormous effort negotiating a complex politics, and I have seen little profit yet. I have a new set of contacts through my wife's family, Tories and Whigs among them, and these must be developed with great caution, as to do business with one set often offends the others."

For all his emphasis on the perils of business, I could see that my brother's profit was first committed to pleasing his wife, and that she was not a person so easily satisfied.

"Sir, you know your business well, and I wish you prosperity in all your endeavors. But Brother, I am quite alone—"

Before I could finish what I meant to say, he interrupted, "Sister, I cannot offer you shelter in our house with your two young ones. I am about to start a family with a new wife. She cannot care for you and nieces and nephews."

"No, this is not what I ask for." I heard myself tell him

that I loved the farm at the foot of the Blue Mountain and that I did not wish to leave it. My loyalty to my farm echoed in my own ears for the first time. "But if my crops fail or my livestock sickens, my children will not have food. And the life is hard, the work is endless, and for one, near impossible."

"Then Sister, what do you ask of me? What could remedy your position? Shall I find a place of service for you in a fine household? It will be difficult for you with the two children . . . but if you like, I will use my connections."

In the end he gave me three gold coins, which I was grateful for. I covered them with cloth and sewed each to my vest as a button. The transaction was businesslike, as he displayed little empathy for my circumstance, and I did not imagine that he felt any. That night, I heard arguing between them. I could not understand a word and was grateful to be leaving the following morning. In the wagon, my daughter told me that she had heard her aunt speak of us to her friend as "Cheeseheads," and what could this mean? I told her it was a compliment about the culinary skills of Dutch women, and she should hold her head proud. "But how could she know them? We ne'er did cook for her," my daughter observed astutely. I said that no, the taste of our good cheese had not graced her lips—and her remark was not empirical but based on our reputation.

I gave the boy a gun. I had little money, but I had gathered what I could from the corners of my house and sold some porcelain and wool. A gun is dear. And more for the powder. But my husband had walked off with his in his hand. I had seen it on his shoulder, pointed back toward me. I had been asking in the village for one since we caught the fisher in a trap. Mr. Stroop said he would inquire when he went to the ships at the Rondout. Muskets were precious, and men held on to them. He finally located a man who would sell, and we had stopped to make our purchase on our return from my brother's house. I know he made a good profit, but we had to have it, and I held my tongue. We had lived well from the garden and dairy through the autumn, but the winter had taught its lesson. We needed a gun. I cautioned my daughter to keep it secret from my son and hid it among the stores we had brought back with us in the wagon.

I surprised him on his birthday and told him he was nearly a gentleman. I could see the delight in the boy's eyes. He begged me to let him go immediately to Mr. Hommelbeens so that a skilled huntsman could show the boy the oil, the locking, and the loading, which he had promised me he would be happy to do. But I made him wait until I could venture with him. I wanted to make my intentions clear and to ensure that our neighbor's promises didn't turn into our indebtedness. I asked Mr. Hommelbeens to take him to the woods and to teach him to stalk game. Again, I got nothing from my neighbor but the most gracious and generous cooperation. Indeed, during all my season's tribulation, there had been not one villager who had not exceeded my meager expectation. Mr. Hommelbeens was no exception and was not anything but kind.

On the walk home, I lectured the boy at length about his responsibilities. He solemnly agreed with me about everything. Now he had a gun. I could see his pride. He pointed it at all the birds and little animals that he had regarded up to this very moment as his friends and made a sound with his mouth of annihilation.

Now all the boy did was wander in the woods. We set traps for small game, and I made him learn to skin them on boards. He did not like it and still did not hesitate to ask me to do it or to beg me to help him. One day I heard shots echo, and he marched into the yard with a turkey. Together we singed its feathers off. Its breast was full of shot, and its legs were stringy, but I boiled up its bones. Soon after we had venison.

I began to see less and less of my boy, and although he often put meat on our table, he attended less and less to what I asked of him.

As the light lengthens my days, I think less and less often of my husband stamping his boots on the doorsill and looking at me beneath the wide rim of his hat, which, not having been of especially good quality and certainly past its prime, fell a bit too low over his eyes, so that his face was in shadow. I no longer waken in the night thinking he has called my name from across the pond, beckoning me into the woods on the other side. His face has blurred in my mind to the shadow beneath that hat.

Now that spring has arrived in earnest and I have sorted

all my seeds and traded for others, they are planted in pots or in the ground, and each leafing is a reassurance. Some of them sprout within a week, and who cannot feel hope when the frailest little stalks push through the dirt and you can see them yearning to the edge of their pot for the light that comes through the barn door.

But the first sure sign of spring, and the one that saves us, comes early at the foot of the Blauwberg. It had signaled us months previously and rescued us from winter's stinginess because all the other signs can come so late. Hard frost and snow and freezing rain are known as late as May and punish all the seedlings, robbing us of their too-early promise. The cold cast of winter can linger with a persistence that defies all hope.

The sign that heralds spring comes as early as March when the sap of the sweet maple starts to run. Even I become part of the village then. For we all tap whatever trees we can find and carry the raw, runny sap to a big cast-iron vat in a smoking shack, and the men of the village bring wood in their wagons and take turns through the night with a jug of warmed jenever while stoking the fire. And then the women come with clean glass jars to fill them, and everyone starts baking again. And the sweetness of life, which has been frozen in the stiff bleakness of winter, is released and remembered. We can smell it again in our own houses, taste it on our tongues.

The run of tree sap staves off April's despair, as April is never as warm as we hope it to be. We pour its sweetness over bread baked on pallets because dough made from Indian meal is too coarse to rise in our ovens. These are the last dull meals we eat patiently before the world turns green and abundant again and spring wheat can be ground at the mill. Now it is safe to set out seedlings in ordered rows, and the promise of their fruit is succor in and of itself.

Mr. Hommelbeens brings a ram called King George for my ewes. And I explain to the girl that they are actually not exactly frolicking. The boy walks quickly away with a turned back. He does not wish to hear such things from his mother.

I have to say I had thought my husband handsome. And not just in his features. His hands and feet were beautiful, and I found the shape of his legs but perfect, like those of a fine horse. He was known as a great teller of stories, which he spun to anyone. Men at the tavern and children were equally delighted. Often a joke was embedded in them that could be most clever. But even as his village audience implored him for entertainment, it was his greater pleasure to procure the jenever and bring it home and spend his hours at the ledge above the pond, speaking to none.

He was gentle and popular with the village children, for what other man would stop with them most of the afternoon to weave a whistle out of grass or to capture frogs in the road ditches after a rain? Yet even all but the youngest children had ideas about industry that were beyond his scope, and when the boys set to mind to build a boat or a tree castle, he would wish them well and wander off. Really, he craved to be alone, with no demands made of him.

Whatever it was that fueled my relationship with my husband—a leaky assemblage of love and fear, bitterness and happiness, dread and longing and intent—was this also the fodder that heated the quaint farmhouses of my neighbors? Certainly there were other women who were not content and other marriages in the village that were hardly peaceful or prosperous. Were other husbands good?

Not that my husband was not good. He had not a meanness or cruelty in him. He just did not like to be asked to do anything. He liked to manage his own task list, and to have very little on it. He had a way of thinking that put any large endeavor to another day, and which let the smaller chores slide into the shadows. But who amongst us did not know that *Langs de straat van straks komt men aan het huis van nooit:* "Later-streets lead directly to never-houses"? You will never plow a field by turning it over in your mind.

And there had been days when he would beckon me to discuss at great length the work he did perform, calling upon me to admire it. After offering my praise and gratitude, if I would point to a method perhaps more efficient or move too quickly to the next need, it would be too much for him, and a great swell of tiresome argument would roll between us. And in aftermath, the silence between us lasted for days, sometimes weeks.

If I were to ask him—when he was eating a chicken that I had fed and cared for and then caught, slaughtered, scalded, plucked, and roasted—whether he held it to be a man's task to behead the chicken and remove its feathers, he would launch into a long discourse about whether I owned the chicken, as I had fed it, and whether he had any say in my decision to cook a chicken today, or whether I had made the decision independently. And as I had not asked him first whether it was a chicken-beheading day, according to his preferences and priorities, which I had not sought or heeded, he was not obliged in the least to the chicken. He carefully worked out these discourses. He was oriented in his effort to speech and not tasks. He was much aggrieved that I found him nonsensical. I should have known or should know now it was not his idea to roast a chicken, and therefore he had no responsibility in bringing it to table—even though he was eating it.

Soon, realizing there would be no roasts excepting the ones I brought to table, I did not mind the breaking of a chicken's neck. The first time was awful. I had selected my favorite for slaughter. The one I called Elizabeth (after the Queen), who came to me when I called her and layed for me so well. Perhaps I should have called her Mary for the Queen of Scots, or Anne Boleyn, or by the name of any other woman slaughtered for the necessity of men.

She had been my very favorite. The color of her feathers and the pattern upon them were as pleasing to me as would be a new gown. I wanted to butcher her first, for if I beheaded her sister before her, she would surely take note, and I did not want Elizabeth to come to me when I clucked to her, never knowing but always suspecting that she might be next. And I did not wish to take her eggs knowing I was soon to betray her.

That is how I often came to have bits of chicken liver on my apron, and down stuck to my cheeks with blood and tears. At least the fisher never got Elizabeth. She had been done in by my own hand. After Elizabeth was in our pot, and after we had eaten her tender flesh, I lost all sentiment to the rest. I gave them a good life, and when their time came, I killed them easily enough.

Today I am glad he is gone. Who could know such a feckless man? Or depend upon him?

Judith Borrows Books

Summer is approaching, and my father has been missing for the whole winter. I pray each night he will come back to me and tell me stories. My mother is so often tired at bedtime. I am too busy in the daytime to remember my father's absence, and no one at school mentions it. My mother says that children can get used to almost anything. I have too many chores to do, and the house is always cold. My mother sends me to the barn to fetch the milk pans. I am afraid to go into the barn, for it is clammy and full of shadow, and the doors swing behind you with a great clap. I have no new clothes.

I look forward mostly to school days. We did have a lesson from that Boston newspaper that my brother had tried to read to me that day at the empty schoolhouse before the term had started. In this lesson, I learned the meaning of the words *gazette* and *massacre* and *unprejudiced*. Mr. Van Bummel read with indignation the account and taught us all its terrible meanings.

The Boston Gazette and Country Journal
NO. 779

BOSTON, MARCH 12.

The Town of Boston affords a recent and melancholy Demonstration of the destructive Consequences of quartering Troops among Citizens in a Time of Peace, under a Pretence of supporting the

Laws and aiding Civil Authority; every confiderate and unprejudic'd Perfon among us was deeply impreft with the Apprehension of these Consequences when it was known that a Number of Regiments were ordered to this Town under fuch a Pretext, but in Reality to inforce oppreffive Meafures; to awe & countrol the Legiflative as well as executive Power of the Province, and to quell a Spirit of Liberty, which however it may have been bafely oppof'd and even ridicul'd by fome, would do Honour to any Age or Country.

Mr. Van Bummel explains everything. Prejudice means when you make up your mind about something before you know what it is about. There was a massacre in Boston which had nothing to do with Indians after all. Soldiers in red coats had fired with muskets in the square in the great town of Boston, and four good men had been killed. And before that, they had killed a boy my brother's age! Murder! That is what a massacre is, except that when there is more than one person killed and they are all uniformed soldiers on one side, it is called a massacre.

I think these newspaper words sound proud, the way that Mr. Van Bummel reads them, and although I have never seen a British soldier, I hope I never will.

The schoolmaster is nice to me and lends me books. Often they are too difficult for me to read, but my mother helps me. If I can catch her before she grows too tired or when she is not pressed by an intention to finish some chore, she will read to me quite a bit. I can tell it pleases her. Reading words on a page seems easier for her than making them up or remembering the old stories as my father had.

Reading in English is difficult, but most of the books are in English, so I am getting quite good at it. The pamphlets and newspapers too. The schoolmaster lends us something called a dictionary, one for Dutch words and one for English. He really has a lot of books. He travels to Boston three times a year to buy them. We ask him English words we do not know and that are not in the dictionaries. He says we have to return them soon.

I still sing Dutch songs but will learn an English song one day. And perhaps one in French.

> *Kortjakje is always ill,*
> *In the middle of the week, but not on Sundays.*
> *On Sunday she goes to church,*
> *With a book full of silver.*
> *Kortjakje is always ill,*
> *In the middle of the week, but not on Sundays.*

My mother says this song is about a lazy girl, and I am not that. I sense it means something else to her, but I don't know what it is. She does not answer, though I ask her more than once.

The morrow is my twenty-eighth birthday—ten months and a hard winter from my husband's disappearance. I have definitely lost weight, and my clothing sags. There is no one to remember it. I want to honor my twenty-eight years, for I've heard tell that the giant planet Saturn will return to the orbit it spun at my birth, and it is during the two and a half years of its orbit that you can reshape all the structures of your life. Your future can be unlocked. A person has such an opportunity but once in a lifetime or, with luck, perhaps twice.

I am loathe to tell the children, who will not remember the day for sure, and who have nothing to give me but what they might find in the forest. I do not want sympathy from the women in the village, because it is so often accompanied by the smugness of the partnered and the pragmatic. If it is not a day of capricious snow but spring in earnest, I will venture to the woods myself, making an excuse to Judith to beg a friend's family for dinner after school and sending the boy to play or hunt.

The day and month of my birth is also the birthday of the Bard. I read this in the introduction to the portfolio of dramas that was written by the English wit and scholar Dr. Johnson. He is the gentleman, I believe, who provided us with the English dictionary that the schoolteacher has kindly lent to us. I have managed quite a bit with reading English, although I still cannot speak it well. And I think to take the poet's precious tale of midsummer to a warm rock in a sea of ferns. This play my daughter also borrowed from the schoolmaster, who has purchased eight volumes at the London Book Shoppe on Boston's Cornhill Street from the famous, fat Mr. Henry Knox. We have had it at hand through much of the winter, and it seems to mock my sorrows. Though I struggle with its English, I can turn the lines one at a time through my mind, as they have such a persistent rhythm. By turning them again and again, and if you imagine the characters, the meaning comes forth. And it makes me laugh. Such as when the women scratch each other's eyes. And when a man grows donkey's ears and yet knows not he is an ass. On such a rock with such a tale, I can wonder if my husband was bewitched by faeries and will come back to me when herbs are set upon his brow. After all, he disappeared on just such a midsummer's night. Or I will wonder how the true love that was Thisbe's, illuminated by the moon and declared by Pyramus through the chink of a wall, passed me over?

I will not be distracted by hunger for my favorite foods and memories of anniversary days when the wheel of the year turned in a world with prospects. Some think of us bower folks as naïfs, but our souls are fed by more than mountains and hard work in the fields. I have turned the lines of poetry in my heart like a lathe, and like a lathe they have shaped me. I speak them aloud for comfort. The poet's sonnets (also a book we managed to borrow) were among them and made me wonder if he had had a wife. Were they at peace with partnership? Or was he distant and dreamy, leaving her to boil the laundry and feed her children—whom he begot and then forgot? His world was a stage, but her shoes touched the ground.

My husband did not give me gifts, nor even remember my day, so why should I miss him now? *Waar de zon schijnt, is de maan niet nodig?* "Who needs the moon, when the sun is shining?" Perhaps I long for him because he remembered the words of great poets and once whispered them in my ear, after his kisses had covered my body. I was most astonished. His comfort in aimlessness was good for winter nights and late-summer afternoons of courtship and for lovely evenings before our son was born. He coaxed my more industrious tendencies quiet, and I would sneak away with him with secret glee and admiration, of course, for his daring entitlement. "Cease your buzzing, Little Bee, and let me lick honey from your fingers." It was only with the spent dowry and the call to prosper by the means of our own labor that he sought as much companionship and empathy from a dog, and his entitlement became my burden.

Today, though, I cannot worry and regret. The rain that falls today won't fall tomorrow. And the rain that fell yesterday cannot fall today. He cannot disappear again. And I cannot be more alone than I am today. Ah, even as my tongue ever turns to the nerve in my tooth, let me immerse myself in the luxury of these verses about finding the truest of loves in the shortest of nights.

PART II

❖

In a woman's education, little but outward accomplishments is regarded . . . surely the men are very imprudent to endeavor to make fools of those to whom they so much trust their honour and fortune, but it is in the nature of mankind to hazard their peace to secure power, and they know fools make the best slaves.

—ELIZABETH MONTAGU,
correspondence, 1743

CHAPTER 4

Blue Stockings

Spring 1777

Independence I have long considered as the grand blessing of life, the basis of every virtue; and independence I will ever secure by contracting my wants, though I were to live on a barren heath.

—Mary Wollstonecraft,
A Vindication of the Rights of Woman:
With Strictures on Political and Moral Subjects, 1792

B LUE. SHE SAID she wanted them blue. Now, why was that? To match her eyes? I had done what I could to get her clothing that suited her. I had pulled out my mother's gowns and traded a pewter candlestick for trimmings and then sent her to Dame Van der Vlieck, who had patterns from Europe, to have them recut with a trade of wool and sheep's cheese. Of evenings by candlelight, we squinted to sew them in a new style with new trimming. We made her a stomacher and a fine Brunswick jacket as well. What would I need of such a candlestick? No one came to dinner. And all pewter would be called up to General Washington's Continental army, no doubt, within little time.

My daughter looked more and more lovely, and more and more she turned her loveliness away from me. I had carded, spun, and knit many a stocking. But the plants I knew dyed them yellow or russet or, of course, grey. It was difficult to get a black to set. And indigo was impossibly expensive—and now impossible to get. I had not a substitute that came close. Our local berries, both huckle and juniper, were more red than blue and faded readily to a dull brown. We used to get the indigo from South Carolina, and it was cheaper then than it had ever been. A woman farmer, by her own ingenuity, had produced enough to export, I had heard, on a bower in the southern colony, with hundreds of slaves that she managed herself. She was supplying all of Europe with her trade and had thus become famous. But by now all that had ended, and we had nothing from anywhere—no dyes, no cloth, no sugar nor salt. And now my recalcitrant daughter insists her stockings must be blue. Only red was more expensive. And, of course, we did not wear the King's colors.

She pulled one of my stockings over her hand and up the length of her arm. "See how coarse these are," she said. "My friends in the village have finer." But I used my thinnest needles to knit them. She stamped her foot (in yellow stockings), and I could see her contempt toward me. I could not contemplate her rudeness in the face of what I had tried to provide—a goodwill, considerable skill, and my industry—all to her benefit. Never mind my mother's gowns. I turned my face away from hers. I did not want her to see the pain in my eyes.

I needed her now more than ever. A strange and cruel turn had ripened among the villagers as the idea that one had to choose sides took hold because our peaceful little life was threatened. As war carried on, a general unease congealed into a neighbor's suspicion of neighbor. With General Washington defeated in the capital of New York, we grew fearful, and fear did not make us friendly. I, for one, felt the village to be icier than it had ever been in any season. One day at market, I overheard some vicious children younger than my own, hiding not far behind their mothers' petticoats, remark out of the sides of their mouths, "Mother. Wait. Trade with Dame Schoonmaker, not this one." One mother turned to her daughter and leaned low to her child's ear to catch her whisper, which was purposefully discernible. "Who would want to eat foods cooked in the cauldron of a witch?"

To my great indignation, the young mother did not correct her nor say anything to me, although I could tell by the look on her face that she had heard what I had heard. I snatched my cheese round that she was turning in her hands and returned it to my basket. My sausages were tied to a string around my waist and dropped long between the pleats of my petticoat, and one of the girls, encouraged by the other mother's tolerance, mocked me. "She has no remains of a husband—or perhaps only one remain," she said, pointing to the stuffed appendages hanging from my waist. "What has happened to the rest of him?" These words spilled forth, and hearing such a daring petition from her own mouth, her eyes widened and her corpus doubled down with laughter.

In the moment's disbelief, I glared pointedly to their faces, and then my amazement turned to defiance. But I was speechless. I tried to summon a suitable invective to match the insult that had been tendered toward me but could not. The children skipped away, shooed by their scowling mothers, who swatted playfully after them, and I could not help but see the flicker of a smile beneath their frowns. They returned to the pending commerce between us and told me to pay no mind, that their children had heard tales they could not interpret and the imagination of children cannot be curbed in these violent times. The women's words were hardly apologetic, but they coveted my cheese and expected their patronage would suffice to make amends.

Humiliated, I removed the waxed wheel again from my basket, placing it in their hands, and named my price. Eyes on the cheese round, they bid lower—a bit too low for a full cheese round salted and cured with the best rennet. I hesitated. It was perfectly customary to bargain at trade, and I knew myself as a buyer that I must start low and come to where I was willing. But bargaining is a game one plays with neighbors, knowing that a mutual goodwill will get to fairness, if not in this transaction, then in another. Suddenly I could not bear these two, to transact with them at all. I snatched the wheel, turned on my heel, and strode away, not looking back. They did not call out to me, and I did not mistake their laughter, which tickled the hairs on the back of my neck as my face reddened in the wind.

Now, seven years is a long time, and what I had ne'er before understood was that the village women's gossip cured and concentrated the flavor of a reputation, as jenever in a tub, cheese in a cloth, salted ham hanging on rafters. The stories about me had become more evil and outrageous as they aged. Their imaginations got the best of them. Now long removed from the actual event of my husband's disappearance, when they spoke about it to one another, their daughters heard them as they worked side by side but could not discern when their mothers' tongues were within their cheeks—wagging as they were like the tails of dogs. Everyone loves the misfortunes of others, and telling them again and again ensures against the odds of having them roost in your own henhouse. For surely such misfortune comes by chance to some and by invitation to others, and not at all to everyone.

When my husband first disappeared, his reputation—and mine through partnership—was already slippery, but we were tolerated well enough. If we had lived on together, the mockery of our marriage would have provided endless entertainment. The worst rumor that I could imagine, and that I had most feared, when my husband vanished was that he had taken up with another wife or a farmer's daughter. However, with no other local person missing, my neighbors did not seem to care all that much about the mystery. They stuck to the familiar village, sent their husbands abroad in pairs and threesomes, and forbade their children to play in the woods. I felt their pity but did not fathom that they may have had other suspicions about me. Had they not ignored me these seven years? Would they have if they really knew what happened in the shadows of our barn? If they could see into the hardness of my heart, would they have let me be? My sense had always been that they interpreted my husband's disappearance as the fate of a woodland accident. My shame had derived from the notion, in my mind and what I had assumed were the thoughts of others, that I had driven him away. But now I understood that some other calumny festered among their discontented imaginings, and I feared that to be named a witch, even by children, was near to hanging.

Judith Bleeds

More important than the war is the bleeding between my legs. I cramp until I vomit and wash rag after rag. How perplexing! My mother brews viburnum bark, which is bitter and dark. She makes me drink it down, but I grow pale and cold and will not go to school.

I was just thirteen when the war broke out and see now that I was then still a child. Now, two years hence, it comes to us. We had not seen it coming. All through the decade, there had been little talk of independence. No one dared mention breaking with Britain. True that an endless outrage about taxation without representation fueled all the debates. We had known the Sugar Act, the Stamp Act, restrictions on colonial trade, rum excises, and the quartering of British troops in the homes of the good people of New York City and Boston. But this meant little to me. And our neighbors could ignore these annoyances well enough, for what did they mean to the Dutch farmer hidden in the upper reaches of Hudson's River Valley? We had been evading British taxes all along with our unwillingness to open our fists to release the very few coins we ever garnered. Ever thrifty and industrious, we would import molasses and make our own crude rum. Nothing stood between a Dutchman and his drink, and the British Crown was no exception.

Now the discourse and its tone has shifted, even among the people of our sleepy village, to the formation of an American nation with its own government; no longer attached to any monarchy or to the notion of monarchy but founded on other principles entirely. All the large and famous Dutch families—the Van Rensselaers, the Schuylers, the Van Cortlandts—have chosen sides, and almost all for the Colonists. Not only that, but our valley had become the strategic theatre in which the British would sear the colonies apart and claim the greatest waterway in the New World. Oh, it is true. Some will not yet believe it. The Van der Bogarts, so long the stalwart influence of our village, clutch an old way of life so singularly Orange, by lion's tooth and lion's claw, and will not believe we are at war. But I know—I can feel it—that my life will be changed forever. Although I do not know how I will be swept away, I long for its unknown course.

I listen to Mr. Van Bummel tell me about the very foundations of democracy. Pericles was the first citizen in a democratic world, but even he had to rage in tears to protect his beloved Aspasia, and he warned, "Just because you do not take an interest in politics doesn't mean politics won't take an interest in you." This was Mr. Van Bummel's way of reminding us that we cannot close our eyes in our sleepy village to the larger political pressures—that the war will change the world as we know it. Democracy is a responsibility. He does not have to exhort me, however, as my mind is more and more enchanted with lofty and romantic ideas of freedom. The break from monarchy seems to have some bearing even on the particular situation of children, but I am not sure what.

I have strange feelings at the tips of my breasts. I think they have swollen, and I purposefully chafe them against the pleats of my corset. I lean over my desk at school and poke them with the end of my pen while pretending to concentrate on my writing. Instead of relief, I become entirely unable to find the next word in two half-formed sentences. I ask to leave the room for the privy and take as much time there as possible. I return only when I think my absence might be noticed.

Mr. Van Bummel reads us a poem written by a slave girl in Boston who is just my age! It was published in a newspaper! Can you imagine a slave girl who writes poetry? Why, she has even gained the attention of General Washington! He actually wrote her a letter! If slave girls can write poetry, then geese can lay eggs of gold, and all is possible. I can become more than a Dutch bower girl. We are American daughters!

The bleeding makes me a more serious student. My mother says I am not to worry. But what girl can be carefree with a war coming and rags wadded up between her legs? I squat over the chamber bowl and weep at the beauty of the crimson of my blood on the porcelain.

At least I don't fear to lose my father to the army. As my mother would say, that rain has fallen.

Talk of the war laced every table and, in fact, was the only lace for the table, as all cloth except for that on our backs had been sold to the armies. The boy worked in the village whenever he could and went to the river to unload boats. Now that the dog had died, he came home rarely, and I could not get him to help me as much as I required. The woodpile was perpetually wanting. My daughter too was not often at her chores. At least the girl came home every day, albeit with all sorts of ideas from Mr. Van Bummel about tyranny and taxation and the perfidy of the Albionic King.

Little could I imagine what all this had to do with us. I had long thought of the British as a primitive people because of their reputation for religious intolerance, palpable greed, unbridled aggression, relentless snobbery, poor performance, limited craftsmanship, and bad food. It was known that typically they smelled. Now all those people I had thought of as British were divided yet again into Tories and Colonists, and even good Dutch people—including my daughter—were calling themselves Americans. She pledged her loyalty to the new colony instead of the Dutch patroons, and went on and on about how the constitution of the new state of New York, drafted by a Mr. John Jay, who she said was famous, was to be adopted in the very town of Kingston, just eleven miles to our south. She insisted that having a declaration of independence and a state constitution forged in our vicinity, a stone's throw down the river, made it apparent that the break with the King had everything to do with us.

General Philip Schuyler, of course, was famous. I guess rich landed families had much to fight for, and it made sense that the old Dutch would never have wished to pay taxes to any British King. Still, in the village and even before when I had lived at the Stone Ridge, I had never thought of myself as anything but Dutch. This was so even when I read the Bard's plays and imagined myself as Rosalind.

It had been a cold winter without much snow, which meant the cold had come into the house, under my wool gown, and into my bones. In February we were depleted of stacked wood. I had to ask the boy over and over again to fell trees and split logs every single time I saw him, which was not so very often. I did not know where he went, and he came only sometimes to dinner and more often to sleep. He looked at me silently and did not answer. I never knew whether and when to ask him, but I needed that wood. Sometimes when days had gone by, I spent my mornings splitting it myself, which was a torture to my shoulders and back, as the axe was too heavy for me. If I asked for his service again, he would scowl at me. "Yes, I am to it. I heard you ask. You needn't ask again." And then the axe could not be found. He said I'd had it last, and I, him. He spurned me. "Mother, you should know that tool—its condition and whereabouts—as well as anyone." Now, what was his meaning in that? We could not buy a new one nor borrow one, and no neighbor had split wood to sell, even if we had the money to purchase it. You could not buy the labor. I thought we would end up burning our furniture.

My son had little idea about how desperate I had become. Although I had been as frugal as ever and went to bed when the sun set, I remember being warm but once or twice. I had longed for spring so I could bathe in hot water and step to my bed without pulling on wool stockings and undergarments.

Throughout the winter, the girl had often slept in my bed, as my room was warmer than hers, with the chimney rising through it. We warmed bricks for the bed in the supper fire and often retired immediately after it. In spite of the heated bricks, the first one in shivered and waited in a knot. The boy had slept in the kitchen and was gone by the time I arose to milk.

As the days lengthened, when winter was reluctantly yielding to spring but not without a fight of freezing, my daughter sought her own bed again and spent more time at school and less time at the farm. Because of the war, the schoolmaster had not traveled this winter to Boston, and to earn his keep, he lengthened his sessions at the schoolhouse. Judith attended, of course, and took on the task of teaching the younger children in the morning, had lessons with some her own age in the afternoon, and stayed late for tutoring in French and the more difficult texts. She was close to fluent in English and not bad at French. She had stopped coming home for dinner but wrapped food in cloth after the morning chores and set off for the day. So I was alone. When the naked branches tapped my kitchen window with ice at their tips, I jumped with a start.

Judith Listens to Her Brother

He says he cannot stay in our little village, especially on the farm. He will see the country with George Washington's army. He will not be a farmer. He tells me he will learn to play a pipe, and he will play notes for freedom. I have never seen someone so fervent and eager to get away, but it is difficult to discern what he is thinking. And I say to him, "Do you not love us? Your mother? Your sister?" He says, "It is not so. It is just that I must get beyond this village—these little mountains with their long blue shadows. I am meant for something else."

"But you may die for General Washington. In the cold and snow. I hear his armies go hungry. And that cannons will blow your ears out, or wipe your nose from your countenance or explode your pate. Mr. Van Bummel says that the British are brutally executing prisoners."

"I will die if I stay here. I must go."

When he sees the sorrow on my face, he says, "But Judy, *meidje* . . ." and I look at him hopefully, that he can find within our familiar the sentiment and duty to comfort me, his only sister. But he only goes on to his own odd justifications. "Judith, I cannot stay. Have you not heard what they say about our mother? Have you not heard the things they say? Have you not noticed that none of our neighbors will buy her sausage?

"They covet her cheeses, *ja*, and despise her *worst*. Milk, *zeker*. Wool, to be certain. Her pickled vegetables. Jam. But have you ever tried to sell her sausage? At any price? I once offered her sausage to Mr. Hommelbeens as a trade for powder. When he saw that *worst* was all I had brought, he insisted on making me a gift of the powder. I saw the look that passed between Dame Hommelbeens and the man when one of his dogs came up to me and snatched the *worst* from my hand where I stood in the yard and engorged it in one gulp. Dame Hommelbeens remarked that now I had given the dogs a taste of my mother's sausage, they would eat anything and everything and howl at the moon for more. But the laughter between the man and his wife, and the joke between them . . . was more than a bit forced."

I ask my brother what he thinks this means: Mr. Hommelbeens's dogs snatching and devouring my mother's hard work, which no one else would have, and the mockery from our most friendly neighbors. But he shakes his head and counters stubbornly with his own questions: "Judith, do you ever think of what happened to our father? Do you even remember him? He was a good man, Judith. He would have come home if he could have. He knew the woods, Judith, like the back of his hand."

"And it's funny, like a peculiar dream, a fog in the clove . . . Judith, I remember seeing him in the barn again on the night of a big storm. I was fevered. But I think he did come home. He tried to come back to us. He must have. I remember him calling out to our mother . . . for her mercy, I think. For her mercy. And Sister, I must ask you . . . Do you think that she had any?"

I press him then, for I find his queries strange, and I cannot discern what meaning I should impute from them. I think hard and do not remember anything about such an evening. But the more I press, the more he retreats, and as I know it might be a long time before we meet again, I want this precious discourse between us to preserve the lighter moments of our childhood affinity. So I let it go and help him pack his meager belongings.

The night before my brother leaves, I have a dream I find almost shocking, except that it comes forth from beneath my own bed pillow. In it I play the part of an Indian maid, taken cruelly from my mother as a slave by a Hessian mercenary who threatens me with a glistening sword as I roll out piecrusts on his table. He barks strange utterances in a language I cannot understand, although somehow I know his meaning. He turns the flour crock with the tip of his sword so that it crashes to the floor. A white cloud engulfs us and transforms my auburn face and hands into the color of ice on the river.

Stranger than the dream itself is that I awake not frightened but steady, with the feeling of being prepared to face whatever the future will bring. I tell no one.

All males between sixteen and fifty years of age are required to enroll under penalty of fine, and regimental commanders are canvassing our districts. A bayonet, sword, or tomahawk, as well as a gun with a pound of powder and three pounds of bullets, must be furnished by each and every soldier. Imagine the expense! Professional men, firemen, millers, colliers, furnace men, slaves, those in public service, ministers, doctors, ferrymen are exempt, as are Quakers. But not sixteen-year-old farm boys.

So the boy had taken the musket, lock, stock, and barrel. We had argued over it. I knew I would need it, and I thought the militia should provide him one. And a uniform. But in the end he had just taken it—as if he had possession of it since the day he was born—with no courtesy to my sacrifice. With a sharp regret, I thought back to the day not so long ago when I gave it to him. It must have seemed like ages long past to him, but I knew it was but a moment ago that I had observed the sweet innocence in his eyes. Now even he spoke of honor—that those that crafted the Declaration had pledged to one another their lives, their fortunes, their sacred honor. That by signing they were traitors to the Crown and would be put to death if the Colonists did not prevail. But I knew what the Bard had writ: "Honor could not take away the grief of a wound. Honor has not skill in surgery. Honor is but a word. And what is that word honor? Air."

He had a new whelp that absorbed his affection, and he took the bouncing dog with him to the field. Though she was only seven months old I could only hope that she might protect him, and I charged her with the task by laying my hands upon her and whispering in her ear. He had but the one set of clothes, as he had grown so fast this past year I could not yield enough cloth to make new ones. His wrists crawled out of his jacket. I traded much to have boots made, for I could not send him forth into the larger world without them. It was too much to bear. I would give up a cast-iron pot to have boots made. He took the stockings my daughter rejected and stretched them thin over his enlarged feet. He did not complain, certainly, about their color. Nor did he particularly thank me.

We had heard much of the carnage at Lexington over two years ago. And had celebrated the retaking of Boston, when Mr. Knox brought his cannons to the hillside above the harbor. Indeed, it was the ingenuity and determination of a fat bookseller that turned the British ships to sail away! Last year the battles were in the big port city that Washington had lost, although he had gained other ground in strategies of movement in the New Jersey and Pennsylvania Colonies. We knew that now the British held the port of New York, they would try to overwhelm the great waterway of four hundred miles—which included the Lakes Champlain and George and went all the way to Canada. While we did not entirely understand all the details of the campaign, we knew that this would cut the northern Colonies in half, separating the East from the West, and contain New England from the southern Colonies. Now it was feared all fronts had moved northward and west, and the North River and its banks had become the epicenter of the drama. We would be ravaged by battles as the British troops moved down the lakes from Canada and then down-river to us. The British Navy would sail up from the port city, thumbing their noses at General Washington's river fortifications at West Point.

The New York Colony had become suddenly war frenzied, and all talk had shifted without a backward nod from unjust taxation to independence. We prepared with an urgency no Dutch village had seen since Stuyvesant had sent a contingent up to fortify Esopus from the natives over a hundred years ago. In April the Provincial Congress paid six hundred pounds to the Ulster County Committee for stockings and blankets. Shoemakers tanned hides and were exempted from service. The commissioners had come through the village buying up the cows and at least the wool from all the sheep, if not the sheep themselves. Also, substantial monies were paid for wheat, flax, hops, and hemp, as well as winter vegetables such as pumpkins, squash, cabbage, carrots, and potatoes. Boots were dear because they could be sold to the army at a good price, even if now the commissaries were paying in script, not coins. Those who could not fight were called to spin wool, and we heard that cloth workshops had been set up in the big town.

Now that all the men had been conscripted, the women were standing in my wooden shoes. We were left to trade with one another, but we mostly had the same goods. My butter for yours. My sympathy to their complaints was aroused over my considerable righteousness. Left alone on their farms with their daughters, as their men marched north to join Colonel Goose Van Shaick's First New York at Cherry Hill, they found that their husbands had worked harder than even they had imagined, and much to their ingrained offense at any wastefulness, hay was left to rot in the fields. At least it was a Dutch officer and a New York Colonial force, or the men would not have marched with any eagerness or marched at all. These farmers had not risked life on the outermost western frontier of the Colonies, separated from New England by the great but unbridged waterway of the North River, without deep suspicions of their mostly British neighbors to the east. Now these Brits were called Americans, unless they still groveled to their English King.

All as young as sixteen had gone. I could not plead that the boy was too young. Although he was. Yes, barely formed in his mind, and skinny and pale as a white birch. I could remember that until he was twelve, he lamented the chickens when we killed them. He cried when I took the sow to town. Five years hence, could he kill a man? He could now shoot a deer . . . but a man? Another boy? It seemed the worst sort of growing up. Once you had killed another man, could you feel free? Is that independence?

I clenched my fists at my sides and pulled at my night-gown in bed at night. To keep my worries from the trials that my son must face, I turned my attention to my daughter. What would become of her? How could she marry? I could not work out how to increase her opportunity and provide her with clothing. Try as I might, I could not imagine a life for her, except one as strangled as my own.

Many of the current conditions of the war I came to

learn at my own dinner table. For when my son had walked away with the musket, I had suggested, in an effort to keep my daughter content, that we invite her schoolteacher for Sunday dinner. He became my only adjunct to the larger world. It was a custom for the village schoolmaster to take Sunday dinner in a village house, but I had never invited him, my husband's absence making it improper to do so. Instead I had sent my children with eggs, cheese, and bread for his breakfast. But now with all the fervor and all the men gone, I would risk village tongue wagging. I had not so much to lose. It was not known if he had managed to pay the enormous sum that was required for exemption. This was doubtful. But when the farmers left, exchanging their strawhats for tricorns, they left without him.

He accepted my invitation with great eagerness and seemed to like it well enough to come most every week, braving the hour's march on the rutted track. Perhaps the women of the village had grown more stingy with their food stores and were feeling less generous with the men and boys gone, though they had fewer to feed. Or perhaps they had traded all to the colony commissioners for script. I, however, was used to the surplus of my own industry and for now was willing to share it.

Judith Becomes a Republican

I loathe the labor on the farm. Now that my brother is gone, it seems endless. My mother impugns me constantly. I have little time to read. Her desperation is palpable, although she reveals nothing. Her worry is a dusting sprinkled on every task. I no longer share with her what I have been learning. I spend as much time in the village, at the schoolhouse, as I possibly can. On Sundays I tell my mother that I go to church, and sometimes I do, but more oft I go to the schoolhouse to read.

At school the little ones refuse the afternoon tea, which, believe me, we are lucky to get. I explain to them that it is smuggled Dutch tea somehow unloaded from a sloep and brought from village to village up the North River. We then dip our bread into our cups and bowls, gleefully slurp, and forswear any taxed tea. We celebrate our stimulant. As children, although I now consider myself grown to a lady, we are naturally and intuitively delighted by the notion that rules can be evaluated by the likes of us. If you find a rule unjust, you can costume like an Indian, board a cargo ship, and toss its contents into the sea, all the while calling it a party. Our justifications become more elaborate and outraged as we play Colonists versus the King's subjects in the school yard. The older children tie up the little ones and mock them as Loyalists until they cry. Our play becomes a way to enact our favoritism. Being quite oblivious to the cruel undercurrents of our patriotic games, Mr. Van Bummel eggs us on.

I have outgrown these games and am more serious than anyone takes me for. Mr. Van Bummel tells me that the children act out what goes on among the people of New York. Everywhere in the Great River Valley, there is dissension and antipathy between neighbors. The Philipses chose the Crown and the Van Cortlands the Colony. But at whatever grade of society, landowners or tenants, families came asunder. Brothers turn against brother, and even more shocking, Mr. Van Bummel has heard that some wives have not followed the politics of their husbands. The people of our little village, to the contrary, and to our merit, I suppose, are all either in denial that a war could ever touch us or staunch for the Patriots. We do not waver.

The movement abroad for liberty from oppression and from bondage is stirring me to think about all sorts of things I have not thought about before. I am beginning to form some inchoate thoughts, mostly through the information that Mr. Van Bummel brings to me. I listen to him prattle on and on. He reads the newspapers, describes the New England and Philadelphia events at length to the men at the village tavern, although except for Mr. Vedder, who can barely get out of bed, and Mr. Hommelbeens, who is now deaf, they are mostly gone. Then in his frustration of finding no audience, he spills it over to the lessons at school. He has become obsessed and bombastic. He no longer attunes to the tenderness of the younger children. But I listen, as he speaks to me. And all of us, including even the very youngest child, are shimmering with new ideas. Taxation informs our studies of mathematics, we recite poetry that cries out for freedom with verve, and we sing "Yankee Doodle" while beating our study tables like drums.

I am no longer a Dutch villager but think of myself as an American daughter. King George, the monarch nobody was asking God to save, seems sullied and old hat. Mr. Vedder has finally taken down the portrait at the tavern, but not before it had been used as a dartboard. King George's cheeks showed the pox of a thousand darts, the end of his nose being the bull's-eye that hardly any drunken farmer could mark.

I am clearly on the side of futuristic ideas and excited by thoughts of a Nation. I notice that Mr. Van Bummel does not speak as seriously about his lofty ideas with the other children; that he seems to have some special intention for me. Now I think often of the world beyond my purview, imagining the path of my brother as he makes his way. How will I make mine? I dare not ask this question aloud, but I cannot doubt that it has formed within my mind.

It is now my habit to stay after school to sweep and put away the books. Mr. Van Bummel says that of course we Dutch have had little allegiance to the English King, in any case, and should not wink an eye to give it up. As a people, we had often been at war with the British, and we have toiled here for some generations now. We have the sod of the New World in our hearts.

So Mr. Van Bummel came to our table when he was not traveling to the big town for newspapers and pamphlets that had come upriver. Trips to Boston had been impossible, but more and more books were now circulating in the river valley. A book trader made delivery from New Jersey in a river sloep whenever he could sneak by the lower river embattlements, and Mr. Van Bummel went to the big town immediately whenever he heard a shipment had arrived, to ensure that he could have his choice of the new material.

I made especial efforts with my cooking and took to breaking one of my hen's necks on Saturday evening so that we would have a Sunday roast, as there was no meat from the forest with the boy gone. That was true in all the village, and my neighbor's tables, as well as mine, were adorned more with cabbage and potatoes than with game. It was easy to entertain Mr. Van Bummel, for not only did he clearly enjoy my food but he also talked incessantly about the most amazing and bizarre topics. He was happy to have a naïve and unschooled listener such as myself. Or perhaps he did not consider his audience at all.

If there were a pause in the dinner's discourse, I had merely to say "Goodness," giving but a little prod for another twenty minutes of rant that would come forth in a slightly pompous, certainly pedantic, and patronizing style. My daughter would blush at my ignorance, which she did not seem to realize was at least partially feigned, and interject her excited opinion to let her teacher know that she was not so unworldly and primitive as her mother. But even I knew that she was as least as naïve as I, but certainly, I had to admit, more delightfully charming. In any case, she too was soon silenced by the torrent of verbiage that poured forth from the orifice of Mr. Van Bummel between mouthfuls of my succulent roasted hen and Indian pudding with cream and maple syrup. He had so much to say, and he relished my food with such lust, that he was often chewing between, during, and after his speeches. I had never seen one person put away so much food.

It was a peculiar and onerous time. Mr. Van Bummel described in overwrought detail the fashion of Pox Parties, those dismal quarantines of those who purposefully inoculated themselves; so that we came to know the color of the pus that erupted upon the faces of the rich. He catalogued endlessly the specifics of the brutality of British soldiers, especially toward women. And barely aware of the effects on his audience, he hurried forth, before finishing his soup, with tantalizing particularity—almost, I would say, with admiration—to describe the fashions of the Loyalist women dressed in red silk who serviced them. This led him to tell of men living in the port town at the mouth of the river, where clean water had become scarce, who drank so much beer that they grew breasts like women and dressed like them to avoid conscription. And then: "Did you know," he went on without meeting my eye, "that there are women so devoted to the cause of our independence that they appoint themselves in breeches and bulky jackets disguised as men so that they can enlist? These women follow their husbands to the field and have been known to stoke and fire cannons." How did he hear such things?

For over a year, he had traveled each week, when he could hire a cart, to an inn in the big town. There he met with a group of men, and they read pamphlets and exchanged books. More than one weekly was available from the revolutionary presses. He returned to the village full of speeches he had composed on the wagon ride. He found that when he came back to our little village from the larger town, he encountered only a qualified interest among the farmers and not the level of fawning attention that he craved. The conversation would soon drift to crops and animals, in which Mr. Van Bummel was not interested in the slightest, unless, of course, he was about to eat them. Now all the farmers had gone to Cherry Hill, and a suitable audience was scarce. I would have to do.

Judith often disappeared, leaving me alone with Mr. Van Bummel, and thus she became the topic of a conversation between us. He sensed my apprehension about my daughter and took liberty to dispense advice without really thinking through our circumstance and what might be possible for her. Thus, some awkward moments arose where I could feel the startle on my face. But I soon came to observe that my responses went unnoticed. "That child is coming up nicely," he said, "in spite of being nearly an orphan." Can you imagine? Children of mothers who care about them are hardly orphans.

He trod on to do even more damage, like a goat in a garden: "She is certainly as beautiful as her mother, with the advantage of the bloom of youth." Was this a remark upon my age? Was he aware of his blunder, and was he trying to make up for it with faint praise? Sadly not, as he went on to say, "It cannot have been easy to encourage her advancement beyond the boundaries of your own learning. To your credit, you do not work her too hard and give her time to read. Not easily done, as times are harder every year. I think she is beginning to understand some of the principles of republican ideals that I have endeavored to impart to her. Her intellect is eager enough, although she refuses to read systematically. She is inquisitive but sweet. The difficulties of running a farm as a widow must have been substantial, and you have not yet remarried." Although I was not by law a widow, I did not correct him.

"Now that the war is coming upriver, will you stay alone on this farm? Will you not move to your brother's?" I told him I was undecided and did not mention that I had not heard from or of my brother since the war had commenced.

CHAPTER 5

Don't Tread on Me

Summer 1777

How sharper than a serpent's tooth it is to
have a thankless child.

—**William Shakespeare,**
The True Chronicle Historie of the Life and
Death of King Lear and his Three Daughters, 1608

IT WAS AFTER the sixth Sunday dinner attended by Mr.
Van Bummel that it occurred to me as I was lying awake
in the first warm evening of May—with the moon pouring through my window onto my coverlet—that I should
marry him. Perhaps that it was soon to be *Pinxter*, also
known as *Whitsuntide,* and a good season for weddings,
put these thoughts in my head. The lilacs were out, and
the roses and peonies would soon bloom to add sweetness
to the air. I was feeling hopeful, like some grand possibility could blossom with the flowers. I usually knew better
than this—any optimism kept in check by hard work—but

hope springs eternal in the human heart and is not easily tamped when the earth is bursting with new life. It was the smell of it that pursued me everywhere and inspired these inklings. I could manage my garden and dairy, as I had all these years. And I could make money with my sheep, my cheese, and wool and lambs. It occurred to me that he could bring in a schoolteacher's trade, and I would have all the books I could ever have time to read. And news of the world, which I was not sure I wanted but which seemed necessary to have in these dire times. Certainly I would not have to talk much, as I was not used to that. He could talk as much as it pleased him.

If Judith married, as I suppose she will, I would then not be alone. Because I could not quite imagine the podgy, blustery schoolteacher in my bed, I shut my eyes to this vision. But I had learned that there is more to marriage than four bare legs in a bed. As he kept visiting on Sunday, I had every reason to think he might be interested. After all, he was a man who must be nearly my age or perhaps a bit older, and had not yet found a wife. He came to my table and ate and smoked and told hours of news. He always brought a book to lend, and told me he would fetch it back and bring another if I cared to invite him again.

The days of dowry were over for brides on the frontier, for my daughter and myself, but this little farm was not nothing, and I had built up my flock and animals. I knew what grew in these rocky soils and when to plant. I could harvest sweetness from the bees and trees and fruits from the berry bushes. I could splice apple trees and set new ones every season so my crop of apples was always sweet and in surplus. I had cider throughout most of the year. My butters and cheeses were still remarked upon in the village, although for some strange reason, my sausage was spurned. You can't please everyone. I could please Mr. Van Bummel, however. He gobbled them up, stuffing both sides of his fat cheeks until they bulged because he could not get them down his gullet fast enough. Yes, as I stopped to think about it, I had much to offer. I still had some things from my mother that made the household more than a peasant's cottage. And the house itself was a fine stone house.

One of the reasons I was happy to keep silent over the bounty of my dinners was that I wanted to feature my talents over my thoughts. I feared my discourse had become a bit disaffected. I knew that I did not have a reputation for gentle speech. I had no idea what Mr. Van Bummel thought or if he had been privy to the village gossip about my marriage. He had only come to our village the autumn after my husband's disappearance. Perhaps it had come to be old news by then.

Now, however, I was so often alone and spoke mostly to my sow, who seemed to listen better than my hens or milk cow. I loved her babies. They were sweet and pink and came to nuzzle when I called to them—something my own babes no longer did. I am now uncertain as to what it means to have a conversation. I was personally involved and had personal knowledge of only the drama of life and death among the swine.

It's true that I had read books and explored the lives in them, but I was not sure it was acceptable to talk about what I found most interesting there—the dark yearnings of lonely women like myself. Or a slave's call for freedom. For I had discovered with some surprise and much fascination that in this strange and wondrous time, even slaves wrote poetry. And if a slave girl could spell out liberty from within her bondage, then it seems at least a possibility that her chains could break. I knew that for myself the very act of picking up a book and placing the soft luxury of its brushed skin cover between my hands and testing the weight of it, opening it then to the title and pondering the mystery of all that would come forth from its pages, had been my only respite. In the moment when I ran my eyes over the pale paper bespeckled with black marks put there by a pen held in the hand of a stranger even from another time and country, that was when I felt least encumbered and most free. But I did not expect that Mr. Van Bummel would understand this, even if I could manage to speak it. And so I let him prattle on.

Judith Steals a Book

My mother is busy making food for our dinner. I remove my clothing from my cupboard to a bundle which I plan to stuff under the schoolhouse entry, hidden behind the steps. There it will wait for me. Its sequester will be how I know that I can and will make my escape. It is a tangible signal to my independence. Packing up my few possessions from my room, I am not reflective. I will leave my old farm jacket, as it is too tight across my bosom to fasten, and I will soon abandon my old apron and petticoat. I am in them for these last days, but they will not adorn the new Judith. Indeed, they are worn to a fray and I will leave them on the floor, where I step out of them. I carefully wrap the leather-bound book of paper, a present from my mother, that I scroll my secrets in, along with French vocabulary and quotes that I wish to memorize. The volume has a lock on it, and I wear its key around my neck. I have a comb made from the pelvis of a cow. I wrap these and my best clothes, a few stockings and shifts, and a pair of gloves in a shawl and tumble it out the window. I will retrieve it from the shrubbery on my way to the schoolhouse while my schoolmaster spins his stories upon my mother's ignorance. I go to the hearth to make them tea and then stand up to look out to the empty road and wait a few moments. As they engage each other, I will walk the track with my bundle to the schoolhouse and play my subterfuge.

On the track, I meet no one. My pace is slowed by the package of my belongings, which are surprisingly weighted for one who has such a little life. Arriving at the school-house, I pry away the wood of a step and shove my bundle beneath it and replace it, tapping it together with a stone. I then quickly take the steps and dart within. I find myself squinting against the light pouring through the well-crafted and glazed windows. I place my boots on the hearth of the fireplace where I often had made the many fires that we children had pulled our benches up to read by in the colder months. I run my fingers on the top of Mr. Van Bummel's table, which we had sometimes pulled our seats around to pen our alphabet with homemade quills and ink. I move between the benches now, laid out as usual in their little rows with an aisle between them, and observe. How min-iature they are! How could I have been so small as to sit at them? And, of course, now that my innocence is tarnished by plans of escape, I take a moment to bid my childhood a fond farewell: "Good-bye, little Judith, and Godspeed!"

On the window ledge is a volume that Mr. Van Bum-mel has left out in his carelessness. I pick it up and open its red leather cover. It is in French—and seems virgin—call-ing me to open its pages. I am delighted to find it, as it is one he had always forbidden me. I know not why, except that he always seems a little jealous that my French sur-passes his. Engraved on the cover page is the title *Candide, ou L'Optimisme* by Voltaire, 1759, and I am eager to know its contents. Mr. Van Bummel had showed me an English translation once that had been entitled *Candide, or All for the Best*, and I was ever curious why I had not been encouraged to read it.

With my hands wrapped around the scarlet cover of

the precious book, I then step to the doorway and pause there. Here I will spend just a moment to ponder my past before setting on the road to my future. But in no time, I find myself impatient. I will not tarry here on the cusp of my girlhood. I am already a woman, with breasts and a beating heart. I stoop to grab my bundle from beneath the steps, insert the book within it, and resequester it for my future. Now I have a valuable book with a red leather cover.

How should I put such an idea forth? I thought I should take some action. I thought a clever woman would know what signal to make, what flag to run up her mast—a flag that even so obtuse a man could recognize if he raised his spyglass. The next Sunday, I was quite nervous and put all my anxiety into making a feast. The garden gave more and more of its abundance for my purpose. I baked bread with wheat; a more civilized loaf than the heavy, crustless Indian meal. I made pudding and apple cake with the last of the apples. The cake turned out beautifully from the oven onto a fine blue plate. The war had made it impossible to get salt or sugar, but I found my food by my art tasted well enough without.

It was difficult to find the moment to speak, for as soon as Mr. Van Bummel arrived, his prattle immediately pummeled through the clouds of my week's thinking. He made his own rain. I laid out my culinary offerings and nervously sat through the discourse on Philadelphia and every tedious conflicting politic of the Continental Congress and every last resolution of the Committee of Safety. The girl had cleared the plates and was making tea at the hearth.

Finally, when Mr. Van Bummel had paused to tamp his pipe, I simply interjected, "Mr. Van Bummel, have you ever thought of marrying?" A nod might be good as a wink to a blind horse, but I was not skillful with subtleties and could neither nod nor wink but must crack directly on the pate. That I should be so forward gave me heart palpitations, yet I did not know how to take a more circuitous path. I watched his eyebrows raise and saw that he suddenly most uncharacteristically did not know what to say. He cleared his throat and pulled on his pipe. He then said that indeed he had begun to contemplate such an action, especially after sitting at my table, and if I would not mind, he would speak about such intentions on his next visit.

He then set down his stained napkin and made his farewell—more abruptly than usual, it seemed. I was relieved, as I certainly did not know how to make small talk in the aftermath of my brazen approach. I said nothing to my daughter, for I feared that she could not understand my dilemma or my purpose. She had sometimes taken to mocking Mr. Van Bummel by thrusting a pillow beneath her apron to represent his girth and strutting about the room, sputtering about the birth of a new nation. "Of the people . . . by the people . . . and for the people!" And, indeed, I could not help but laugh heartily and aloud.

A day can stretch out like an eternity but can mark endless time so indelibly that seven of them can tell of all that needs ever to be said. Did not God make the world with such a plan? And does not the marking of the seven days paint a picture of the world? The great book where this is told is often the only book we study. Surely the holy week is a practical convenience so that God can establish his provenance and demonstrate that all that came before is but a fear-driven chaos and all that comes after is a blaze of glory—a refuge from the painful events and suffering or even from the monotony of those days.

Is there not a rhyme that teaches us the character of each day and prepares us for a capricious fate somehow tied to the week's day on which we are born? "The moon day's child is fair of face." Had I not taught it to my daughter so that she too could mark time? For elsewise, it will get away from us all.

Surely that is why, out alone on my small farm, I have found that time shifts about among the shadows, and the days and weeks and months had disappeared into years. Here at the foot of the Blauwberg, seven days can fly by and blur with all the other days of a month or a season or a life—forgettable and lonely. My husband has been gone for seven and a half years, and it seems that only three days ago I had spittle on my lips from rage at him. And only a few days before that, he made laughter bubble in my heart.

But even before his disappearance, days at the farm could stretch into a dry desert of loneliness. And then after that midsummer's eve, he was simply endlessly absent, and I could no longer hope that any Monday he would walk through the shadows of the evening to the kitchen door, or that on Wednesday he would be spotted passing the sundial and taking dinner at the tavern, and I would hear about it from my children.

The thought now of a future filled with books and with a person to talk to, or who talked to me, seemed like a pleasant dream, unscarred by all the hard work of days. Such an enticement stretched out before me to the east like the sky toward the river. And contrarily, such a future might imprint my life with the comfort of a week's pattern and diminish the long shadow that the Blauwberg cast before me to the west. Up until this moment, it seemed that I had no future except what my children would carry forth beyond my reach.

On the Saturday before Mr. Van Bummel would be coming for what was to be his last Sunday dinner with us, I dreamed that I was standing behind my husband as he faced away from me at the laundry trough. His white blouse was removed and billowing beside him like a sail where it hung from a hook against the wide grey planks of the side of the barn. His back was so familiar in its shape, the snake of his spine crawling out of his pantaloons toward the nape of his neck at the hairline. And the color of his skin was a precise tone that I would know anywhere, as I knew the markings of the animals in my barn.

I held a washing cloth, and it was such a dream that I could feel its warmth and its wetness. With the greatest of tenderness toward him—a tenderness I had no idea could be called up from within me—I washed the expanse of the back of my husband and the crevices of his arms with the soap I had boiled from ashes. His ribs were solid beneath my fingertips, and I slid my hands around his frame toward the softness of his belly. There I knew exactly where the soap would slide, crossing the border to where the hairs on his chest would lather.

Upon waking, I was embarrassed by such intimacy and such a remembrance and quickly set it aside. But not before I noted that I yet could not recall the features of his face.

Judith Plots

I have begged Mr. Van Bummel to inquire about a position and to keep his inquiries between him and myself. I will inform my mother in good time, I tell him, once a position has been secured. I do not wish to arouse her concern just after my brother's departure. Can I leave my mother? What faithless daughter have I blossomed into? Has she inspired faith in me? Hardly! Stubbornness, perhaps, but not faith. My father? My brother? I am to be just another departure in a legacy of absconding. Perhaps my mother has inadvertently conferred me with fortitude. And now I contemplate employing that fortitude toward a life without her—a life of considerable remove.

My ears had perked up when she said it, but I kept my face to the fire. What had she asked? She had put to Mr. Van Bummel whether he planned to marry. Does my mother consider becoming the wife of a toad? What a vulgar and unappealing notion. I am repelled.

It is clear I must make my escape before the plot grows too thick and my clogs root in the cloying mud of the farm. I will not live the life of a farmwife, nor that of a schoolmaster's stepdaughter, and be throttled by this war. I will escape in stages. How much longer can the war really last? Surely General Washington will prevail. Everyone says so! Except those that don't. Who knows . . . I will earn my wages and by my charms will make my way to Amsterdam or Paris.

The schoolmaster has told me these several months that he would look for a position for me as a governess of the young daughters of a French family in the Huguenot village two days' journey south of Kingston, and at last he has made inquiry, and a family has sent word that they wish to meet me. I long for such employment. I cannot bear to linger here, although it is all I have ever known. Yearning for more, I would be more. Desire is everything.

Hearts and minds have awakened these months, and so have mine. I am not just a bower girl. The times will ne'er be the same, of this I am sure. My courage has gathered into a knot on a rope that I will climb upon. Seeing from a height, I will carry forward. Nothing can stop me now. I feel my determination in my hands and feet.

I dare not tell my mother, for she will scowl and rail. No doubt. Or beseech me? Surely my brother's departure has infected me like a scourge. I cannot bear to be left here alone. Mr. V.B. has become tiresome, and my mother I can no longer tolerate. There is not a soul to talk to.

I duplicated and expanded my efforts to provide a gracious and abundant table for the following Sunday. The hens were laying, and the cow had plenty of milk. With less trading for eggs that the war had brought, many chicks had hatched and grown to hens I could spare for the roasting spit. One of my ewes was providing milk for cheese as well, if I could chase her down at night. And the garden was new and bright with greens. After a rain on the rock shelf, I luckily found puff balls, which I knew to be tasty sautéed with garlic. I funneled my nervousness into industry and baked pastries with butter and wheat flour. I had but one remaining jar of applesauce I had hidden from the children over the long winter months.

So I was setting my fine table when Mr. Van Bummel strolled up the long road at the usual time. He eyed the fare with obvious anticipation but seemed so excited with stories of the British encampments under General John Burgoyne and Washington's counter strategies that he launched immediately a lengthy discourse about the recent developments along the river. General Burgoyne has announced that he will arm the slaves and has money to do so. If the British Navy gains control of the North River and the waterways from the port city to Canada, this will strike terror in the Southern Colonies. Much of the human trade had been moved from New York to Charleston. Surely the Southern Colonies would be likely to surrender with a condition to keep their slaves.

Mr. Van Bummel was particularly concerned because

this month there was rumor that all exemptions would be revoked and all men fifteen to sixty years of age would be called to service or to pay up. You could buy your way out of conscription upon a payment of more than ten pounds, but a schoolmaster did not have such a sum of money. In the end, his anxiety and excitement did not stop him from eating, however, and I watched my offerings disappear into the ever-wagging cavern of his mouth. A rather constant dribble of globs of gravy ran onto his shirt ruffles and vest. Certainly marriage to such a man would bring more washing.

Finally, I interrupted his dissertations and took the moment's pause to say to Mr. Van Bummel that I had something of import to say to him. Would he care to walk to the vegetable garden? But he ignored me and did not get up from the comfort of his chair. Finally, I insisted that he stroll with me.

"I will not survive this war alone, and I no longer feel safe on my farm. If I move to the big town, I have no house, nor a place for my animals. And I cannot sell this house."

"And why not?"

I hesitated to tell him that if I am widowed, it is my son's house, and if I am not, it is my husband's. So I said, "In these times, who would buy it?"

"I see. I see."

"I have traded off almost all that I can spare. I wonder if you have thought of what we spoke about last week and whether you have decided to move to the big town."

"'Tis an excellent idea, I think my only choice, to live more closely among others and to seek protection. Although I may soon join a regiment. Can you but imagine?" He prattled on as if we were exchanging recipes, as if I had not spoken of my diminished choices and my fear, as if he and I were equally vulnerable. He charged past me without a nod to my situation and my confidence in him. Then I heard these words as if from a great distance fall upon my ear:

"This past week, I have often thought kindly of the mention you made of my domestic situation. If you think it is a good idea, I would be honored to have her."

"Have her?"

"Have her as my wife."

"Who, Mr. Van Bummel?"

"Why, your daughter, of course. She is grown quite lovely, I think . . . If I join a regiment, I am sure to be commissioned as an officer and should have a salary and a fine blue jacket with leather buttons. I could set her up in rooms in the big town. Behind the stockade. More than one hundred families made a life there—she could teach the little ones."

I stumbled on a clump of dried root-ball and used this as a way to keep turned away from him, but I could not bear his bumbling past me, his stupidity, his ridiculous self-importance. I nearly ran back to the kitchen and once inside picked up dishes of what little remained of the food on the table and set them down again. He huffed through the doorway, and I looked directly to him, as if seeing for the first time the man he was. I said nothing, and he continued to try to regulate his breath so he could speak, opening and closing his mouth like a toad gaping. Then he looked up at me, and I now stood still, my eyes locked to his, and there was no way, even for such a stupid man, to mistake what was in them.

But he was slow and long in the custom of having the floor. He would not be stopped by the look in a woman's eyes, even if unsubtle. "Certainly . . ."—he finally paused—"you were speaking of Judith?" His question followed the answer to it, which was plain upon my face.

"Then of whom did you speak?"

I had not gathered my thoughts before my tongue came out of my mouth with a sea monster upon it. What fills the heart will flow over from the mouth. "How dare you imagine yourself the husband of my daughter? You are old and blustery, and with all your schoolteacher knowledge, not even so very clever. Your belly hangs well over your cod. You think of yourself as an officer, but could you even stand at attention? My daughter is coming along? Hah! She has twice your intellect. If only she would read more systematically! If you read each Greek and each Roman all in order, you would be lost to the nuances of her mind. I would not have your pudgy hands tarnish her beauty. Have you not partaken of my economy with the expectation that you would have her hand? I am closer in age to you than she. But perhaps I misspoke."

My cheeks burned. And besides admitting that I had misspoken, I knew not what to say. But I felt a rage within me, and it rose up like a tide. All of a sudden I was drowning in hatred. A hatred for my loneliness. A hatred for my pride. An instant and insurmountable hatred of him, who was so insanely full of himself to not even notice my hatred.

After my outburst, I resorted to my customary position of watching him bluster and fixing my attention on the spittle on his lip. And finally, I saw the dawn upon his face, a flicker of recognition, of amazement. A brief moment of clarity touched his features before they clouded over with horror and disbelief. "Madam, you did indeed misspeak, for your reputation of shrewish habits and ill temper precedes you. Did you think I am Petruccio? Certainly you are Kate! Do you think that it is not known among the good people of the village that you drove your husband from your farm with a tongue so sharp you have cut yourself? It is known that you can hardly muster a word of kindness to anyone. First you drove him to the blinding comfort of juniper and second to the mysteries of the forest. What woman drives a man from his own hearth? It is even said amongst the village women that your husband endeavored to return to you. But that you pursued him with such violence, he was done in."

My eyes darted around my kitchen. I felt the danger of exposure, but a delirious and luscious urge swelled upward out of my loins as I squeezed them in my rage. I could not resist its temptation, though I knew its dangers. I wanted more than anything to strike fear in the man and knew the tool to do it.

"A risk it would be even to marry the daughter of such a woman! Do not such tendencies follow generations? Judith's sweetness may be only beguile. Her hunger for learning, now seeming so innocent, could readily emerge as unbecoming. 'He that would the daughter win, must with the mother first begin.' Have I not but followed the custom of the country? Though I feel the sensible trepidation of entangling myself with a termagant!"

He insulted me pompously, for he has had nothing but the fruits of my labor and the courtesy of my ear. And my daughter! First he teaches her and then berates her for her learning. He comes to seduce her and then chides her for her guile. But he so liked to hear himself that he rattled further. "Yes, I've noticed that she has a tendency to independent thought . . . so awkward and indelicate in a young woman."

I flung the remainder of the pudding at him but clutched its bowl, which I then set upon the table as I moved around it toward the hearth. I swallowed hard on my words. I ached to hurl plates. I was sorely tempted to aim at his forehead, but my cherished porcelain was too valued for such service. I was satisfied to see the glob of pudding meld with the drips from the other table food that bespeckled his vest.

Slug of a man. You sot. You, who have come smell-feasting my table and my daughter are worthy of neither! Scoundrel! Cur! I screamed within my mind but uttered naught.

And then I felt my hands wrap around the long, curvaceous handle of my axe, which I had leaned against the hearth when I had brought it within to shave a log for tinder. I stepped toward him and heaved my instrument above my head. For once, he was speechless, and I was glad that I could observe the terror in his eyes. The dawn of his recognition, I thoroughly enjoyed. He backed through the heavy Dutch door, his girth portal-wide, and slammed the lower half shut—a stumbling retreat at a desperate pace.

My legs shuddered as I rushed the lower door and hung there, leaning out after him, calling out invective and insult across my yard.

"You bedpressing bellygod! You slug, you!"

He turned on his heel but twisted to keep his eye to me and lost his shoe, which he swiped dramatically from the pathway, his fat buttocks spreading between the tails of his coat. He limped to the gate, letting it swing after him as he set himself, one-shoed and ridiculous, upon the track. For effect, I came out to stand at the gate after him and held my weapon above my head and shook it in my fists. He looked back but once as he fled with an ultimate speed that I could not help but notice and appreciate.

Trembling, I turned back to the table purveying the remains of its fine fare. I then set about to erase the evidence of his company and my efforts to please him. The late afternoon shadows soothed the flush of my rage and wiped the stain of resentment from my brow, leaving a hard, cold apathy. Woodenly I cleared the dishes and heated water. I inhaled the sweet smell of the animal pen across the breeze of the late afternoon. The red sun would soon stagger between the trees along the edge of the sheep meadow. The shadows of this long and awful afternoon would vanish in time, and I would welcome the evening, relieved to have my shame shielded by the night. I called my daughter, but she did not come.

Judith Bites

Grasping at the air of a crisp autumn day, I walk to the village in less than an hour and go directly to the schoolhouse after dinner when Mr. Van Bummel has trapped my mother in his unrelenting discourse at her table. School has been suspended, as Mr. Van Bummel is plotting his own escape from our little frontier village. In any case, his remaining pupils, girls and the younger boys, are needed for harvest and putting up the winter's food, since all the men are gone. The single room is empty and silent, which is just how I wanted to find it.

I stand in the doorway with a restless eye on the track. Where is that blustery schoolmaster when I need him? We have agreed to meet here after dinner, and surely he will have tired of my mother, eaten every morsel, and lumbered this way by now. I wait with little patience, and finally, after what seems like an eon, I see the man shuffling along at a faster gait than I am used to seeing him move. His stockings are dusty, his hat askew, his coat flecked with mud, his cravat twisted, and the ruffles of his blouse stained.

He approaches and greets me, and I return his salutation. He brushes past me into the room and, drawing me away from the entrance, firmly closes the door and then stands with his back against it, as if he were fortifying a barrack. His usual style is sanguine and talkative even as he is self-absorbed, but now a nervous quiet emanates from him.

I ask him for news. He launches into what I had heard

before at table. He repeats the rumors that the British are coming, down from the North, and perhaps upriver as well, if they can manage to get past General Washington's West Point fortifications. We are to be squeezed from both sides and perhaps pressed and flattened. Although this was enormously shocking, I shut my mind against it. I will not take in such a threat, for its great inconvenience. Catastrophic news of war is not the news I seek, and I refuse to be alarmed. We had talked war these past two years as if it were an excitement. I had yet to perceive any violence, and from my sheltered existence, I feel no imminent peril. The prospect of invasion seems simply beyond anything I can fathom. Who would want to come here to this sleepy village that is not even yet marked on the maps of the region? How can we figure in world events? When it comes right to it, in my stubbornness, I am willfully blind. I do not want news of the nation if it is to interfere with my destiny, which now rises in my mind to greater import than the Republican Cause. I cannot let the movements of the King's armies interfere with my plans.

I cast a net for the man's attention. I draw his eyes to me. "I ask you what of the family? What of the Huguenot town? Do I have a position? Will they have me? Can I go?" I press him 'til he turns his tack. He asks me, "Will you leave your mother, then?" I reply that yes, I must. I will establish myself and then visit her. I will unbind myself from her venue and thus escape my Blue Mountain bower girl fate.

"Yes, child, they said they would like to meet you." Oh, happy words! "But it is dangerous to travel now. And yet I am not sure you should go home again either." What is he on about now? It is not in my consideration to return to the farm.

"I cannot. I will not. I won't." I do not quite stamp my foot but stiffen my knee as if I might. "I am not a child," I add.

He is startled by my vehemence, and I imagine him taken aback. I have ne'er openly challenged him, and the lack of favor for him I have found growing within me I have kept to a private mockery. The wool has been easily pulled over the beady eyes of this one, and it has not been so difficult to protect what is useful to me in our acquaintance. I shall be careful not to risk it now.

But I feel an impertinence rise up in me. I cannot have such a foolish man telling me what to do. I have not previous to this moment felt the pleasure of such an unmitigated disrespect. "You must give it me. I must have their name, and you must direct me to their town. I implore you to keep your promise." Now, I can't say that I have ever heard him promise me that it would be so, only that he often told me that he has both the society and the wherewithal to make it so. I believe that he has increasingly tried to elicit affection from me when the idea occurs to him that he has something that I want.

"Judith, Judith, do not speak to your elders with such fortitude. It is unbecoming. If you are to make an impression as a lady and gain a position, you cannot be so forward as to say what you want."

"Why should I not want? You encouraged me to find such a position, and your word was that you would help me!"

"You may want, my dear, but for the sake of your sex, you should not speak it, and you should submerge your desire within the wisdom of your betters. You may have desires in your heart, but it is unfeminine to call them out. To speak so forwardly is like a farmwife, not a lady. Of course, you have but eaten what is offered at home." He shakes his head with a pity that I do not find sincere, and I turn my sneer into a smile and tamp the fire in my eyes. He is easy to fool, as he has no clue as to my intents and purposes. My cheeks blush to the defense of my mother, but I keep quiet. I do not want her to be a subject between us. I do not wish to be tied to her with any string, or to think that my apple has fallen from her tree, or to dwell on her for even a moment. I tilt my face to my shoulder hoping he will not perceive my annoyance.

He does not and carries on, as usual blowing his trumpet. "As you had implored me, I penned a letter that recommended you as a children's governess." He first goes on and on about his own credentials, introducing himself as a great scholar who has educated me well. He continues with how fresh and bright I am due to his cultivation, how I have been planted amidst hardship but flowered nonetheless. "I submitted that you had a proper education for a lady underneath a proper supervision of an educated and discerning scholar. That is me, of course." I humor and agree with him. "Oh, to be certain, Mr. V.B."

"No Latin, no Greek, but a good deal of French; English, of course; poetry. We dared to read those lovely sonnets. Suitable classics in translation, no politics—I told them no politics. A bit of arithmetic, but nothing advanced or abstract. And that you can converse on only subjects becoming the distaff company in the parlor of any respectable household. Unfortunately wanting in music, for I could not instruct you, and your mother did not, but able to sing with a voice that is clear and feminine. Oh, don't think I have not noticed. And most important, not a Catholic or Church of Englander or a Quaker, but with a proper religious upbringing in a Reformation Church."

I begin to wonder if he has been paid a commission. For these are all exaggeration and wishful thinking—almost lies. Did he think that I cannot detect prevarication? That I have forgotten or will betray what my eager brain has taken such pains to absorb? We have colluded in this, him and I. The pompous schoolmaster has few promising students, and in his disappointment at not capturing the attention of the village men and their sons—who were often more interested in bowers than in books—he has perhaps encouraged me to study beyond the prevailing conventions concerning the wisdom of educating girls. His male students often scoff at him not so far behind his back that he does not know their opinion of him, and, not finding any male apprentices, he compromised by finding in me his most enthusiastic and patient pupil—an audience—an eager mind that soaks up ideas like a sea sponge absorbing brine. A crusty residue of the salt of knowledge remains, but now he wants to find in me only a cloying distaff sweetness, washed clean by a pure rain.

And I *had* studied. Has he not observed that I had taken the neglected grammars home with me—for he is not such a scholar that he missed them—and I then committed those declensions to my learning? That I had memorized the histories? That I had scribbled those unknown terms in lists and later combed the classroom dictionaries? That in order to save paper, I had committed to memory additional lists of words I did not know? Oh, soon enough I knew them. How could he not have noticed that I had gathered every political pamphlet strewn about the classroom and pored over every claim to freedom, every promise of the Rights of Man? I had committed to memory the poetry of the Revolution, and ignored the poetry of love and obedience.

How is all this not to inflame a young girl's mind? And yet to me, my mind feels deliciously warm, like my body, warm enough to share with others, even children, and not so hot as to raze my femininity. Somehow, if the temperature in my brain is a wick to a flame in my body, or *vice versa*, and one seems to fuel the other, what is the peril in this? Will I fire like a cannon? Explode into fragments in the sky? I know intuitively that if I confess this purview, it will be considered somehow exceedingly controversial and hardly welcomed.

He holds the letter before me and waves it between our noses. I notice he is sweating, and as he steps forward toward me, I can smell his rank. I back along the aisle between the pupils' benches toward the table that he had sat behind these seven years, leaning back in his armed chair with his belly protruding toward us between his legs turned out and spilled wide ever more each season, pontificating at me and the other children. True, he had unlocked my mind and taken it on journeys not often offered to girls. But now he is notably unsure that this has been the prudent course. However, he so much still wants me to be his work, a consequence of his pedagogy—I can feel his eagerness to have his product fully admired by others. Yet I am not quite willing to represent him.

Suddenly I snatch the letter, which surprises him; I can tell by the start in his beady eyes and the drop of his jaw that he hardly expected this of me. His pinch slides to the edge of the folded sheets and hangs on, the gaze down his nose rivets to what is between us. I tug but do not wish to tear the paper or smudge the ink of the words, as I have a dire need for them to be interpretable. "Necessity never makes a good bargain," my mother would say. I need the name of the family, the time they would expect me, and the town where I am to appear. I know none of this, and I count on him. I have only once ventured beyond this village, and certainly never by my own devices. Oh, bother . . . needs and dependencies!

I switch tactics. I let my body soften and my voice, but do not let go of the letter. My eyes drop to the floor. "Sir," I whisper, leaning forward from my waist—not quite a curtsy, but a physical entreat. I can feel my breasts fall forward in my shift at the rim of my stays, and I notice his leer drop against them.

"Please. I must venture. I must go."

He says, "Judith? May I ask you something?"

"Anything, Mr. Van Bummel. Ask me anything."

"Did you ever . . . consider . . ." He pauses—uncharacteristically. He seems even to reflect. I have no idea what he is after.

"Judith?"

Nor do I particularly want to know. "Yes, Mr. Van Bummel."

"Am I? Do I? Would I?"

What is he on about? Why can he not complete his question? Yes. No. What answer can I make? If the question cannot be formulated, any answer will do.

"Judith?"

"Yes?"

"Have you ever . . . ?"

"What, Mr. Van Bummel? What?"

I do not lose my perspective on the letter. Is it not my goal? I continue to perceive him as an obstacle, where formerly he had been my friend; someone who had some vague interest in my advancement. I must move him. And while moving him, I must escape any expectation he may have had of me and any obligation he might call in.

I had learned from this man—a transfer of a certain kind of knowledge had occurred—yet I found now and in a new way, I did not admire him. I was having trouble mustering any gratitude. What is knowledge, if not infused in wisdom and creative goodwill? He is clever but not wise. And certainly not empathic, which is the better part of wisdom, I would venture. But I had better not say as much. He does not *move* me. No. It occurs to me now that if I were to look into my heart, I would but find disdain for him.

He stands before me, blubbering, unable to formulate his question; or if formulated, he cannot bring it forward. He seems large, amorphous, and soft, and if I had been a sailor, I would see a white-and-pink-fleshed whale. Oily. I am afraid and yet not. I think the condensed pith of my youth—my intelligence—can get around him. And I desire it so. I do not want him. I want to be free of all his inclinations. I am done with him. Like the village I am done with and wish to flee. But I need what is in that letter, and that letter itself. My calculations are ongoing, with my fingers still attached to the page.

"Judith, do you feel any affection for me?"

I start, not expecting him to suddenly find himself. "What do you mean—any special affection?"

"Yes, exactly . . . I am asking you if you have any special affection for me."

"Mr. Van Bummel, I have to say I do not." I can see he is miffed as he stiffens.

"Do you mean to say that you have no gratitude?"

I realize that I must circle or lose the cause. "No, of course not, Sir; that is not what I mean to say. That is not it at all, and that is not what you have asked. Is gratitude a special affection? I thought you meant else." I do not ask exactly what else he might have meant because I do not wish to know it.

"Mr. Van Bummel. Tell me—is there a family that would have me?"

"Yes, I believe there is. Judith, if you choose to go, I shall visit you there. I will not come back to this village. I am bound for a career in politics after we defeat the British and gain our sovereignty. There is much work to be done. Voices and scholarship like mine are needed. I shall find a position in the new government of New York. I will find some way to rise."

"Good for you, and Godspeed, Mr. Van Bummel. I wish

you well. You have much to offer the State of New York, I am certain. Now may I have the letter?"

The blowing of his own horn inspires him, as he suddenly relinquishes his pinch of the paper, and lunges at me, grasping me to his belly with the swoop of his arms pinning mine and pressing the fat of his sweaty and stubbled cheek against my neck. He takes two long strides, nearly lifting my body against him, until my back is up against the front table, and I arch as far as I can away from him over the flat of its top, while trying to keep my feet grounded to the floor. As I pull my face away from him, he sweeps his coarse whiskers across it and latches his blubbery lips upon mine and sticks the glob of his swollen tongue between them and down my throat so that I imagine I am going to choke.

I do what any fair maiden would do in the circumstances and use my teeth to great effect. For as I bite down on the soft slab of the organ that fills my mouth, I taste blood, but I do not unclench as I press him with my arms at his chest away from me. The moment extends itself, and our rabid gazes meet, with our eyes as wild as tethered bovines just before slaughter. The shock of recognizing each other in the whorl of agitation in which we find ourselves makes my mouth open. Upon release, he then finds his lungs to bellow the coarsest, most anguished roar I have ever before heard from any living being. I am satisfied. For I feel a hatred in me now. And as he bends double in the agony of his torn tongue, I slide to the side away from him and around the benches and out the schoolhouse door.

I run down the lane, and looking back over my shoulder, I see him bent and hanging at the door frame. He shouts after me, and through the thickness of his tongue, I am surprised to hear him beseech me, "Judith, do not go home. Whatever you do, do not return to your mother. You do not know the spectrum of her evil!"

At least Mr. Van Bummel left me with a good book, which he had forgotten when he stumbled away huffing and puffing. And the irony was not lost upon me that it began, "The various accidents which befell a very worthy couple after their uniting in the state of matrimony will be the subject of the following history." And that it was the story of a wife in distress with the name of Amelia. So something good came of our rupture. I had been but fooling myself to think I could live more than a day with Mr. Van Bummel. Had not my husband often said, "May those who love us, love us. And those who hate us, may God turn their hearts. And if He doesn't turn their hearts, may He turn their ankles, so we'll know them by their limping"—his eyes twinkling with this last aside.

And I could spend my lonely hours with Amelia, and look up in Dr. Johnson's dictionary the words I did not know. There is a good deal of consolation just looking at words on a page—how there are so many of them laid out one after the next, each to be contemplated, each holding its own secret. The mind follows them one after another and sticks to them, and recedes from the present moment and the tasks at hand. Sometimes you can return to them again and again—and find them on their place on the page. There they are in the same order, just where you left them, although you might not remember they were there. What comfort that they do not change. Coming upon them and reading them again, they can leap out and then echo with a meaning you did not discern before.

I know that a life must be lived as a book is read, page after page, unfolding in order. The character is little known at the beginning, the way I knew so little of myself when I first came to the farm. The nature of Amelia, which has been heretofore cleverly hidden, is suddenly revealed in a word, letters strung together, little blotches of ink. A sound hums in the mind as the letters of a word on the page jiggle up against each other. And the eyes move across to another until the relentless vibration transfixes a vivid experience, and your fate is joined with that of the character's. And in that relief, the pain of living your own life becomes only a weakness that departs from your body. No wonder it is frowned upon for women to read novels, and slaves are forbidden to read at all. Did not *Robinson Crusoe* describe how to survive when all is lost? How to carry on with nothing but solitude? How can I know what my future holds except that it is joined to the fortunes of all women scorned? Turn the page, turn the page.

"Mother, what did you say to Mr. Van Bummel?" The evening prior, she had come into the kitchen long after Mr. Van Bummel had waddled down the wagon path, disappointed that now he would have to infiltrate another household to dine. The evening had slid out of the cloves across the sheep pasture and curled itself around the house, so that when the sun removed to below the rim of the mountains to the west and no moon had risen, darkness was sudden and replete. Having done with the evening chores myself

and drawn down the crossbar on the barn door with finality, I was sitting at my kitchen table with no candle at a cold
hearth. She started when she saw me, assuming, I am sure,
by the dark house that I had retired, but she said little, and I
did not have the fortitude to ask her where she had roamed.
She went soon to her bed, and I soon followed to mine.

The next morning, the relentless sun was boldly tickling
the flowers in their pots and tapping the animals on their
noses through the stall windows, as it could be counted
upon to do. Like any other morning, the animals and hens
began to bleat and cluck with anticipation of the break in
the long fast of the night. And I went to them as I always
had. Their dependence and their insouciance cheered me.
When my daughter came silently to work beside me, my
heart expanded ever slightly in my chest. My breath eased
and followed only itself. I was doubly cheered to see the
cast of sleep upon her face, as it reminded me of when her
countenance was curious and innocent with childhood, the
younger self who had looked to me to interpret her world.

Her question startled me, and I looked hard at the
young woman before me, backlit now by the sun at the
barn door.

"Daughter, I must ask you to tell me the same thing!
Did he speak to you of marriage? Has he courted you?" I
was relieved to hear my daughter snort, "Marriage? *Marriage!* Why, I had sooner be a toad than marry a toad! And
live upon the vapors of a dungeon! I cannot imagine the
curse of marriage to a blubbery, barrel-bellied schoolmaster who loves best, next to filling his belly, pontificating
over it! To hear himself bluster about liberty so he will not

be asked to defend it. Or live its course. Can you, Mother? His discourse about the Rights of Man is but a discourse and has not the merit—not even the possibility of a transformation to action—for that would require courage." She paused. "And surely he is wanting." She paused again. "His promises of a better world are not authentic. I look to him for no more than his books and pamphlets. That is his only use to me."

She sounded sure of herself. At first I experienced a great relief at her words, a sense of pride. I could feel the blades of my shoulders lower in my back toward my apron knot. And then just as suddenly I was flushed with suspicion. I could not see her face, but it occurred to me she might be lying. Suddenly her demands about the color of her stockings and the style of her gowns, and her wrapping food up for dinners taken at the schoolhouse and her sauntering home through the darkness of evenings, took on a new meaning. Had not the stirrings of my own heart at that age drawn me toward whatever, and whomever, was beyond the sphere of my family? Had not I myself been plotting an escape from my ordinary circumstance with opportunism and guile? Had I not been able to tamp my natural repulsions to invent a man who would make the world right? My younger self had only just misjudged my opportunities or my ability to inspire my vision in others. That is all.

But my daughter would not be beset with problems similar to my own if I could but prevent her from curtailing her opportunities. Her youth and beauty would inspire many a man, and I could even foresee these fortunate accidents as a ladder to a new social station. Her years on the farm had not made her coarse, like some bower girls, and she had a reasonable education, which she had taken more seriously than her peers. Surely there are some husbands who value an educated wife. Nor had she succumbed to the casual courtship of the village youth. She did not pine for any who had marched north. She had not seemed to think the attention of the village sons as worth cultivating. Perhaps she mimicked my remove. Or although she could but little remember her father, perhaps she still held her head above the rest without a mind to anybody, as he had done.

"Daughter, I have questions of my own, and you will answer to them before I answer yours. I think you are not entirely forthright. Have you been intimate with this abominable man? What kinds of learning have you engaged in . . . from your schoolmaster?" I could see a shock on her face, as if she could not believe she had heard correctly, even as she could not mistake my tone. But in an instant, no trace of the sleepy openness brought to the barn from her bed remained on her face, and a veil was drawn over her eyes.

Immediately, as if by instinct, she turned the table. "Mother, what do you accuse me of? Your own fantasy? Your own longing? Your own foolish plans?" The knowing child had come uncannily close to a truth about me I could not then bear to bring into my own admittance. I whirled around and lunged toward where she stood at the barn door and smacked her hard upon her golden cheek.

Judith Flees

Away! Away! Away! I stumble down the track with my braids flying out of my mob cap and the motion of my arms propelling me forward as rapidly as an insect scurrying once the rock has been lifted. Even so small a beetle, though unable to take long strides, compensates with a flurry of motion, employing every leg and wing, turning about to bead a direction and make an escape before she is crushed or devoured.

I know now that my plans must go forward and that I will move out into *the World*! I will leave my Dutch mother and this Dutch village, and my life will forge an American tale. Not Dutch nor Palatine, nor Hessian, nor Huguenot. Certainly not British, nor Scottish, nor Irish. My mother will regret her brutality. I will not linger at her door. My heart beats hard against my ribs, and I can feel the flash of my eyes gazing forward toward my fate. My boots slap the puddles and spray grit up my legs into my skirts. I have not yet soaked their leather in mink oil, and wet as they are, I will not have an alternate pair anytime soon, conditions being what they are. I had left my mud-caked farm clogs in the barn. "Get thee to a nunnery!!!" sayeth the Bard. "I say we will have no more marriages. She is away." Better that I am as well. I will find a nunnery rather than to live here. I am beginning to understand how things are in Denmark. How a family, which was everything, could collapse upon itself. And insanity can seem like the truth.

Who knows what my father had done to my mother?

Or she to him? Who knows what bed of justice they may have lain down together in? Or risen from? How was a child to know? Perhaps my brother, two years my elder, had known something that I had not. Could not. He knew her handiwork with an axe, as he often snidely remarked upon it. His commentary on our parentage was ever demented and disrespectful, and he seemed ever more confused. However, he was more than circumspect—guarded. I could never get an explanation from him. A shadow veiled his eyes, and he hardly spoke, hardly considered himself of our farm. Then off to soldiering.

Well, soldier on, Brother, soldier on. I hope to see you when the war is over and the revolution ours. Fare well in General Washington's infantry and come back to us safe. I know for your own reasons you had to flee our little farm—to desert our bower—at the foot of the Kaaterskill Mountains. "Seven days in a week . . . seven locks in a life!" Is that how she would put it? Oh, I can't remember her *exact* words. But best to forget them!—before I find they turn my feet scuttling back along the track to hide among her skirts as I did when I was little. "Find the key! Find the key!" That is the matter now at hand. I know I failed to listen to you and defended Mother against your barbs. I thought her more than you could ever make of her. Is not my fate entwined with hers? No, best to forget her admonishments and her philosophy . . . look at where she landed! In this moment, thinking back on your warnings to me and the sting of her hand upon my cheek, I am not at all certain of her integrity. I would say I have little sympathy for her presently. No . . . I am well beyond that. I am no longer polishing *that* stone. Indeed. Look at me now . . . I have put my flannel cloth away.

Here I am, my beetle self, scurrying along the pathway to my future. I have taken myself south of the village, to further remove from the farm, to the River Road, and I must race the plunge of the autumn sun, which comes quickly enough to the edge of the earth and falls behind it to darkness. I have but five and a half hours at a relentless pace to arrive before evening at my night's stopover. Mr. Van Bummel told me six or seven, but I know I can be as quick as he is casual. I am thin, and he is fat. I have but two legs; but now conjure six and propel these new appendages rapidly upon the hardened dirt of the road.

The leaves are as passionate as you ever could believe; their ravishing yellows and reds are not at all calming and egg me on. But I am walking too fast and hard to be truly anxious. I tamp down the worries in my mind so that I can ignore them. And I do my best not to let my mother in. It is not a time to have an ear to her or an ear to what the schoolmaster has said about her. First my brother and now the schoolmaster. What could my mother have done to make them so reticent in regard for her? And even fearful?

But as these questions rise up within me, I think to my own boldness in my encounter with Mr. Van Bummel. What would he be saying about me now? Nothing complimentary, to be sure. My only hope is that he will be too distracted by the calamity of the times to write again to the family in New Paltz, with retraction of his opinion as to my suitability to be a governess of children.

So I walk with the vigor of pent-up youth, and make an

effort in spite of my turmoil to fully endorse the violence of my escape from the schoolhouse . . . and the farm . . . and the little village that had been a great stage for an innocent bower girl but which had shrunk to a tiny platform, a cage, and a gaolhouse. A stage it will be no more. How brave and clever I am! I am not defeated by my own temerity! And will not be! For this is my most tenacious fear, that I would give in to uncertainty and run home to the hen house of my mother's bower. But no! I had acted like a bold heroine. I am my own queen. Like Maeve. Like Boudicea. Like Camilla.

The first regiment was sent to support General Schuyler at Fort Edward in July 1777, and I believe Mr. Van Bummel went with them. It was hard to imagine such a man fighting the British or his Loyalist neighbors. Subsequently, I heard rumors that he became a commissioned officer in The Continental Army, no less, but this I could not believe and took to be a product of the usual Dutch inflations. I, having had the man's character revealed to me, could only imagine that he would as soon try to talk the King's men into going home and leaving the country to us—and their food stores to him. That man could outcant the Babylonians.

I did not hear of him in the village through the rest of the summer. This was not unusual, as the school closed during the harvest months, and he had often been absent during the summers in the past. Needless to say, summer was a time when the children were needed to work the farms. And now with all the fathers marched north, the children were haying with their mothers.

What happened to my daughter, I do not know. From the barn door, she had spun away, and as she stared at me with astonishment, she said words I would have cut my ears off to have never heard. In the moment that she spoke them, the world became a brittle place, cracked and parched. "Mother, I can no longer bear you . . . You deserve the lonely existence you have created for yourself on your pathetic little farm."

She then had stamped to the well-worn track beyond the farm gate and followed the footprints that led only away. As I watched her body leaning into the wind of a determined, rapid departure, I did not call out to her. Had I known what was to follow, I would have, of course. But we do not always fathom what comes next and therefore do not measure the consequence. I watched her vanish around the bend at the end of the sheep meadow, as her father had, her shoulders clutched with blame and disappointment. But it was well beyond my ken to understand at that moment that it was the last time my eyes would rest on the shape of her back.

It was much later I found the gowns that I had remade at such cost and most of her clothes removed from her room. When had she removed them? Had she all along been planning to depart? Was I so naïve that I could not discern the play's meaning until after the actors had taken their bows and the stage went dark? Could I not follow with my eyes to beyond the length of my own nose?

CHAPTER 6

Appeal to Heaven

Fall 1777

*Het zijn niet de slechtste vruchten
waaraan de wespen knagen.*

"It's not the worst fruit that is eaten by wasps."

—Dutch proverb

I SPENT THE MORNING in the kitchen, boiling every-thing. Vinegar and dill weed. Beeswax warming on the hearth. The abundance of food satisfied me. I did not need to eat when I could count. I baked for a fine dinner later. Today I treated myself with yeasted wheat bread. My cider jug is full. I have butter and cheese plenty and would soon take it to my usual customers. Except for that one, of course. Pumpkins ripening on the vine would be ready in a few weeks. I will stew them with apples and onions. Every day I have gone to the orchard with the wheelbarrow for apples and picked it clean. My husband's trees were from seeds, so the fruit was mealy and sour, good but for cider.

Since he had departed, though, I had grafted the trees of my neighbors for eating apples, crisp and sweet. I spent a day making applesauce. Shredding cabbage, and slicing cucumber and summer squash for pickling, are my tasks for this fine morning.

Berries and blossoms had been put up earlier, and the jars lined my kitchen sills and shelves. Bunches of dried flowers and herbs had been tied to the kitchen rafters. Last week I took my corn to the miller and had him bring it out the track in his wagon so I wouldn't hurt my back in carrying it. I had such a large crop that there was enough to trade for the milling and delivery, and I had four large sacks sealed carefully in my best barrels. I laced dried tansy through the barrel-top handles to deflect worms and pests.

I miss my children with a sudden longing I had never expected. Not the ones who had left me, restless and silent, whose lanky bodies I no longer recognized and who told me next to nothing. But the little round ones full of laughter and stories. The ones from before who liked nothing better than to describe some triumph to their mother. Or the twelve-year-olds. Those who fell into a rhythm with you, who worked at your side with a complete confidence that you supported their greater good. Once, they had listened. And I had found no greater pleasure than listening to them. What had happened? These seven years when I had spoken mostly to them and (when I did speak to others) of them had galloped by like a horse across the moon. What did my mother used to say? You cannot shoe a running horse—unless it stumbles and falls. We had formed a charmed world together, with the richness of the little farm, its rocks and rainfall, the sun-baked garden, the moon's reflection on the pond. I had blinked, and now that world was unpopulated, and the seasons would go by unremarked.

Industry and planning save me from the darker reaches of my loneliness. Today I rejoice in the abundance of my garden and dairy. Today my bower feels like a domain where I alone am sovereign and replete. Contentment smoothes my brow. Ah, but I am flushed by the hearth heat and will wander out to the pond for a bit before my dinner. On the way back, I can bring in the butter to package in swamp cabbage leaves.

I wandered through the ferns to the water, still and dark among the slate blue of the stones. All those years ago, it was the softness and depth of these mosses that kept me alive. I knew the mosses' comfort once by lying prone to put my face among their stars. It was the last caress the skin of my cheek has ever known. The lost child would be just six, and I would have the comfort of a young one, with the others gone. But I cannot constantly touch my sore tooth with my tongue; I am getting old enough to know that the hardness of a bitter heart is forged from one's own repeating thoughts more than from any circumstance. I lifted my face to the sun. I would be grateful to lay in this place for a sweet little nap, and so I bent down to test the mosses' dampness. It was dry enough to lay upon, which I did, arms splayed on the padded quilt of the mosses.

It was within this very moment, when I had surrendered to the seduction of afternoon sleep, that I heard the pig squeal. The note drew out longer than the road to the village, and something in its length and pitch made it seem not of this world. At first I was not alarmed but curious with a quick and steadfast attentiveness. A serpent sliding along the crossbar of the pig sty? But no, she would root it, stomp it, and eat it, if I but knew her. A wolf lurking toward her trough? My husband come home? In the languor of that undeciphered moment before the world would change forever, I could feel laughter froth across my face. I stood up and listened, only to hear another eerie screech that was probably her last call, both frantic and wildly indignant, for my aid.

Still, my heart was abruptly pounding as I slinked toward the long, low house. I stayed out of sight on the wooded shelf. There were three men in the yard, one holding six horses. Another two horses hitched to a wagon were at the gate. I had ne'er seen so many horses in one place, and their largeness and their beauty filled my little yard. The steeds were nervous, pressing against each other's flanks, turning to nip and snorting. Two wagons stood in the track open at the back, the one already full and the maw of the other filling fast.

What I then took in with my eyes filled me with horror. One of the men had a pig sticker in one hand and had hoisted the pig tied by her hind hooves on the wagon post to bleed her out into my best kitchen bowl. She seemed yet alive, squirming in the hoist. The sow had been my dearest friend of late—although to be honest, I had planned to kill her myself this season, in any case. A man came from the barn with two piglets held by their hind legs, one in each hand. Another came out of the kitchen with a grain barrel, chewing on a fistful of my newly baked bread. My cider keg was already on the wagon bed, next to the bled-out sow.

I watched as they went from wagon to house to barn to garden. The wagon was piled with food; enough to feed an army. Ah, of course. To feed armies. These men were either Cowboys (the Tories) or the Colonists known as Skinners. I could not tell which or who these men could be. I knew only that they were the devil himself come to rip me out of the earth. Most likely they were middlemen, those profiteers from both sides who were set to find supplies and sell them back and forth between the two opposing armies. A market is a market. But surely the British army could not be so nigh. We would have heard of it. These cads must be profiteers for Washington. We had heard he was desperate, out of cash, imploring the French for aid. They wore not red or blue. They flew no colors on their wagons. I listened, though the sounds were washed over by the rush of my blood in my ears, but other than that they spoke English. I could not hear the accent or recognize a name.

Revolutionary or Loyalist? A nod is as good as a wink. It did not matter a whit to me. And my sympathies, my loyalties, my sensibilities were of no consequence to them either. I had goods, and they were needed—so men could go to slaughter with their bellies full and so the soldiers who had slaughtered them could be warm at night after their rampages. No, none of it mattered. What dawned on me to matter most, I realized yet again out of the extremity of my confusion, seemingly as if for the first time and simultaneously as I had known it from the first night of his departure—my husband would ne'er return to me.

He was gone forever. And I countenanced for the first time since they had left that my children would not return to me either. *Oh, you can't take anything from me,* I thought, *as I have already lost everything.* Suddenly the war did not seem so noble, so foreign, so dreamlike. I had been blessedly fooled and in this moment became unfortunately wise. A cold and singular droplet of sweat ran on my skin to the waist of my dress.

My eyes were drawn to movement in the upper loft under the low roof. In a few moments, a man emerged from the doorway of my house completely covered in my bed linens and blankets. Two others followed at each end of my bed quilt drooping to the ground with the contents within. I heard the crash of breaking china. My eyes were sucked toward the barn door, where a man emerged with a sack that I knew by its sound and movement contained my chickens. Another was chasing the ducks and geese about the yard. I saw yet another rounding up and collaring the cow. I had always felt blessed by the ease of catching her. Now I wished that she were far less cooperative. He tethered her to the back of the wagon, which was now piled high with the fruit of all my labor, with the fruit of my life, with every sweetness I had ever known or would now ever know.

They worked with the efficiency of a barn raising. One of them kept barking orders like a dog. Mounting their horses, one of them opened the pasture gate across the track and entered to herd my six sheep through it. They trotted behind the cow tied to the wagon. Suddenly my legs and arms lost their stone-like quality, and I hitched my skirt to run toward the yard screaming. I had been too slow, and the ground to cover stretched before me, a greater distance than I had ever measured.

I turned the corner of the house and stopped, throwing up my arms. They were well on their way up the track by then. And so I stood solitary in the yard howling Dutch venom in the teeth of the wind. The poison in my bitter heart cultivated day to day and which I had thought a canker, a weighted mass, was paltry, light as a duck's feather compared with what I drew up from my viscera now. I had not enough hatred in me to curse them with the cursing they deserved. Curs! Louts! *Honden! Klootzakken!* Evil balls of dogs!

The men standing on the wagon bed or sprawled atop the contraband finally noticed me as I raced after them along the track. They raised their muskets and scoped down the barrels, but seeing only me, they lowered them again. I was not worth their powder. They looked back and mocked me, calling out, "Come with us, fine woman! Gather your harvest in your skirts and bring it to our beds!" But the commission plodded on before me, and they laughed at me as I hurled myself forward and spit the dust they had kicked into the air. That very dust settled on my hair, the foam of a gritty spit upon my lip, a searing dryness in my eyes, my own rage wafted back upon me. The loaded wagon wended so casually onward and away, the wheels turning so inevitably. I sat down in the path that the wagon's wheels had only just imprinted with the weight of the modest cargo that was my whole life and clawed at it, rubbing fistfuls of grass onto my cheeks.

The sky above me was azure and unbesmirched by any cloud on the autumn afternoon. How could that be? How could the sun still disperse its heated and desultory beams to touch my face and light the day? How could the trees still stand upward alone and in multiple to make their shape against the sky? How could the leaves have the fortitude to attach to branches? How could the soft blow of the wind push and pull with such a persistent gentleness? How could the blades of grass still form waves across the meadow? How could the track still lead out and meander toward the world? And how could that very track revert? For it reverted only to . . . nothing.

Nothing was indeed all that answered me. And it was by nothing, in the choking dust of the track, with a face striped green with the claw marks of my own nails, that I came to know that the life at the foot of the Blauwberg was done.

The kitchen table was white with flour that had spilled from a broken crock. Other than that, it was empty of pickle jars and any other thing. My cast-iron oven and other pots were gone, as was every utensil. What had been warm upon the hearth had been dispelled from its vessel outside the door. I stepped across the threshold to the other room, which was unscathed, the high backs of the well-hewn chairs neat against the walls. I sat down in one, folding my hands in my lap.

When I looked up again, no shadows brushed the walls. I went to the window and looked at the moon's sliver, and

I knew it could rain no more. I stumbled up the stairs, not bothering to latch the door, and shivered in my unquilted bed. At the dawn, I awoke with a start and realized I could lay about. No need to milk. No chickens to feed.

Though my present life was done, no new life called to me. I lay in bed for most of several days under all of my clothes, which I piled high. I guess the army had little need for women's gowns. They had taken everything but spared my mother's gowns. Loss is but the wound of loss . . . but shame is the scar that curls over the wound and adheres to the innocent and adjacent flesh, tugging at its softness as a constant reminder of the injury. Scars itch. The sun rose to mock me, for what could I do under the light it shed? I pulled my apron over my head and turned my face away from the door toward the wall. Cold blossomed as the shadows shortened. And as the Equinox had passed, the nights fell suddenly and hard against the earth.

I got up but once to walk to the garden, which had been stripped of any late harvest. I dug around and found a few potatoes among the barren rows. I stumbled to my orchard and scoured the ground for the last of the half-rotted apples. Only a few days before, I had gathered up all the fallen apples and made mash for the hogs, and there was not one apple left on the trees or the leafy ground. I remembered how the pumpkins had shone like orange suns from the back of that wagon of thieves. I stood for I do not know how long, staring at the habits of the trees.

Finally, turning my back to the mountain, I willed my footsteps toward my house. Coming through the forlorn gate swinging on its hinge, my eyes roved the yard for the difference. But my mind was a brick. Some change of import was waiting to be noticed, was begging for attention. My attention, alas, would not muster. At last, with a great effort, I paused, purposefully willing my gaze to the surround. Something was different in the yard that was not only the shift of shadow. And then I knew—the woodpile. They had removed the wall of wood. They must have loaded it first while I was dreaming by the pond, and I had not observed it underneath all the foodstuff and animals that had been strewn atop it.

In these several days, I had not once made a fire in spite of the frost in the late-September evenings. The days I had lain in my bed had been warm enough. The emptiness, the whitish expanse of the long wall against which the dark logs had been stacked, was now flickering in the early dusk. How could I have ignored the dimension of its absence for so many days?

The height and breadth of stacked logs are a measure of winter, and if winter can be measured log by log, then it can be survived. I had come hard by the wood. With the boy gone, I had none to saw and split, and I had forced myself to do a little each day. And patiently, persistently, day by day, I had built my challenge to winter. But I could not help but worry that I would fall short—there would not be enough. And the anxiety of it had gnawed at the satisfaction I found in my harvest. Such a shortage had been the biggest threat to my life on this bower, and it was what had prompted me to seek another course to going it alone. Now all that preparation and planning were no matter, and all my hope for relief was dead on its vine.

Time that has no tasks in it does not move forward. And the empty present was unbearable. I stepped to the kitchen and sat at my table. I brushed the spilled flour on its plank into a little pile. Salt and water would make a pancake, which I suppose I could heat on a stone. And then I remembered the wood and that there was no salt at all.

I wrap up my mother's gowns in a bundle as I prepare to walk to the North River. There, under cover of darkness, I will quell the shame of my burning cheeks with river water. My apron has deep pockets for stones. I dread most the passage through the village, and plan a detour, but in the end I am too weary and walk right on the main road at dusk. The village is quiet, and I pass but few, and no one stops. When I get to the rise on the river side of the village, I look back at the shadows of the Blauwberg. I know those blue shadows like the veins in the back of my hands.

One shadow of that mountain is the measure of love that had stumbled across the doorstep of my childhood home just upon the verge of my womanhood, with its promises and kisses. And then its loss. But to be honest, perhaps the brief love I had enjoyed was more than many are ever allotted in all the years of a lifetime. Perhaps I am as fortunate as any other woman in that regard. Perhaps growing old with someone causes love to desiccate and fade, and you are left with a memory that you must cultivate together lest it whither to nothing. And if one does not water and till, then what?

Yet another specter is the boredom and loneliness of my solitary industry. Yet, mistake me not, I had enjoyed and been satisfied by my labors. The bluest shadow, deeper and longer than any other at the base of that mountain, puddled there like a dark pool, conceals from me the whereabouts of my own children. I left a note for my daughter underneath a flowerpot. I have little hope my boy will return.

If I am but simpleminded, poorly educated, and given to complaint, I still know this—I know there is as much tragedy in children growing as there is in death coming. The seasons do not stand still for us after all, even if we are not prepared for them to pass and cannot face what is next. Time is a hungry maw yawning, and we all roll before it with no hope of escape. You cannot shoe a running horse. At times I accept this without any kind of resolve; just accept that moments have passed that will never come again. I can respect that each moment is changed in remembrance and lost forever in its original form. Children must grow up, and every being that has lived will perish. Sometimes I am not afraid.

Often though, acceptance and the mind's peace keep their distance and cannot be summoned. Once you started seeking it, making a meal out of it, mixing it in a bowl and placing it to solidify on a hot stone, it becomes an entirely different pancake, cold and chewy, barely palatable. I cannot bear that the children whom I had brought down upon this earth and loved—and with whom I had created a tolerable world—no longer exist and had vanished these past several years into the future's fog. Not my future but their own. Where I might not be welcomed.

So frightened was I of the coming days with only my-self as company that I had plagued my progeny and made a pox upon their hopes. These new adult persons, though in close proximity—indeed, in the next room—were some-how cruelly unknown to me, leaving me to wonder about them as I wonder about the woman who now wears my mother's garnets around her neck. My worst suffering, however, is the realization that I had not noticed that they were grown; had not wanted to, had clung and clutched so tightly in my mind to a past.

Now I could see that often I was overcome and enraged. Who am I? What kind of mother? What kind of wife? Am I darkness? I am that mother who fathoms my children sliding perilously and irretrievably into a future I will never reach myself. And while I imagine I wish them well, I grasp with claws at their hems and coattails. For who would not?

Could I have been so deluded to think I could keep them? If I had noticed their intention to remove, how would I have stayed them? As they slept? Indeed, I had watched the breath of their sleep so many nights—their fingers gently curled around their dreams—could I have smothered the hot breath of their innocence with a pillow? Is murderous rage a part of love? Had I slewn my marriage? With its own tools? With an awl-like tongue and an axe?

What have I done? I squint. A congestion captures my chest and shoulders, grips behind my eyes, squeezing the salted droplets of onus out upon my cheeks. They are meager, as of a drought. I am soon dry. The pit of fear plunges from behind my eyes to deep within my midriff like a stone at the bottom of a creek, impermeable, with the waters of life flowing over and above it. Those waters, in their scurry, do not flow deep or fast enough to ever dislodge that stone from its bed. And the weight of it drops deeper in my groin. The fear of time passing is lodged in my groin.

I have always loved the gentleness of dark and spurned lanterns and candles with a preference to shuffle about in the velvet of night. As the dark pitched into the river, I plodded step by step to its shores. I knew the directions well enough, and my eyes and feet adjusted to the night. I tossed my bundle on the beach and waded out from a stony cove to stand up to my knees for a long while. I did not wish to live. This I had seen written in the wood grain of the rafters above my bed. But to end a life is not a casual thing. To think of it ending and to wish for it are not the same as extinguishing it, which requires determination, if not courage, and a particular kind of ingenuity that I had run short of. I knew I no longer had in me what had once ended the life of that fisher, so long ago behind my barn.

I thought the river might embrace me, reach out to me lustily. But it ignored me and rolled on by, completely oblivious to me. Shall I gather up stones? Would my guilt and my grief sink me? I tried to inch further from the shore. A strange inertia beset me, and I stood there through the hours as the moon rose. Eventually—because I became languidly aware of a weariness that did not allow for further standing—I turned my back to the river and lay down. The water supported me, and I floated. I thought eventually, with patience, the water's weight would enter me, and I would be sucked below. As the current moved me away from the shore and into its great succulent heaviness, I would not be able to recover. I was yet filled with calm.

As I was drawn on the surface of the water toward the center of the great river, I heard a sound that had a rhythm. A water sound, somewhat familiar—a bob and swish—but I could not fathom what that sound could be. A clatter of wood against wood could not be interpreted. An oiled iron clanked. But then I heard someone say, "Oh, my goodness," in a voice that was low, just above the sibilant water. A curiosity sparked in my brain but seemed removed, as if some other person might be curious, enjoying the airy tone of the voice and the pause after its utterance. I did not respond—indeed, could not—and the voice followed as its own echo. "Oh, my goodness." I felt something hooking into my skirts at my waist, and I could discern a long gaff across the darkness. However I did not turn my head, as I could not draw my gaze down from the stars, which had suddenly exploded like faery dust across the sky.

And now I was being guided, pushed, pulled, and steered. The length of my body alongside a skiff.

"Leave me alone."

"I cannot. I cannot."

"Why not?"

"I see your sorrow, Madam I see your sorrow."

"Then let it be."

"I cannot. I cannot. We all feel it, Madam. We all feel it."

"I feel shame."

"There is no shame in it, Madam, sorrow only. No shame in it at all, only sorrow."

I heard his words and wanted to believe him. Why should I feel such shame? What had I done in life besides work and wag a sharp tongue? Was I a thief? A murderer? Would God forgive me?

"No shame in it," he said again. "I watched you. I stayed my course. And you did not. Now we are one." A naturalness infused our conversation, as if we were taking tea together and speaking of all that is ordinary. As if this discourse out upon the dark and astonishing river were taking place in a parlor or on the corner of a street.

I could not remove my eyes from the stars. I was so weakly motivated and strangely inert, given over to the current of the sorrow in my heart, and now hooked like a fish. My petticoat and apron billowed about me. The gaff urged me down some, and then I was fastened to the bow and drawn. I heard the sounds again—a slurping, a swish, a creaking lock. Now I knew the sound—an oar. A pair of oars creaking in their oar locks. By its rhythm. All had slowed and receded. An interval between each of my thoughts was luxurious and pleasurable. The muddlement, the clutter, the condemnations—the racket and rattle within me of the previous days were subdued. No . . . more . . . it was cleared away. I did not have to defend against its clamor, and I could rest. I observed that I felt a deep cold, but somehow I did not mind. All that had mattered suddenly did not.

And after a time, we came to a cove, and as he swung the boat toward the shore, my head was hit, but the hurt of it seemed far away. He jumped into the water, which was chest high to him. When finally I turned my head toward him, I saw him. I took him in, and I was afraid. He was black, and his teeth and the whites of his eyes shone out of his face like beacons, much brighter than the stars. A big black man. He lifted me up in his arms. And though it occurred to me that I should, I could not crawl out of my stillness to resist. Our wet skins were cold and stuck together. I could hear and feel the beating of his heart, and beneath the cold tack of the surface of his skin, I could discern underneath it the deep warmth of being.

To be plucked from the river, with the water pouring out of the weight of my clothes, to be held in someone's arms, stuck against a someone—and such a large someone; someone twice the size of me—and as strong and supple as the birches in my sheep pasture. To hear the heart thump of another, like a drumbeat on my head, it was all too much. Yet not enough. I had not experienced such a thing since I was a child. And when then? I could not recall except by the sensation which seemed familiar enough to be called home. So I was a child in the arms of a stranger. Comforted. And this constriction, this bundling in a receiving blanket of powerful arms, encouraged me to awaken from my dream state and talk to the man.

But then I looked at him, and I was shocked again to silence. For he was not at all like my birches. Smooth, dark sycamore bark covered his frame, and I could barely make out the border of his body, so merged was he with the black of the night.

I was afraid.

A strange question came to my lips after all, and I heard

myself utter it: "Are you free?" Although it was almost a whisper, he heard me too and answered just once: "I am free." And it was not 'til much later that I knew what I had asked and what he meant in reply. Then, under those stars, in the state of that river dream, I did not know what I was asking. But he knew his answer. "Are you free?" Did I think that an enslaved man would be safer for me, having his master to answer to? The foolishness of such a thought did not occur to me. I was wrapped in my own concerns. But he did not reply again or take up any questions of his own.

He set me down at a log on the beach and pulled his skiff in to tie it. We walked as the dawn rose up. Every time I tried to sit down, he upped me. "Please, Madam. Please, Madam. Susanna will take care of you. Susanna will take care of you." His voice was lilting, encouraging, and insistent. Each time he spoke, my fear subsided, and I returned to a kind of indifference, as when I was merged with the water of the river. As he insisted, I obeyed, for to think for myself was beyond me. I saw some buildings and a shipping dock and on our approach to them a cabin by the water. We trudged over the rocky shore to the cabin, and he backed against the door to open it, and I walked into a pleasant little room with windows facing the water.

"Susanna! Susanna! I caught a big fish. I caught a big fish." The woman, Susanna, pulled up a chair and set me in it, but I so nearly slid off it that she lay me on a cot underneath the window. She then went to a hearth that was set through a portal in another room and soon brought me hot tea. I took one draught and set it down and lay back to oblivion.

When I awoke, I was alone, and my petticoat and vest were hanging on the back of the door. Through the dullness of my senses, out of habit, I counted the cloth-covered buttons that I had carefully sewn to my vest so long ago and found that all three were attached. One. Two. Three. I could hardly move but needed a chamber pot, which I found beneath the bed with great relief. I hardly knew what to think, and when my mind moved backward over the previous days, I felt sick and dizzy, so I quickly brought my sensation forward into the present time. But as my mind moved toward the future, I instinctively knew this too should be avoided. Finally, I brought my thoughts to the moment in this cabin and would not let them budge at all but stuck them to this place. I used my eyes to explore the quarters, which indeed were spare but had a certain order that I always looked for in a room. And immediately I found a comfort in it.

Soon I was slumbering again until I heard a door open and the woman came into the cabin, with some vegetables in her apron. I kept my eyes shut when she turned toward me and gave me what I thought might be a hard look, from what could be discerned furtively from behind my eyelids. When she went to the hearth, I watched her. I thought she was not so much older than myself, and there was a clarity to her face and movement. Her dress was grey homespun, and her apron and cap, white, which made her dark face shine. I coughed. She then came to sit on the edge of the bed, but she did not speak, and I knew not what to say. My eyes met hers nervously and then fluttered away. But hers were steady. She waited and looked right at me, so I sat up.

I thanked her for helping me. She looked at me.

"How long have I been here?"

She did not answer. She got up again and went to pour the kettle into a pot. She then ladled from the pot into a cup and brought the cup to me. She said, "Trink," or maybe she said nothing. And I was glad to. She seemed to have no questions for me, and I was not sure what I would get from her. Somehow she gauged that I was not ready, and she went about her labors and let me rest. I slept, and when I was not sleeping, I rolled my back to the room and stared at the sill of the window.

She came again and again to feed me mash, or soup with bread—different from the fare of my kitchen but not at all bad. On the second day, she walked me carefully to the privy without a word. And she held the covers as I climbed back to bed and pulled them taut to make them comfortable. The blankets were coarse but warm enough.

That afternoon, I told her about my farm and my son and daughter and the disappearance of my husband long ago. She shook her head slowly from side to side and replied that she was indeed sorry for my sorrows. It didn't seem to her, she said, that nobody had them. "Everybody does, you know. The cauldron is full, and the soup within it seasoned with sorrow. Everyone eats that soup." Although she seemed kind, I could not make out whether there was any particular sympathy in her remarks.

I asked her what should I call her. And the man who rescued me. She told me they were brother and sister and that her name was Susanna and I should call her that. And his was Obadiah or, sometimes, Thomas. They were slaves of a well-off Dutch family, and Thomas had been here since he was eight years old, but she had come much later after she was already grown.

"But Thomas told me he is free."

She frowned. "Oh, he is free. It is just that everyone does not agree about it. Our master comes, but not so often. He has not been here in a few days. You can stay here. We have food. Then when you are better, you can walk to the big town and your people."

"They are not my people. I know no one there," I told her in a dull voice called out from my body with great effort. And added a bitter afterthought for myself: *nor anywhere.*

I lied, as I thought my brother could, in fact, be found, and some whom my father had conducted business with would surely remember me. Mr. Van Bummel might even have taken refuge there. And Judith? I felt sick. I brought my mind back to this room, where it flickered to the gold beneath the cloth of the buttons that now were my only friends. It occurred to me that I had left my mother's gowns in a bundle on the riverbank and now was entirely bereft of the substance of my former life. Except for three buttons.

She went on. "The bird in the berry bush eats berries until there are none left. Then he flies away to another world. Your farm is like a berry bush. Sweet berries once but no reason to go back there. Now you are free too. There is work, and you can find lodging," she said. "The few families who support the British have abandoned their houses. A few have been taken and made into workshops. My master will help you. He is starting a stocking and homespun workshop and needs women to weave and trim. General Washington needs stockings for the army, and the Colony is paying. All the farmers have brought in their sheep, and no one eats lamb or mutton anymore. Here at the wharves, the sheep will be sheared, and once the wool is dyed, carded, and spun, it will be shipped on the river, and every soldier shall have New York stockings, if not blankets."

The thought of working for pay intrigued me, and suddenly the thought of the future was no longer accompanied by nausea. The easeful way she talked about the transfer from one life to another inspired me. I was almost a little curious. The war might bring opportunities that had not yet occurred to me.

"Obadiah, he unloads boats. He guards this warehouse. He serves food that I cook to the men on the sloops. We stay here, and our master comes sometimes down the Rondout or brings a wagon from the town. We load it up, and he usually gives us something, for he is not an unkind man, if he is obeyed.

"There is one thing, though, Madam. If you tell him that Obadiah was in a boat on the river, he will be removed and locked up at night; perhaps whipped and chained. If you call him Obadiah, he will be severely admonished, for they call him Thomas. So call him Thomas. His master does not know that Obadiah has a skiff and goes to the river at night. We keep that to ourselves."

She waited, and I noticed she looked up at me from

what she was doing with a little squint. She wanted to know if I was catching the import of her words, but she did not wish to sound an alarm. Now I know what it means to keep secrets for survival, but she could hardly have been able to discern that I did. "Can we thread our words together into one rope and tie a little knot, without altering the meaning of what has happened to you?" She spoke a strange, lilting Dutch that was hard to make out, but she looked me directly in my eyes with confidence and waited, and somehow her meaning unfolded before me. I was wondering how it could be that she would trust me; before, I thought it was that she had but little choice.

I slept fine on the little mattress under the rough blankets. The two of them worked all the time. He made ropes, and she spun like a demon on a wheel in the corner, when she was not busy making food. I stared out at the river. It was very interesting to find myself the least industrious of the household. One evening when Obadiah had gone out, I asked her, "Why do you call Thomas Obadiah?"

"He takes that name. He is a prophet. When he was a boy, he asked his master to teach him to read. He liked that big book. But the master say no time to teach him to read, but he could teach him the words of the shortest book that he should know them in his heart. And so that he could call them up as he needed them. So he did. That book had twenty-one verses. And it is the Book of Obadiah, the prophet.

"So Thomas took the words into his head and then into his heart. And I think that his master was surprised at Obadiah's quickness to learn and his appetite. And it did not please him. And he would not teach him another, longer book. And then Thomas took for himself the name of the prophet. From the only book that he knows. And that is who he is. They don't know. But I know. I am his sister. They look in the book, but they can't see the truth in the book; what is right in front of them and which they can read." It was the most energetically I had ever heard her speak. But she then quieted herself abruptly, fearful perhaps that she had been imprudent.

I thought on this story. I did not find the silence awkward between us. And she obviously felt comfortable in the lapse without words. I, for the life of me, could not remember the book of Obadiah nor any of its verses. I knew only that the servant in *The Life and Opinions of Tristram Shandy* was called Obadiah, and remembered that he was part of the fun and foolishness and the mockery of relations between a servant and his master. I sensed that for Susanna the matter of Obadiah's name was of utmost solemnity and had a great significance.

I wished to draw her out. I could not help but think she had knowledge that I needed and hoped she would trust me enough to impart it to me. "I must ask you . . ."—I faltered—". . . why does Obadiah say something and then say it again, repeating the same words?" She gave me a look as if I were a child for whom the world must be interpreted.

"What he tells you once is what people say . . . or want . . . or what might be. Once is plausible and likely yet to happen, but maybe not. What he tells you twice is possible and probable, and most likely to happen. But you will not be shocked if sometimes it does not. What he tells you three times is true. Is *true*. And the way that truth is beautiful, if he says it three times, it is also beautiful in that way. I mean truth is scary sometimes, will make you fall off your seat, keep you up when you should be sleeping, but when he says it, you know it can no longer be distorted. Or denied. When he says it, people know it even if they can't hear him and can't say it themselves. He can. He is a great prophet. I have not heard him often repeat a notion thrice. Not much happens in this world that has truth embedded in it. Little truth abides in the words between one person and another. And little is said about anything that happens at all that is actually true," she added as an afterthought.

"Obadiah thinks his finding you in the river is of great significance. He will get out his bundle. He will throw the bones tonight. He will speak a prophesy. He will say it three times, and we will know what is true. All it takes is to listen and believe." I don't know what I thought of her words. I know only that she seemed very certain. She spoke straight and directly, but seemingly not without forethought, and I felt an excitement that I had not known until this very moment and that I had been longing for my whole life.

Obadiah was on the beach at the confluence, down the kill from the cabin, where it joined its waters with the Great North River. The night had come quickly, but the moon was on the rise. The wind was blowing off the water, up river and creek, as the water charted another direction underneath it, making its escape to the sea. It was a night for extra shawls and a warm bonnet, and we had to go back to the cabin to get them before we headed toward him. The beach was stony, but he crouched atop an overturned skiff and spread feathers and beads upon its flat bottom, soft of rot. He had a wild look about him, with his tricorn smashing his hair down on his head and an old overcoat buttoned all the way to his chin, but Susanna said not to be afraid, and so I was not. He watched our approach and nodded his head in welcome before he began to speak. He had built a little fire on the beach, and the flames reached up to light his face from below.

"The men in red coats say they will free us. They say it. We are not at all sure. We are not at all sure. Their reasons are not good ones. Their words are not true. These are uncertain times. These are uncertain times. Appeal to Heaven. Appeal to Heaven. That's what the others say. That's what the others say. Join or die. Liberty and justice for all." He paused. He looked from right to left. He looked behind him and then turned back to look past us. He looked up to the sky and then squatted before us, and as he was atop the boat and we stood on the beach, his eyes were at our level.

He commenced in a conspiring whisper, "But this is what the sovereign Lord says about these people. We have heard a message from the Lord. An envoy was sent to the nations to say, 'Rise, and let us go against her for battle.'

" 'See, I will make you small among the nations; you will be utterly despised. The pride of your heart has deceived you, you who live in the clefts of the rocks and make your home on the heights, you who say to yourself, *Who can bring me down to the ground?'*"

I shivered at his question. I knew not whether he still spoke of the politics of the day or if he had entered another realm, or was he speaking of the arrogance in us? The arrogance in me? I was no longer afraid of this man because he was the color of a crow and the size of a horse, but he was strange to me, and I had become attuned—that I might hear a word from his mouth that would set me where to go next and what to do, for I certainly had no idea myself. He calmly waited in the silence and then after a time began again.

"'Though you soar like the eagle and make your nest among the stars, from there I will bring you down.'" His eyes rolled up to roam the sky, and he stabbed his chest with his thumb. Was it he who would bring us down?

His voice enlarged in his throat and gained a cadence as he swayed on his feet from side to side, supporting himself with his hands. "'If thieves came to you, if robbers in the night—oh, what a disaster awaits you—would they not steal only as much as they wanted? If grape pickers came to you, would they not leave a few grapes?

"'But how Esopus will be ransacked, the hidden treasures pillaged! All your allies will force you to the border; your friends will deceive and overpower you; those who eat your bread will set a trap for you, but you will not detect it.'"

Now he stood again and looked beyond us, projected outward as if he addressed a crowd. The timbre of his voice deepened and engorged. "'Will I not destroy you, men of understanding in the mountains of Esopus? Because of the violence against your brothers, you will be covered with shame; you will be destroyed forever. On the day you stood aloof while strangers carried off your brother's wealth and foreigners entered his gates and cast lots for bounty, you were like one of them.'"

I shuddered and drew back as if accused. How had he drawn me into this? I fingered the buttons on my vest, which he seemed to be peering at, as if he could see through their cloth covers to the value of gold underneath. Surely I imagined this. Then I found myself clasping Susanna's arm and pulling my body close to hers and turning my face into her shoulder. This astonishing intimacy was awkward and improper, but I could not help myself. And she stood steady.

"'You should not look down on your brother in the day of his misfortune, nor rejoice over the people on the day of their destruction, nor boast so much in the day of their trouble. You should not march through the gates of the people in the day of their disaster, nor look down on them in their calamity in the day of their disaster, nor seize their wealth in the day of their disaster. You should not wait at the crossroads to cut down their fugitives nor hand over their survivors in the day of their trouble.'"

And now the cadence of the speech acquired magnitude and rang beautiful in his deepened voice, and he found the rhythm of the words as he had found the rhythm of the oars when he rescued me. And again I was guided through the cold of my ignorance by a gaff that he purposefully set into me. I felt nothing but a strange consolation as he continued.

"'The day of the Lord is near for all nations. As you have done, it will be done to you; your deeds will return upon your own head. Just as you drank on my holy hill, so all the nations will drink continually; they will drink and drink and be as if they had never been. It will be holy, and your house will possess its inheritance.'"

Suddenly he turned to me and grabbed my arm, which was crossed on the front of my body beneath my shawl to interlace with Susanna's. I stiffened again with terror. He locked my gaze and said to me specifically, with severity, "Your daughter will have what you have not. She will know all her people and remain in their security. Your daughter will have your inheritance, and her daughter will carry it forward as all women will for two hundred years. Her inheritance is a story—your story . . . and her story—written in a book. She will turn seven keys to know that book, but she will find the truth in it. Feel no sorrow for your daughter, for she will know her own truth. And that is all we can ask for in this life. Your husband you will never know, for he is dead to you. You have cut him from you, and you must now cut him free to his own fate. He stole from your profit even in your sleep, and his dreams overwhelmed him, and he cannot ever again lie with you in your bed. He sleeps, instead, alone on the side of a mountain above Hendrick Hudson's river, a victim of his own imagination. So he will remain for twenty years. And you will not know him again, even as he awakens."

And now he turned and spoke again to his sister, looking directly into her eyes, with steadfast gaze and kindness. And she swayed in silence as she absorbed his deliberate words, each one crafted for her and received by her. And he spoke to her comforting words about the whereabouts of her sons and daughters. But I could not perceive his message to her nor comprehend anything more than the astonishment that he had spoken *to me* with a knowledge of my circumstance that I had ne'er given him. How could he have known my very secrets?

He then turned his face again to the sky of the night and proclaimed, " 'All the houses will be afire and all the houses will be enflamed; the houses of Esopus will be stubble, and they will set it on fire and consume it. There will be no survivors from the houses of Esopus. The Lord has spoken.

" 'People will occupy the mountains of Esopus, and people from the ships will possess these rivers. Deliverers will go up to heaven to govern the mountains. And the kingdom will be the Lord's.'"

He stopped and was silent. His sister said nothing. I had no idea what I had witnessed or what it meant that I was standing on a river beach with strangers who spoke words from a book that I had studied as much as anyone but could not understand. The truth was that I had never connected well with much in that book and had been repelled by its messages as much as enticed. Listening tonight was the closest I had ever come to absorbing its mysteries. I was still on the brink—understanding but little and grasping at straws. Yet Obadiah's delivery had moved me. I had never heard such passionate elocution, and its deranged sincerity made me long for sleep.

The wind was up, and suddenly they quit their positions and turned back toward the cabin. All was ordinary again except that the wind was too warm for this late in the season. While I pondered and struggled to comprehend the messages of the evening, I soon found out that what it meant to them was that they must leave this place and warn their masters. They went immediately to the cabin and began to pack. They brought knotted blankets full of what they had to a skiff on the river. Obadiah then walked up the creek and tied the loaded skiff among the reeds. While he was gone, Susanna told me we would spend the night in the woods, and tomorrow we must walk to warn the town.

"What is happening?"

Again she looked at me as if I were a child. "Did you not hear him? They will come. They come now. They are coming."

After several hours of packing, in which I took little part because they would not direct me but seemed to think I should know what to do, we climbed a hillside where we had an unencumbered view of the cove and settled down in the woods. I asked a sequence of worried questions that they simply did not answer, and so I stopped my queries. A cold and cramping slumber settled on me where I sat. But even Obadiah, who had insisted that he must keep watch, did not see the unlit soldier ship out on the river until the cabin and warehouses were ablaze. As the fire roared and enlarged in the dark hour before the dawn, we heard men shouting. Obadiah watched and did not move, with a look of horror fixed upon his face. When the fire had burned all that it could, a smoky twilight settled on the land even as the sun began to rise.

We then stood and turned our stinging gaze to the west and saw a smoke pillar billow and bulge above where the town ought to be. We knew now that we would issue no warnings to those people. The moment for warnings had passed. Obadiah moaned and wept. And Susanna held him in her arms.

The cold comfort of dawn had come as it does no matter what. We walked a trail toward the smoke. The stockade was a charcoal rim that we had to climb over to get to the streets, and the houses upon them were shells. No roofs, no floors. No stairways. No beds. The fire buckets still hung in the entrance halls of the stone houses. You could see them there because the doors were burned. The church held ashes instead of benches, and smoke poured from its steeple, as the stairs to the bell burned. No matter how well built, the wooden barns were felled inward into piles of smoking hay, but there were no charred animals and no stench of hair, even as the flames still flared in the wind.

We picked through the desolation, avoiding the streets where we saw soldiers. They were easily espied in their red coats. Each useful item that Susanna picked up—utensils that had not burned, stray tools that had been left on doorsteps—Obadiah firmly took from her hands and placed on the ground. What practical person would not be tempted? I did not understand his prohibitions. For now they had less than nothing and would soon be in need. That Susanna would attempt a harvest of goods made sense. But he repeatedly muttered the same question: "Would grape pickers not leave a few grapes?" Finally, the meaning of his words of the previous evening that were floating in my brain and making me dizzy in the sooted air broke through to me. He meant that we should not profit from the misfortunes of others, not even our enemies, and this was his instruction.

There was hardly anything, in any case. It looked as if the houses had been emptied of goods and furnishings. No animals had perished in the barns, no corpses were smoldering in their beds. The people of these houses had been warned after all—if not by their good slaves, then by others—and they had fled with their stuffs. By necessity, Obadiah and Susanna had been left at the confluence of creek and river to their fate. Could they have been simply forgotten, and would they have been burned in their beds as they slept if not for Obadiah's prescience? Their abandonment seemed to puzzle and disturb them, and they whispered together, pondering its meaning. Should they seek to find the masters who had abandoned them? A strange dilemma for persons who were property, to be sure. And what of me? How could I either figure in or impede their plans?

I knew the shock of the sudden demise of the circumstances of the present and of finding the future an empty, meaningless expanse. Having survived one such shock and having taken refuge with strangers beyond my borders made me think to seek a path that led even farther out. Some pudding of thoughts congealed within my head. I found my voice and gathered the two, and implored them to return to their cove and the skiff of supplies tethered at the shore. We could embark and ponder our fate once out upon the river. They ceased their conspiratory whispers and seemed to awaken to my entreaty. In this moment, we noted our lack of discretion and moved to better hide ourselves.

A single house remained untorched, and the Redcoats gathered there. Susannah said that it had been owned by the town's most prominent Tory until he was driven out of town, his home converted to a factory that turned out goods for the Colonial Army. We saw them from afar. We brushed embers from our shoes so that the soles did not burn through, and stumbled over the slag of the fallen stockade to find the road back toward the Rondout. Our eyes were burning. Obadiah led us to the path that ran through the forest along the kill off the wider wagon track, and we pushed ourselves along it.

We soon came upon the confluence where it widened to the river. Several large ships were tied offshore, and the small beach near the burned cabin was an encampment swarming with men in red coats. Finally, too tired and dismayed were we to hide from the soldiers, so we spilled from the trees into the open. And when we came upon an officer with his men, we approached them. They had found the skiff in the reeds, and the blankets were emptied of their meager contents, which had been tumbled over the stones along the shore.

"I wish to speak to the commander of this ship."

"And do ye now, Madam? And who are ye?"

"I am the wife of a Loyalist from a tiny village on the frontier upriver, and I have no knowledge of these conflicts. I have lost my farm, and all its goods went willingly to feed Loyalist soldiers." Although I doubted the truth of this, it now seemed the most opportune interpretation of my little tragedy and one which I did not hesitate to exploit. "I am here because the rebels failed to warn me and abandoned me where I stayed, knowing that I am loyal to the King. God save him." This was true enough in part.

"And who are these two?"

"These are my husband's slaves." I was careful how I put my words, but my approach came easily enough. I lowered my voice and turned my face away from Obadiah and Susanna, as if there were no need of conferring with them as I took the captain's arm. I pushed my mind to make a plan and knew that I must sell it to these soldiers. Not knowing what it was did not stop me, but I was not sure I wanted Obadiah and Susanna to hear my words. My tongue was thick within my mouth from the smoke and my own lies.

My mother's gowns were spread out over the stones on the beach, for I had asked Obadiah in the days after he pulled me from the river to travel back to retrieve them. We had tied them with the cabin goods within the skiff. One of the soldiers had slipped on a textured jacket and donned a petticoat over his breeches, and was cooking over a fire. Many of the soldiers were drinking beer or cider from a barrel, and I could see others tippling from flasks. There was tinder in this company for another fire, as the mood was raucous and confident. A victory without a fight. But I decided to play the upper hand of a woman wronged, and so I boldly walked to him and demanded he remove my mother's gown before his officer returned, or I would make the matter one of theft and impropriety.

It was not General John Vaughan who reported here but another lower officer. With haughtiness, I immediately asked to speak with him, and when he came to me, I took him aside.

"I must get with my slaves to the port city. I cannot stay here, or I will starve. I am a Loyalist, faithful to the monarchy, and gave all my goods except my husband's slaves to undermine the American traitors." I even managed to mutter, "God save him. My husband may have died at the hands of the Revolutionaries, and I must return to Europe. Will you, can you, help me?" I did not know where these words came from, but they were not difficult to forge, and I appealed with urgency, "Sail us three down the river. I will cause no trouble, and my slaves will perform whatever domestic service might be useful to you and your men."

Luckily, he deferred to General Vaughan, who was not present. We would have to sail downriver a bit to find him and gain permission to carry passengers. I had to convince Obadiah to get on the ship. I went to them, who were standing together at the rim of the activity, as if they were thinking of blending their corpuses between the blackened trees and removing themselves from the scenario. I said, "I claimed to own you—I thought it was the safest tack—but, of course, you are not mine; you can do as you wish. I myself can only see that the most prudent course is to arrive at the largest city where none of us is known. Surely the chaos of war would prevent those who would seek us from doing so, or if they did, from finding us."

It did not occur to me then that my point of view had aligned with theirs in such congruence that I did not realize that my proposed action would not only make it difficult for slave owners to recover their property but also for a daughter to reacquaint her mother.

I looked at Obadiah, whose face was full of fear. I recognized shame in his eyes—a deep shame that was familiar to me—and I knew that his reluctance came from that. He was owned, and he felt a duty toward his masters, and a fear of them, even as a taste of freedom had been introduced by their tragedy. I took it upon myself to entreat him, "You must leave with me. Our fates are now entwined. As you plucked me from this river and guided me here, I can also set you on a new course. And I will. You once told me there was no shame in it—only sorrow. You said it twice. Now I say it a third time, back to you. I will not let these soldiers harm you. I will not let any man believe that you have abandoned your duties or unlawfully escaped your station. We must go."

Prophet or no, he was not used to making decisions for himself, at least in the public domain. He could hardly proclaim (to whom?) that I lied. Yet I could see he was acutely confused and afraid. And this saddened me. Susanna whispered to him and took him by the arm and counseled him to trust me. And thus as the dawn rose a second time amongst the dissipating smoke, we boarded a boat full of soldiers in red uniforms, suddenly more courteous than threatening, as commanded by their officers, who were as easily our friends as our enemies. As the light shone from the east against the mountains in the west, we found ourselves on a ship of war—the ship of the navy of a faraway king. The morning tide lifted the cradle of the vessel off the sands. The soldiers, now sailors, chanted to haul the bowline and heave the sheets to tack into the current. The colors flattened out behind the mast, and the sails billowed above where we sat upon the deck with our eyes on the scintillating river.

Now the devastation of fire was in the minds of the soldiers, and as we met up with the other ships, they cut directly across the river to land on its eastern shore. The soldiers disembarked and marched north to burn the Livingston Manor house, to destroy its fields and fodder, and to wreak havoc among all the Livingston tenants. We were left on board with the ship's guards. The soldiers returned within a day, raucous, with a good deal of loot, ashen uniforms, and eyes as red as their jackets. Obadiah was horrified and very frightened, and he shook whenever a soldier came near him. But the soldiers, for the most part, ignored us, and we were left to huddle amongst the sailcloth piled upon the deck.

We soon learned that any plan to sail north and meet Burgoyne at Saratoga had been scratched, and it was only later that I came to know of the great colonial victory that proved the British failure to claim the strategic corridor of the Great North River and to split the Northern Colonies apart. The British soldiers did not speak of these events, as they were probably not informed of this disheartening news by their officers. The seven ships departed, drawing into the downriver tide, and over two days, we sailed through the highlands and skulked through the eastern eddies, past the fortifications at West Point without drawing any fire.

Obadiah, Susanna, and I whispered on the deck together. We needed new names to set our story, and I knew that common British names would be best. I advised Obadiah not to choose Obadiah, for I did not want his name to echo at all from his past. I put forth that he select a common English name that would mingle with all the names of New York City, and I suggested Samuel Johnson. I told him he was a man of considerable wit who knew the power of words, as Obadiah himself did. He might well learn to read them if he had such a name. I could see that this appealed to him, and so they became Johnsons—Samuel and Sally. I told the officers that Johnson had been the name of my Loyalist husband. Mr. Van Bummel had complained at considerable length that Dr. Johnson, although a great scholar, was an avid monarchist, which he could not forgive him for at all. But Dr. Johnson's name was as useful to me now as his dictionary had been in the past. And as we were now deep amidst Tories, why should we not wear their clothes? I thought it a good fit with a measure of safety. Although we did not know who would win this war, we needed to survive it.

I would soon revert to my Dutch maiden name, but for now I was the good Mrs. Johnson, wife of a Tory landowner. So together we made up a story with chapters that would be a suitable past for us all. We tied our threads together in one knot, as Sally would say. Lying was surprisingly easy for me, and I came to enjoy it, gilding lilies each time I told a tale. Doing so not only enlarged my little unembellished life but freed me from its constraints and losses. I found to my astonishment that I enjoyed playing to the sympathy of others, and that they lent their ears eagerly to my saga of misfortune.

I had never before sailed on a high ship through the long corridor of the great river and knew not the extent of its magnificence. While Hudson's River might have some infinitesimal beginning, as do we all, such as a tear squeezed from a sorrowful eye, far north in the lake in the clouds—when the waters gather girth and speed in the middle of our valley—the Great North River is already great: as roiling, massive, and wondrous a water course as any eye could ever behold. We stood on the deck, mesmerized by the golds of the autumn season and the curvature and color of the shores. And finally we sailed into New York's shimmering harbor, chock-full of the Royal British Navy and commerce vessels of every type. Our excitement could hardly be contained, even as we could not know our fates.

I thanked the British officer who had made our voyage possible for his gallantry, and it was clear that he was happy to be rid of me, lest anyone take him to task for granting us passage on the King's ships. A week after the burnings and pillage, we found ourselves on the busy streets of the great port city, searching for a businessman who would change my Dutch gold coins for British shillings.

We rented lodging in a house where a shack in the back served as the quarters of Sally and Samuel Johnson, and I had a room upstairs. I had pulled one of the three coins from my vest covered in cloth as a button, and we lived on this money. Happily, I bought a new whalebone button from a seamstress as a replacement. These buttons would readily have served as dowry for my daughter or to purchase my son's conscription if either had known or wanted such a thing from me. Now they would serve another purpose, and once I had it in mind, I did not find myself conflicted.

As soon as we were settled, I asked my landlady how I might find the offices where I could seek help to set upon my task. She sent me to the customhouse near the harbor, and I searched the office windows for a sign with a Dutch name engraved on it. A gentleman informed me that I would need title to the two before I could gain them legal status as freemen at the King's offices of the colonial government.

So I set about getting papers of ownership by insisting at the town office of the Royal Commander that all bills of sale had been burned by General Vaughan's troops and that the British government was responsible for giving me papers that would protect my husband's property. I insisted that there would be no witnesses to be found here or anywhere to attest to my husband's ownership, as my neighbors were traitors and would like nothing better than to seize his property for their cause. I was careful how I worded this. I led them to ambivalence as to whether my husband had perished or was alive from the fighting in the North, sure that I risked diminishing what little authority I had as a wife under British law if I admitted to being a widow. I was well used to that uncertain status and understood its perils.

I appeared in the waiting chambers of the command offices every day with a new confidence, and I insisted on being seen. Finally, by extending several shillings on several occasions, I received a title for each of them that referenced records kept in the Ulster town where I said the sale had occurred—and that had surely perished in the fire admittedly caused by the actions of the British Navy. I think they finally executed the documents in order to curtail my persistent visits.

The town was ragged and upheaved, full of red-coated soldiers, and it was God Save, God Save everywhere. But when the soldiers were on parade or drunk at the taverns or asleep in their barracks, there was much fearful talk among its citizens. Many Republicans had evacuated, but all sorts and types had stayed to claim abandoned property and serve the soldiers. The strange sounds of many languages were heard in the streets. Chameleons were everywhere. Now everyone was whispering about Burgoyne's surrender at Saratoga and why General Vaughan had, in fact, turned tail with his ships. Critics charged that Vaughan was but a vengeful coward, tardy in his aid to Burgoyne and selecting encounters where no defense would be mounted. Perhaps the British would not prevail after all. Each New Yorker was inventing a story to tell with a certain style to the King's men, but in such a fashion that it could be easily flipped over like a pancake on a hot stone if it should happen that General Washington were to win.

I soon discovered by chatting with my landlady that I was not the only one telling upriver tales, and I was somehow delighted. It seemed that General Vaughan was reporting that at Esopus he had faced hundreds of windows with muskets pointed from every one. I guess there was not enough soldier's glory in demolishing a town where no resistance had been mounted because the rapscallions had fled.

Once I had obtained a title of ownership, I then set about manumission—that process by which the bonded become free, and persons who are the property of others come to own themselves. And in the few days between these accomplishments under title of my fictitious husband, I owned two human beings, a man and a woman. Four hands, four feet, twenty fingers, not counting my own. And two heads, one set in a tricorn and the other in a white cap. Who were these people and how had they suffered? How did you think about yourself if you were property? Even British wives could not be sold at auction. Why should I find now that the measure of their safety was on equal footing with mine? I could see why my husband had abhorred this strange institution—it was not only that he thought work an inconvenience, but forced work for anyone was most certainly, at least in principle, an anathema. His thinking about justice did not extend, however, to me or to the imbalance of our collective labor. To his credit, he was adamant that the idea of owning another person was deeply awry. For humans to own humans like animals, this could not be the natural order before even the cruelest God. Men had got to be fooling themselves to think it. Had not Mr. John Jay come to Kingston to argue against it? I could now sense that my husband may have had an upright moral commitment, outside of any social conventions, and long before the war brought such issues to bear. Surely he had a keen nose for hypocrisy. He would have had an ear for Dr. Johnson's comment on the Republican effort: "How is it that we hear the loudest yelps for liberty among the drivers of the negroes?"

I now sought papers at a colonial office run by those appointed by the British, who did not question the legitimacy of the newly sealed titles issued with the waxed imprint of the Crown. Most of my mornings were spent in waiting rooms, waiting to see this official or that in his chambers. I told the clerk that I must return to Europe and could not take two slaves with me, and it was not within my consideration to sell them. I had heard that those in bondage who set foot in Britain were freed under the common law. "In any case, I stand to lose my property," I said, feigning indignation. Besides, they were farmworkers, and I had no intention of farming. I could not afford their ship passage and was not certain how they would be received at my destination port.

My prevarications flowed easily off my tongue and loosened my brain. My lies meant nothing to the clerk, but they enchanted a notion in me. Why had I never thought that I too could be free? I had enough in my remaining coins for a ship's passage. My mother's sisters had returned to the old country in decades past. Perhaps I could find my aunts in the ringed capital of my mother's birthplace, and perhaps a life different from the endless labors of farming awaited me there.

Sally and Samuel must have sensed that I was up to something. But if they did, they did not press me about it. I was not forthcoming, in case my scheme came to naught. It was only in my efforts to obtain their liberty that the patriotic struggle and all the squawking about the Rights of Man touched my heart at all. I realized that my conversion to freedom's advocate was awkward, as I had thought little about the conditions of slavery prior to my time at the cabin on the river in the company of those who in spite of a desperate circumstance and perhaps with a disregard to their own peril had cared for me with respect.

We found a seamstress and brought my mother's gowns to be cut and remade in the current fashions, as I had done for my daughter. Two for Sally and two for me. One had been lost and was probably now adorning the sweetheart of one of General Vaughan's soldiers. Although the fabric was old, it was still quite fine. We purchased sturdy merino for lengthening, new sleeves, and inserts into the skirts. With a pang for my daughter, I bought indigo stockings and drew them high upon my legs.

Samuel was restless, for there was never a time that he had ever not worked, and he did not know what to do with himself. We walked to the wharves and found him wage labor as a shiploader at a rate of three shillings per day, which was paid to me at the end of the week. I kept his coins in a purse and wrote daily entries in a ledger that I had bought, along with pen and ink and candles.

In the evenings, we worked at letters and numbers until Samuel could write his name and discern the dates and earnings. We practiced English. This Samuel Johnson was adept and quick. He could recite from memory what he had heard but once. We drew a calendar together. We counted out the money into his hands and matched it to the ledger. We borrowed an English Bible, and before I knew it, he could recite in English the book I had heard in Dutch verses on the beach. All twenty-one of them.

One morning, Sally asked me for permission for Samuel to invite a guest he had met at the docks for supper and an evening in their room. It seemed odd to me that she looked to me for this authority—a habituation, I suppose—and rather awkwardly I gave my encouragement. Once asked, I could not pretend that they did not think they needed my approval. During the day, Sally brought more than their usual frugal repast and spent some time in the back court-yard in preparation, setting a pot upon a small cook fire and stirring it often.

I ate at my landlady's table and retired early to my room. When I sat upon the window sill, I could see across the back courtyard to the shafts of light spilling out from the window of their room, and I found that a peculiar curiosity arose within me. I had seen their guest, a tall, dark man with trousers at midcalf and wild hair to his shoulders bristling out from under a tri-cornered hat. He stepped with enormous feet jutting below the narrow poles of his legs. He, however, was somehow dignified in a black frock coat as he ducked beneath their door frame. Mirth wafted upward toward me on the stippled light hanging with courtyard dust, and long hours of excited conversing ensued. I could not make out their words, but I knew they were now gesturing with the full force of their life's experience, amplified and emboldened by the process of retelling it.

The very cadence of their speech and its vocabulary were entirely altered from the polite evenings we had spent at accounting and the alphabet. By this, I came to know how much they reserved from me. I suspected that Obadiah would not speak augury to me again. On that beach by the river, he had called advisement from the depths of a realm that I had not the wherewithal to enter. And never would.

I thought back to one evening when I had stopped to collect his wages from his employer, as they would not put the money in his own hand, and we were walking together back to our lodging. I had asked him about my daughter. If his prescience could be applied to the movement of entire fleets of the King's ships, then surely he could apply it to the whereabouts of my daughter. He had the habit of walking a bit behind me, so I slowed to address him.

"Obadiah?" I asked him, wanting him to inhabit the role of prophet so that I could recover my ability to trust in everything that he said.

"Madam, my name is Samuel now. You can call me Samuel. I am at your service."

"Well, Samuel, then . . . Do you remember on the

beach by the river when the wind was wild, and Obadiah told me that my daughter was secure with her people and would have her inheritance and carry it forward for two hundred years?"

"Madam, I cannot remember all that I said to you on the beach. The fire that followed . . . the devastation . . . it was too much for me."

I sensed in him a deep hesitation, but I continued to try to draw him out.

"You told me that my daughter would have a legacy and that her legacy would be a story—my story—written in a book."

"It may come to be, Madam, it may come to be."

"But what did you mean by that? What book? What history? Which author?"

"I do not know the particulars, Ma'am. I cannot see the future. I am but a man—and not yet a free one. A man who is not free cannot see well or think well. Bondage is a confusion."

"If I tell you, Samuel, that soon you will be free, would that help?"

"Well, what do you think, Madam? If I can believe it, you know it would. Freedom is everything. But free or no, I am sorry, I can't tell you more about your daughter. I suspect you might have to let her go. That would be her freedom. And yours."

"How can I let go of my own flesh and blood? My only anchor to this earth?"

"Well, now or later it must be done. You can choose when but not whether. That is all I can say."

And indeed, he would not say more on that day or any other. He committed to nothing he had said previously, no matter how I pressed him. He said only "But Madam, I do not know your daughter. How could I tell her destiny or understand anything about her? I am but a laborer, and all I know is from my work." The mystic on the beach had retreated into the skin of an ordinary man with ordinary notions. Had I imagined a prophecy? Had I coughed up the stones of my own heart and spread them on the beach that night and arranged them in a pattern? Was I mistaking strange ritual of a foreign people for illumination?

We lapsed into silence, and he fell behind me. I heard his soft voice with his final remarks on the matter: "Madam, how many times did I say this about your daughter?" I told him, but once.

He said, "Well, then, Madam, I apologize."

So without any further confirmation or guidance, the power of Obadiah's prophecy waned. I still clung to parts of it and felt the power of what I could remember. Some of it had faded, so I read the verses of Obadiah again. But when I took the book to Samuel and asked him what they meant, he said only this: "But Madam, it says just there, 'Do not rejoice over the people on the day of their destruction nor look down on them in their calamity in the day of their disaster, nor seize their wealth. You should not stand at the crossroads.'"

And so I knew by his recalcitrance that he would not interpret my life for me or set me in a direction. Now I must do that for myself. I had not profited from the misfortune of others, but nor could I cast my lot with those who were so enigmatic and different from me. I did not fathom that Sally and Samuel, having helped me once, could help me now. It would be a grievance to expect it from them. Yet I needed help. I wanted to know so desperately that my daughter was safe, but I could think of no way to find her. The misfortunes of the Johnsons were cut of different cloth from mine, and we could not truly understand each other. Our futures would soon diverge. I lay on my bed in a strain of eavesdropping to their kinship and knew my utter solitude.

Each afternoon with great eagerness, I explored the streets. Sally was content to walk with me in the city, which was full of people of all sorts from everywhere. I asked her to do the shopping and watched her ask for prices and count change until I knew she could be quite shrewd. We walked of a day, down to the harbor—the Battery, they called it—and looked out upon a port full of fine ships. The large and handsome vessels of the British Navy were clustered, and several were moored to docks on the east side. Smaller sloops with sails, such as were once owned by my father, stippled the wider waters to the west. They leaned out toward the shores of New Jersey, a land it was told that General Washington had recovered by his cunning after losing purchase on this island. These ships would have an appearance of engagement in peaceful commerce if it were not for the minions of soldiers. Even with scarlet everywhere, all seemed of an ordered beauty and not of chaotic war—at least today.

We sat upon a bench, and as hope insinuated itself upon the morning, I drew inward and away from it. Had I not planted all my hope in my children? And now, finding them gone, I could not let it bloom again, no matter how bright the sun. Any optimism that I could call mine was once and truly dashed. Best it should lay aground and fallow. I began talking of my daughter to Sally Johnson, beside me on the bench, about how the loss of the child felt like the death of day in me and how the great weight of a dark water had seemed my only course in the wake of losing all that I had once held so dear. How are such losses borne? Now that Samuel Johnson had plucked me from the Great River where I had been drawn in the current but not plunged deep enough soon enough, I must wake up every morning to the day. But I did not know how I could without my daughter. I had foundered in the shallows—not a fish, not a bird. And now what? My feet of clay must step on land again. But how? I had asked Samuel for advice, and now I turned to his sister. I could not face the decision to abandon my children to their fates. I needed a kind of permission, and I sought it again here.

Sally said nothing but sat beside me with her gaze out over the expanse of the water and her face shining out of her white bonnet. I carried on and told her again, in greater detail and with more honesty, of a lost husband, the conditions of my marriage, a perplexing son, and a ravaged farm. I went on and on, plodding through her quiet and telling each sorrow, wending through each dismal trail where my sorry shoes had trod. She listened with a straight back.

Then when I was spent, she waited with an undaunted

patience until my words had dried a bit and thinned in the warmth of the sunshine. "Did you think that Samuel and Sally are brother and sister? Yea, Madam, it is not by blood. We were born of mothers from different parts of Africa. But we were taken from them. We ne'er knew our fathers. And in this sorrow we became brother and sister. Do you think I have not been here before? In this city? On these ships? At this port? Do you think I have not lost children and do not know the desperate, cloying tar pit of that loss? I have borne seven children. The first one had skin as light as yours, and the youngest was yet as dark as Samuel Johnson, and all the others were shades in between. And yet they all had the same light spill out from behind their eyes into this world. They all set forth laughter that hung on the breezes.

"Now they are gone . . . lost to me, and I know them not. But I remember them, those seven, as seven precious gifts, a good I have given the world. And do I think the world deserves this good? A good brought forth with effort from my very loins? Do I think that this is a world where light coming forth from behind the eyes of children and a child's laughter on the breeze matters? Well, sometimes I have to guess about that. But when I am with Samuel Johnson, he make me feel that it was not for naught. So he then is my brother. And I for him. I am his sister. You must find a brother or a sister to help you know that it was not for naught. We all need that aid. That is all."

She became quiet again, and I knew she would say no more and would tolerate no more desperation from me. She did not want my pity and afforded me the dignity of having none for me. When we walked again with a silence between us, I thought to become porous like a dry sponge from the sea dipped in a bucket, so that I could absorb the salted waters of her wisdom and reconstitute my shape.

In subsequent days, I pondered my future. I picked at the lock of it. I searched for a key. I walked more alone and left Sally and Samuel to their work and their evenings. It was walking about alone one afternoon that I saw the sign on the side street. There in green lettering on a red oval were the words *Book Shoppe* hung above the door of a wooden frontage with windows wide and short and so low you could not see into them. Impulsively, I stepped up to knock but then just tried the door, which swung into a dim, low room. I stood still at the entrance until my eyes adjusted, as I saw no one, and found myself at the top of a set of steps looking down upon a room with a long table at its center and shelves along the wall. Cautiously, I stepped down one at a time, and when I was on the third step, I called out hello in English. What slowly crept into my consciousness is that the table and every shelf were stacked with books, in towers on the table and spines outward on the shelves. Quite a few precarious vertical piles of them arose from the floor.

I had never seen so many books together in one place. Suddenly I was nervous. But a young man greeted me— "Good day, Madam"—and invited me inside. I stepped down from the stairs to the floor. He said I could peruse as I wished, and if I wanted any one book in particular,

I should but ask him. I said that I would like to browse amongst them if he did not mind. "Not at all." He then lit some candles on the table to enhance the light.

I peered at the spines of the tomes piled on one table. I lifted one and ran my fingers over the embossed leather of its title, then opened its pages to follow the strange iconic letters that must have spelled out Greek. I sensed the shop-keeper's eyes on me and quickly replaced the volume on its stack. But when I looked up, he was turned away, busy shelving in some order the books from a crate beside him in the far corner where he had squatted before the lowest shelf—taking books off the shelf and putting them on the floor, and taking books from the floor and putting them on the shelf and shifting their order from right to left and left to right. I had thoughts of fleeing, although I was as embar-rassed to leave as to linger.

Without looking up from his task, he asked me if I read Greek or Latin. I said that sadly I did not, only English and Dutch. He said he had few works in Dutch, only histories and philosphies, but everything in English. "You have a thirst?" I thought he offered me cider or tea, which I, of course, declined, as to accept such an offer seemed confus-ing. My "No thank you" was met by a long look that in turn gave me pause. I explained that I was not thirsty. He said nothing, and a long silence followed in which I kept my gaze upon the volume in my hand.

"You like to read then, and you are dry with wanting it?"

"Well, yes, I savor whatever book comes into my hands."

I did not tell him that the few books I had been able to

get my hands on had been my greatest solace in times of trouble and my most stable influence. I did not tell him that I taste words on my tongue. Or that characters in books have been at times my only companions. Sitting down with a book has been my only rest and words contrived by others and set upon a page my only charter.

"Have you seen this one? A novel told in letters." I saw the author's name and thought it was familiar to me. I wondered at a life full of letters. My own life had been so constrained in this aspect, with only three friendly missives from the midwife and then the miserable, cold, and uncomprehending correspondence from my father followed by only essential business from my brother. I imagined a life of letters with connections and appointments, multiple permutations of the same view, shared thoughts and sentiments—my life amplified in letters.

Now I recalled that Mr. Van Bummel had brought me *Pamela: or, Virtue Rewarded,* a life told in letters, but I had found it too irritating to finish reading it. At the time, I had not been able to explain my annoyance to Mr. Van Bummel or to my daughter, who had mocked me with sanctimonious impertinence. Now, looking back and remembering Mr. Van Bummel's lascivious designs on my daughter, I found the story of Pamela and her virtues especially unappealing. The stuffy book, the story of the life of a resolute servant girl armed only with her virtue and domestic purity, was much praised by the hypocrite Van Bummel because she repelled her master's seductions again and again. To me, her zeal for housewifery seemed entirely artificial. And the undisguised moral message that a girl's virtue is a commodity, although no doubt a common sentiment and perhaps true enough, I found an insult and a bore.

The bookseller's recommendation was soon revealed as a test of my mettle, for when I hesitated and could utter nothing enthusiastic in regard to my recollection of reading *Pamela*, the young man reached to an upper shelf and pulled out a slim volume. "Then perhaps you will find this of interest." He handed it to me, and I saw its title: *Shamela. An Apology for the Life of Mrs. Shamela Andrews*. What could this possibly be? My curiosity made my hands turn the pages, because I could not make out why he stood before me grinning and watching with amusement how I might react.

He must then have witnessed the turn on my face from puzzlement and trepidation to tentative comprehension when my eyes turned to the first page. It seemed he could wait no longer for my response. "It is by Mr. Henry Fielding, who has writ a great parody! How amusing to see the conventions of British society being taken for a ride down a country lane."

The pleasure of my afternoon extended with the shop-keeper's ill-concealed delight at showing me book after book. He seemed ever pleased as I paged leisurely through his collection. But the prices—I dared not to ask. On the table lay a ledger with titles and amounts. Each book was so very costly that it occurred to me that Mr. Van Bummel had been generous to us beyond belief. I could almost let myself feel kindly toward him. With some embarrassment, I divulged that I had but little money and could ill afford a purchase. If the man were dismayed, he did not show it, and as I took my leave, he invited me to return again. "You and I both have the thirst, so come to drink when you may."

Eventually I obtained a certificate of manumission, and I brought it to Samuel and Sally to read aloud. I saw Samuel's eyes fall upon the parchment and the pink of his forefinger pointed to each word in the script, which he read with difficulty but without any hesitation.

Certificate of Manumission

November 2, 1777

Know all Men by these Present that in Confideration that my Negro Man Servant named Samuel Johnfon and my Negro Maid Servant named Sally Johnfon, who have been good and faithfull Servants unto me are now defiring to be made free.

I do therefore by thefe prefent Witneffes and for Myfelf fully and abfolutely free Them and difcharge Them, the Johnfons, to act for Themfelves.

Then, keeping his eyes on the page and not looking up to mine, he ran his finger over the seals of the British governor and took Sally's hand in his own and ran her fingers over the document.

I had paid the expense of three copies and filed one in the office of the attorney of law (although which laws would prevail was yet to be determined) as well as the British registry. I bought a leather folder and put a copy in it, and I needed not to tell them to protect it with their lives. We walked by the attorney's chambers near the Custom House so that if they ever needed a copy, they would know to call for it there.

On this day, I ordered a special meal for them and brought it out to the back quarters from the dining room. I brought new candles, and we sat together. We had little to say to each other, but I could ascertain their gratitude, and their unspoken curiosity loomed within the silence. They had not asked me about my errands nor commented on what I had accomplished. I would not know how to answer them, in any case, for I could not have clearly spelled out my motivations. My actions might have been uninterpretable to them, as they may have been even to myself. I did not wish to speak directly to them, so I let the topic of their impending autonomy hang between us lest it would require us to discuss their enslavement and its humiliations.

I was not confident of what had driven me in my endeavor to free them and feared they might find my motivations wanting, worth only one, or perhaps, at best, two repetitions, in Sally's accounting of what made something true. My desire for their freedom was only vague and sentimental, a need in myself to do some good in the world, in contrast to what it could only mean for them—the consequence of having been born into bondage and now at liberty to act for themselves.

I recalled that night not so very long ago when Samuel had pulled me from the river, and I had asked and he had readily declared to me that he was already free. I was beginning to understand what he meant by this, and at the same time, I understood that it was not enough for only one man to think so. It was but only that he had made it clear to me, from the very outset, what he had known since he was a child, and I had not learned until midlife—that slavery is as impractical as it is abhorrent. We all must come to think it.

So this is how I came to be certain that I was deeply satisfied with every action I had undertaken and knew that they had made my freedom possible as much as I had enabled theirs. I was not so foolish that I did not realize that I was under the influence of my own purpose, and under altered conditions, I might have left them to their fate without even looking over my shoulder. I knew now that they could and would find their own way. My time with them was near to done.

Perhaps I was learning at least and at last that to clutch or grasp, whether at a coin or companionship or children, not only did not serve but was its own cage. Better to release all the fingers of your hand—pry them open if you have to—and wave Godspeed to all you most desire. You find freedom, after all, only beyond the fringes of the fear of losing everything.

After our celebration, life seemed to go on as before. Samuel kept working. Sally sewed and cooked. But we three knew everything had changed. Shortly thereafter, Samuel told us about a village across the river in Brooklyn founded by slaves, now free, that he had learned of from the loaders at the wharf. If he and Sally boarded a ferry and walked a day, they would find themselves among an entire village of free Africans. It was between the Waal Boght, or Bay of Walloons, and Fort Putnam, a redoubt built by General Nathanael Greene but abandoned by Washington's army a year ago, during the battle of Long Island. Samuel now had some earnings, land could be leased, and fishing boats could be put out on the bay. It would be as safe as anywhere, and there was no reason for them not to go.

And that they did. They came to me and told me and then without hesitation or delay prepared rapidly for departure, packing their few belongings in the blankets from their beds. I stood at the ferry and waved my handkerchief at them, wishing them well from deep within. As I turned away and walked along the bustling street from the docks back to my lodging, I used my handkerchief to dab at the moisture of my eyes and told myself that the wind and grit of these city streets were no longer tolerable.

As for me, at first I had easily accustomed myself to idle hours and so much company, but now on my own again and accountable to nobody, I grew restless. The late-autumn days were lovely, and although the streets were full of mud, I walked them. I stopped again at the book shoppe and with much excitement permitted myself a purchase. It indeed proved difficult to choose one among all those tomes, even with advice from the seller, and my visit extended for all the hours of an afternoon. In the end I chose by the count of pages, as I needed a friend for the weeks—not days—to come, and by the prospect of absorbing myself in a tale of adventure. Tobias Smollett's name intrigued me, as did the hero of his *The Adventures of Peregrine Pickle.* Would I not now become such a rover? And hopefully, by my wits and experiences, not so much the fool. As winter was rapidly approaching, I asked at the docks when the next ship to the Netherlands would depart and exchanged the entire value of my last button for a place on board for one.

PART III

✣

Thus it would seem that knowledge and genius, of which we make great parade, consist but in detecting the errors and absurdities of those who have gone before, and devising new errors and absurdities to be detected by those who come after us.

—DIEDRICH KNICKERBOCKER,
A History of New York, 1809

CHAPTER 7

Now Found

1790

Make women rational creatures, and free
citizens, and they will quickly become good
wives; that is—if men do not neglect the duties of husbands and fathers.

—Mary Wollstonecraft,
A Vindication of the Rights of Woman:
With Strictures on Political and Moral Subjects, 1792

M Y MOTHER WAS a good, industrious woman. It's
true that she did not get on with people very well,
but they did not know her, and perhaps saw her at her
worst or assumed the worst about her. But how many
times can a woman be forsaken before she is permitted to
complain? And if she complains, what will they make of
her? A scold has no place in the world and is often accused
of darker aberrations. Does anyone listen? No, they do not.
Even if they know that they themselves might have the

same bellyache and that her position may have merit. Or perhaps especially so. No, the upright citizens, with their overactive spleens, take their own discomforts, their own misdeeds, and their own unease (which they don't like to admit), and put these afflictions on her. She speaks for all with her evil tongue, and so they don't have to. And what does she get for speaking? Tsk, tsk, tsk. They push her into the village well, and she cannot rise again. At the very heart of the society, within its depth, as her little life decomposes, she fallows to poison the water from which they all must drink.

I remember that my mother's heart was kind, not cold, and her sharp tongue could both amuse and tell the truth. Although the last time I saw her the words were not gentle between us, I do not blame her for this. I wince when I think of that day, and the regret and sorrow weighs down on my soul when I remember it. How could I know that the whim to leave my mother's farm and the determination to be independent would cost everything—that a whole way of life would vanish?

Live free or die, they were saying then. How was I to know that as a girl of fifteen this did not apply to me, certainly in terms of citizenship? And in terms of personal liberty, it meant death to the freedom of my childhood—that innocent time of laboring side by side with another; that time when my mother and I were partners in unconflicted industry and intellect. I for her and her for me.

Years were lean after the war, with steep taxes to pay to the new State of New York to foster its economy. Over these years, though, the mid-river valley became a prosperous place to settle and more secure than it had ever been. My husband was able to get Tory land near New Paltz at quite a price, which he held and then resold at a profit so that I could move north again and return to the foot of the Blauwberg. I had a yearning for a garden and a dairy and was tired of speaking French, with its singsong. I wanted to speak a more guttural tongue and I longed for a closer view of the mountains. He wanted a trade more than to farm, and had established several businesses along the river. I had the good fortune that it was my husband's desire to please me, so he had a stone house built for us, and when my children were yet quite young, we packed up our household goods from the Huguenot town and moved north to the village where I had been born and where I had not set foot these thirteen years.

Oh, I looked for her. Don't think I did not. That is, I sent my future husband to. His diligent kindness was how I knew he would be my husband. In the spring of '78, he rode north, through the burnt town that they were then rebuilding, all the way to our bower and found it desolate. None of the village wives admitted to knowing anything about my mother's whereabouts or what could have happened to her. I wrote to my uncle at the only address I had for him in Albany, yet I never received a reply. This did not surprise me, given that my mother had told me about his business with Loyalists—after the war, he would have had to reinvent himself or disappear. My husband then rode to all the settlements and towns—Hurley, the Stone Ridge, Marbletown, all up and down the river. But it seemed she had vanished as mysteriously as my father had nine years previously. Perhaps she was off to join him in the vales. But I could not imagine it. My heart ached again.

Twelve years later, when we occupied our new house in the village, we asked our neighbors, many of whom were from other places, but not even any of the old-timers had any remembrance of what might have happened to her. And not long after we settled, we stopped inquiring.

We had never traveled much when I was a child, but now the world had opened up, and even the Blauwberg did not seem so remote. I promised my husband we would visit the Huguenot town often, which we did. We traveled through the big port, which was built up again after its burning, to visit his family, and my children knew their cousins, and their second cousins, and their cousins' friends. It was a gay potpourri and staved off loneliness, these threads of connection along the river with a great confluence of tongues and customs.

While I had learned the French way to cut shortening into flour for a fine flakiness and how to make particular cheeses for which they preferred the milk of goats instead of cows, and how to grow the string-like beans that they insisted upon at almost every meal, I still sometimes preferred fermented cabbage and *snert*.

The settlement had grown considerably since the war, as many farmers were no longer afraid to be so far west of the river, and new towns were erupting everywhere, even up on the Blue Mountain. Our village had a new hotel, a new schoolhouse where my children studied with a schoolmaster, several sawmills and clay works, and ever more citizens arriving upriver. In the winter, there was iceboating, and in the summer, a festival of flowers. All the towns grew with French and Germans and Belgians, as well as all the English speakers. The Jonnies settled down, moved to a new place, and forgot they were ever loyal to a monarch across the sea. They were quiet about their old politics or reinvented themselves as Revolutionaries simply by telling stories again and again with themselves in their neighbors' clothes.

All the talk of liberty and rights had led some slaves to think they would gain freedom, and some were set free, but only because a few private citizens thought it honorable to do so. Most labored on in bondage, even as the talk of "liberty for all" echoed around them. John Jay had tried to abolish slavery in the new State of New York when he first drafted the constitution in the meeting house of Kingston, but business interests had prevailed. Thus men could still own men—and women and children, of course. So not everything had changed.

People hung on hard to the old traditions and com- plained bitterly about the challenges of democracy, now that life, liberty, and the pursuit of happiness were all we had. Peter Vanderdonk, the oldest inhabitant of the vil- lage, and a descendent of the historian who had written the earliest accounts of the province, took it upon himself to gather up the pamphlets and documents and penned as many oral histories as he could. He found that among the Dutch families alone—the Stroops, the Wyncoops, the DeWitts, the Schoonmakers, the Van der Bogarts, and the Hommelbeenses, there were so many contradictory ver- sions of significant events that the task of summary soon proved beyond him. If the events were insignificant, their details were even more controversial, and he found himself mediating disputes late at night. He eventually claimed his need for an earlier bedtime and gave up his attempt to document and interpret the pre-Revolutionary society.

Nostalgia is a disease, however. And it was not only Mr. Vanderdonk who suffered from it. So he applied to a scholar from the great port of New York, whom he had heard was writing a history of the reign of the Dutch governors. This Diedrich Knickerbocker was a famous historian who had trained in the great universities of Europe and who took interest in the old Dutch way of life. However, Mr. Knickerbocker's landlord replied by letter to Mr. Vanderdonk that the good gentleman was immersed in his research and the writing of *The History of New York, from the Beginning of the World to the End of the Dutch Dynasty,* which was a very important endeavor, as it was the first attempt at an authentic American accounting of the times. Such a scholar could not be distracted from the import of such a noble project and most likely could not spare the time to venture upriver. So I am not sure Mr. Knickerbocker ever actually came to our village or interviewed the good people here until much, much later. Probably too late, when many witnesses and participants in the old Dutch life had not returned after the war, or had grown so old that their memories twisted through the years and could not be allocated to one period or another.

The time before the war now seems romantic. And people reflected back upon it with endless reminiscent fervor. In their remembering, they made life like a faery tale. Although the bower life had been tranquil enough, the people forgot how hard they had worked and recalled in a reverie the inconveniences, which they now referred to as the old good times. It is true our little village had not much trouble from the Indians, because unlike some other villages, we had kept our juniper liquor to ourselves, and that did much to ensure peace. We had also used our Dutch sensibility of good trade and land sovereignty, which, at least, recognized the Indians as a people with land tenure. We were just a bit fairer than our British counterparts, which does not say all that much about justice, tolerance, or equity, and in the end we were most likely just as greedy—or even greedier, given that we were Dutch. In any case, the Dutch laws were now dismantled, first by the British and then by the new state government, and our customs mocked and ignored. Even so, we had yearned as much as any people to see the conditions of our endless toil set upon the stage of world events. Who would not? And the war had offered us such an opportunity.

Looking back upon our old life, you may think, as Mr. Knickerbocker did (for he did end up writing a considerable amount about us), that we were a simple people wanting a simple life. You might romanticize the thunder in the skies of our mountains—and quip, as my mother would, *"Als de hemel valt, krijgen we allemaal een blauwe pet"*: "If the sky comes down, we'll all be wearing a blue cap." You might succumb to the charming cadence of voices from the past and their telling of amusing old tales of Hendrick Hudson's sailors rolling ninepins. You could idealize the wide lines and sloping roofs of our stone houses and the stature of

281

our barns. You could insist on the especial innocence of the rosy cheeks and wide blue eyes framed by the starched bonnet of a young blond girl with thick braids. But might I make the suggestion that perhaps it would be a mistake to underestimate the concordance of the girl's heart pulsing in her chest with the drums of time beating across the globe with the Republican Spirit? We were not as naïve as we looked.

My case might be made in point. You may have thought of me as an innocent bower girl, concerned only about my milk pail and my prospects of marriage. But I was attuned to the foment and contemplated my place in the world. My introduction to the serious consideration of the condition of womankind began when the schoolteacher first came to our village, and I began to read in earnest. Once the thirst had awakened in me, I had to drink. I was encouraged by Mrs. Adams, who at that time was advocating for the education of girls. She wrote in a letter to her husband that she regretted the narrow, contracted education of the females of her own country and connected this poverty of learning with the conditions of our servitude.

I now thought of all sorts of possibilities for my daughter that I knew my mother could not have dreamt of for me. You could say perhaps that the unintended consequence of my reading was that a wild imagination like my father's erupted within me, and you might consider imagination itself to be unfeminine. But perhaps it was not my education but the shock of my father's departure that had first caused my mind to bloom.

I was most certainly a woman of the times, as well as

a girl who evolved out of the personal circumstance of her childhood. Who could tell what cart was before which horse? It was just at the time of my father's disappearance that the schoolmaster came to our village. And with him came the wider world. He traveled to Boston at least several times a year and returned as often with a supply of books. The schoolmaster departed for the entire endless summer, when I was left without the distraction of daily lessons—only a miserable English grammar to study by myself, and the tasks of carding wool and churning butter on the lonely farm.

In the early years, he had brought mostly European classics from Mr. Knox's famous bookshoppe, which he lent me as part of my daily lessons and which I struggled through. I learned that Pericles was the first citizen of the first democracy. But he also brought newspapers and pamphlets that suggested democracy and citizenship for us all. To my great surprise and delight, I discovered that some articles were written by women! In any case, woman or man, we dissected every word. We set them in the context of what we had learned of the histories of Greece and Rome. And we had no doubt that the expounded principles of liberty and justice applied to us.

When I say *we*, I mean mostly Mr. Van Bummel and I. For while there were many other pupils, and some of them older than I, they were often not serious about their studies. I soon observed that Mr. Van Bummel did not find them quick. I came to know that he discovered in me an especial intellect, which he believed he had implanted, and took credit for. I was certainly interested in learning, and he, therefore, gave me a particular attention. As I grew and learned, he sometimes asked me what I thought of certain passages, ones he himself was not quite sure of. That is how I came to know that although he could not quite admit it, he depended on my intellectual development.

My aptitude did not make me particularly popular with the other students, but I did not care so very much. Perhaps I had learned not to concern myself about what others thought of me, given my father's disappearance and my mother's way of coping. I enjoyed that special privilege of having books lent out to me, sometimes for months, and this more than compensated for not having first turn at jumping rope.

It was not long before I started to spend more and more time at the school and left more and more of my work to my mother. I took my cue from my brother, who barely came home to sleep, although it was a mystery how exactly he spent his days. He was not so much of a pupil. I could hear my mother become sharper as she grew more tired. And as her complaints became both a greeting and a fare-well, the less I wished to listen to her peevishness. *"Ikke, ikke en de rest kan stikken"*: "Ah, me, me, me and the rest can choke." Now I regret my disrespect.

My brother had decided to join the New York militia, and the night before he marched off with the musket my mother had given him, we had stayed up talking about our destinies in grandiose terms. It was clear that he thought little of the consequences his departure held for her, so entirely absorbed was he with the expectations of General Washington and whether he would get a uniform. Indeed, he assigned me to break her the news, and I wondered how my brother would fare against the British if he were not even brave enough to tell his own mother his plans. I think she had anticipated his departure in any case but could not face that losing him then might be forever. So instead of pleading with him, she turned inward and withdrew into her work. She expected me to do the same. But I felt only helplessness in the wake of her despondency, so greatly increased by his absence, and I escaped as often as I could from the farm. A girl, however, cannot march off with a musket, so I had bided my time and fretted.

Of course, I did not then think of myself as selfish. We wanted only to speak to injustice. I wanted desperately to take part in the new America. I could hardly do so at the foot of the Blauwberg. A great excitement had fevered my brain, and I, like my brother, could no longer bear my mother, her provincial fears, and her little bower.

So how was a young, quick girl like myself not to become heady? And how would I know that it would come to naught? That I would find myself so very glad to settle myself again in this very village—that I would miss her so. Perhaps I should have no regrets. It was a radical time and a time for radical hopes, even as they bordered on delusion. We appealed to heaven with every expectation that heaven would answer us. And in certain ways, it had. It pays to petition your desires. Sometimes it pays. I was not now one to scoff at my blessings. But still.

Fantasies of independence were fostered in many, not just foolish bower girls. I have even heard since that the famous first lady, Mrs. Adams, had written yet another missive (one of many I am told) in those times to her husband at the Continental Congress, entreating him to remember us. "Do not put such unlimited power in the hands of the husbands," she had implored. And given that our future vice president and president replied by laughing at her, mocking his acclaimed "friend" and "advisor"—his very words—we were not mistaken in our thinking, only in our hopes. We did not misinterpret the words that were shouted and printed on the banners. Perhaps it had been a mistake to teach us to read them. Did the good gentlemen of the new nation think we would not notice the distance between their words and their willingness?

When I arrived in the village, I discovered that my brother had been returned for seven years, and I was so glad to find him again. He was much changed, and my mother would have mourned the passing of her son from an unformed youth into so haunted a man. War changes men, and they are never the same, I am told. So it was with my brother. He refused to speak Dutch to anyone and was a man of few words in any language. He lived in a room at the sawmill, for which the town was now named, and had some role in keeping the wheels turning there. He lived alone, as he had never married, and he seemed to have few friends.

When we first came upriver, I soon heard that he lived nearby, but I never saw him among the town's society. So I made an effort to visit him at the sawmill and found him dressed in the rags of his old uniform. He wore a coarse cloth coat of his old regimental colors of light brown with blue facing and a white linen cravat. Both were torn and stained, and no buttons fastened the jacket. He wore a buckskin waistcoat and breeches of drilling, which were stretched and falling down so that they had to be held up with twine. His home-knit woolen stockings were so full of holes that they could have been made of the cheese of the Swiss, and his low shoes did not match and had no buckles or straps. A felt hat with a low crown and wide cocked-up brim was smashed over his long hair and awry on his head. But I recognized him immediately and was overjoyed to see him again.

In his reacquaintance with me, I learned that he had come back to the village at the end of his long journeys. When he had signed with the Ulster militia, the Third Yorkers, he had first been sent to defend the western frontier at Fort Schuyler, also known as Fort Stanwyx. But he arrived there after the British siege had been broken and had spent most of his time drilling, building mud fortifications, and serving officers tea. So he then volunteered for the Sullivan Expedition of 1779 and had walked farther west to the land of those narrow lakes, where he had helped roust the four tribes of the Iroquois from their own land. After only one battle against the British, he had walked with Sullivan's troops quickly from settlement to settlement, slashing and burning over forty villages and the crops in their fields with the rest of the soldiers. If you can't shoot a Redcoat then an Indian will do.

Only later did we learn that a whole way of life had been destroyed. Those who had survived the razing starved or froze to death outside of the British Fort Niagara that winter, when the Tories would not share their winter rations with their Indian allies. Fair-weather friends, I guess. Given Sullivan's quick withdrawal, it was now clear that the obliteration of a people, and the entire manner in which they lived, was surely the very purpose of the endeavor. Killing two birds with one stone. Listening to my brother, I was reminded again about how fortunate we Hudson Valley Dutch had been to live peacefully on our farms for over a hundred years. I was glad that my grandfather had not sought his fortunes on the Mohawk River, like so many other Dutch settlers. But after the war, there was no more trouble with the natives, thanks to Sullivan and his men, with my brother among them.

By late fall of '79, my brother had marched south, and by winter, he nearly froze to death while camped with the New York Brigade in New Jersey. Then he walked all the way to Virginia and back with the regulars of General Washington's army. For two more years he marched, and when the Third disbanded, he joined the First New York led by Goose Van Schaick for another two of stomping around New Jersey again waiting for the treaty. Finally discharged when the war ended, he found that the new State of New York was in debt and that his pay vouchers were worthless. When the borders of New York were drawn, he was offered farmland in the West—which Sullivan's massacre had made permanently safe for settlement—as wage compensation. But he did not wish to farm. After all his marching, he returned to the village penniless, and he did not seem to be able to forget all those steps he had taken.

I learned all this when he invited me into his room, which was attached to the workings of the mill. It was windowless and dark and dank. The wheels were cranking loudly with the cacophony of the stream, which made it difficult for us to converse. But I soon found that this did not matter. He listened not to any discourse or reply from me. He turned all threads back to the battlefield, the hardships, the witticisms of those he had once known. My brother was not living in the present. He was still on the march. And whatever he said was about the men in the regiment, as if I had known them, and as if they were part of our present society. It did not seem pertinent to my brother that he had a niece and a nephew, and he seemed not to know my husband or care about my family at all. Oh, Soldier Boy, Brother. What happened to you? I am sure I will never know.

I found him unwilling to play the role of uncle or brother. I felt injured by his vacancy, as he was the only blood family that I could know. So I left him to his sawmill and forged ahead in my new life, and found sisters and brothers in my friendships in town and among my husband's sisters and brothers and joy in the intimacy of my own household.

Village life, now as we scuttled onward through the first decades of our new nation, went on as ever but was enlarged and enriched. With the greater society, the winters were not so long nor quite so lonesome as they had been.

Traditions mixed and melded—as in my own family, when I found myself baking my New Year's cake instead of frying it round with a center hole. I still used my mother's cast oven, though, a triumvirate with a curled lip. I had retrieved it from under the floorboards in the barn at the old farm, where I knew my mother hid things, along with a felling axe with a perfect blade. I was so very glad to have an emblem of the old life, and such a weighted one as that.

I found that I had learned a thing or two from her before we were parted. A place for everything and everything in its place. Looking back, I was grateful that she had insisted upon an ordered house and that she had kept it herself, with much industry and intent. What else did she have to fortify herself in this uncertain world? Now that I was no longer a child, I imagined too that she was a woman of passion. Did not her love of books spell an allegiance to a world of imagination that was removed from her days? After long hours of work she could indulge in a reading life, of an evening before she drifted to the world of sleep and restoration. She also loved to sing, and does not music come forth from an awakened heart? At times the silliest of ditties rollicked her with laughter.

> *Hyder iddle diddle dell*
> *A yard of pudding's not an ell.*
> *Not forgetting tweedle-dye,*
> *A tailor's goose can never fly.*

Melodious laughter, pleasure in reading books, well-cooked food, and silly songs were the parts of her that I endeavored to pass to my children, although they never knew these were from her. Somehow I did not wish to call their attention to the absence of their grandparents, which I might be called upon to explain but could not.

Life was good at the foot of the Blauwberg. I made cheeses, but unlike my mother, I no longer milked cows and sheep. There were hired farm boys to do it. I made them both in the Dutch way—the way my mother had taught me—and in the French style of my mother-in-law, and they became quite well known in the village, and in other villages too, for their quality and richness and how well they kept. I had a workshop behind my house, and a lovely fenced garden with fragrant herbs and a vegetable plot, but also roses, which, when they bloomed, I cut for the table.

My husband's businesses prospered, and we had money for cloth and books and few worries. We enjoyed each other's company and admired each other's work. I made friends among the women in the town, and my husband was well-liked and respected among the society of men. We settled well in the village, as it came alive in its slide toward a new century.

Thus I was startled and dismayed to hear the conversation of two young women on a day when, accompanied by my daughter, who was just eight years old, I found myself picking over a new selection of buttons in one of the new dry goods shoppes. These were two wives, probably my age, who had not been born in the village but had come here after the war. They did not know the old families, nor did they know the old ways. They were looking out the window of the shoppe when one commented upon the long blue shadows crawling to the rim of the village, down from the Blauwberg and spilling onto the river plain. "Oh yes," said one to the other, "the devil slides down among us upon those shadows. Oh perhaps not all the way down to the village—for he is repelled by the gatherings of goodwill at the tavern and the singing of the hymns at the church. He stops at the old abandoned bower at the base of the clove. It is there that the devil does his work."

"What work is that?" inquired the other. "No one is idle in this town, and idleness is where the dominie says that the devil finds a foothold."

"Well, he stomped his boots on the fields of that farm, for certain. He has left his footprints. That old bower with the fall-down house is where a farmwife took a hatchet to her husband and clove him in two because he would not do her bidding. And she bound and rolled his cleaved body into the barn, where it lay frozen in the pudding of its blood and baled in hay for the entire months of winter. When the snow melted and the lilacs blossomed, she put each of his limbs through her meat grinder, turning its handle one orbit at a time. And she salted and herbed the ground meat for sausage. And used the skin of his stomach to roll them up and the string from his gut to tie them. She then fed them through the summer to her children, with the best pickled cabbage with caraway seeds. She made *tête fromagée* from his head, which she fed upon herself and washed down with the remains of the juniper; the very white lightning from her husband's own staved barrel. And she then went mad. And her children ran from her. That's what the blue shadows will do if they fall upon your bonnet day after day. They will make dark ravines in your mind, and your heart will plunge into its crevasses. Those devil's shadows will drive you to a lonely delirium where your husband is your most bitter enemy and your felling axe is your only friend."

I looked up from the buttons and stared blankly at the women as they whispered at the window, not believing what I had heard. "Let's leave the purchase of buttons to another day," I told my daughter nonchalantly. I had already clamped my hands over her ears and now steered her out the doorway and into the street, where I hoped the bustle would distract her from that gruesome exchange.

But she had heard everything, as children will. As we walked, I could hear the questions formulating in her wide-eyed silence. And after but a few minutes, she asked me. "But Mama, why won't you buy buttons? What did those Damen say? Who? Who, Mama? Who chopped up her husband and made blutworst of him? And fed her children with it? Mama, who? What farmhouse? Which barn? Which children? Are they Dutch? Do we know them?"

I tsked. In my urgency to quell my daughter's imagination, I kneeled on one knee in the street for emphasis and grabbing her sleeves drew her eyes directly to mine. "*Meidje*, don't believe those lies. Those women tell perversities for vulgar amusement. For the purpose of alarming us. And themselves. They do not really believe what they say to each other. Perhaps they are a little miffed with their husbands and suffer ennui. Perhaps they are bored by the labors of their days, and turn to the dark cloves of their minds for a bit of mystery and maliciousness to speed the beating of the blood in the arteries of their necks and the veins of their wrists, to make the time pass, lest they fall asleep in the dullness of their daily lives. They fear the blue shadows of the mountains, but I grew up beneath them, and there is nothing to fear. I promise you. Those women do not have the courage to look into their own hearts, to understand that a woman's love for her husband and children is not only honey but hard work and boredom. And such a tempered love is the stuff of survival. For everyone."

I could see the anxiety recede in my little one's eyes. She believed me. I could feel her comfort in my authority and her willingness to move on in her attention because the matter was settled with certainty. Staunch is what children expected from their parents. And truth telling is what they expected of their mothers. I amazed myself at how easefully I concealed from her my horror and my doubt.

Living in the village again evoked my mother in my thoughts in a way she had been missing. I grieved for her, and there is nothing as tender as a guilty heart. Had I been an ungrateful child? I could see now that I had been wrapped up in my own shawls. I am now disheartened to know that she never will meet my children. She would have loved them and spoken Dutch to them and fried up *oliebollen*. I had written to her with the pen and ink I had removed from her writing desk and sent it to our little village so she would know my news. That was after the big town had burned, and I doubt my missive had found her. I feared that the letter was mislaid by the chaos of the war. The last time we were together had not been sweet. And now she would never know that her daughter still loved her and had grown safely to make a marriage and bear precious children.

I now contemplated whether she had perished in that vengeful fit of burning by the King's soldiers. I had no idea that she might have ventured through that town, but no one I asked seemed to recall her fate. At that time, I had fled farther south to the Huguenot town, which remained unmolested. It was Kingston that was marked as a hotbed of Revolutionaries and a nursery for almost every villain in the country. And all perished there: one hundred sixteen houses, one hundred three barns, two schoolhouses, the academy, forty-six barracks, seventeen store houses, the courthouse, and the church. We had prepared to flee from New Paltz as well, but, miraculously, the British ships had been called south again, when, with the news of the American victory at Saratoga, the threat of local battles disintegrated in the autumn fogs.

But dead or alive, I was dismayed about how my mother was remembered by others, for I doubted what was said about her could possibly be true. Yet these were the tales that were told, and there was little that I could do to influence them, and, indeed, I had no sure knowledge to restore her reputation.

I missed her. I had lived these long years without her, yet she had shaped me more than I had known. And I was just beginning to realize that now. It was not too many years before the fateful day when I left my mother's house that I had begun to even sense the outer world. Up until that time, we lived at its precarious edges, and my mother interpreted and filtered daily life and its meanings, as I did now for my own children. She clearly had my well-being in mind when she insisted that I spend as much time as possible at the school, even as it meant more work for her and even as I was involved in learning she could hardly comprehend. But had she also lied to me? The way I lied to my own children. And for the same purpose? To protect them from who I really am and the harshness of what I really think.

The more I wondered about her, the sadder my heart. How could I come to her aid when I knew so little about her? How was I now to know . . . now that she was encircled by the pettiness of rumor and no longer here to defend herself? I could *not* believe she was a woman who would take a hatchet to her husband. No matter what. That was too much and betrayed the memory of my childhood. And the tale of the sausage? That was also too ridiculous. So clearly a figment of little idle minds. There was no way to rescue her or to rescue her reputation. So I remained silent and let them talk. To protect my children from ridicule, I could only hide my connection to her, which was easy enough. With my new name and the way we spoke French in the family, I believe not too many of the newer residents realized that I was not really one of them but a member of the quaint society of Dutch elders. And while the dark rumors circled about a certain woman at a certain farm my father's name had been all but forgotten, as was hers.

And my old neighbors . . . what was there to distract them? You may think that the people of an isolated village on the frontier that was the midland alluvial plain of the Great North River would be ignorant of the currents running through what was thought of as civilization. At one time, this might have been true. But now the villagers and the farmers thirsted and paid more for news than they did for beer. Indeed, they could make their own beer. The local news, however, was not usually as bubbly as the mead and often became stagnant by its repetition, even in these modern times. So gossip and rumor and lies were still our theatre—and no admission was charged.

Ah, and I began to feel that I was quite a bit like her after all, which I admitted to myself more and more as I felt the cloud of my deception settle behind my eyes. My failure to defend her reputation was not without shame. But in a small village, gossip is a green-eyed monster that eats everything, and I could do but little to stop it. So I hid in plain sight: in the shadows that slid from the mountains and—contrary to what ground in the gossip mill—did not stop at the outlying farm but drew all the way to my own door.

Now I thought back more and more about how she must have perceived the events of my departure, and I felt the pangs of my former impertinence. My mother seemed to think I was running off with or to Mr. Van Bummel, which was silly. He was too old and very pudgy, and all he sputtered about were the separation, the Safety Committee, the Rights of Man, the state constitution, and a new world order. It was all exciting, and I was given to learning, but political education is not necessarily romantic. Once he put his hands around my waist at the schoolhouse, but I promptly set them off me and took great care to ask other students to stay with me, so as not to be alone with the man. I began to leave promptly with the other pupils. By then I was studying quite well by myself, and he still lent generously from his library.

Mr. Van Bummel did help me to find a position, but his behavior on the last day that I saw him was reprehensible, and I had already determined to sever myself from his acquaintance once I had called in his favor. True, he had instructed me with great care about the dangers I would face and what to do and what not to do, as if he were sincerely concerned for me. I had noticed that he seemed a little reluctant to give me the information I needed, but in the end he did not insist that I stay at the farm. And at the point of our violent rupture, he had said what was hardly comprehensible. He left the village that day himself and departed earlier than I. It was rumored that he went off to join the militia, although I could hardly imagine him as a soldier. In later years I heard he became a congressman, so I see that his political passions served him, although how they served the people still remains a question. In any case, I am not unhappy to have never encountered him again.

In the days before we both quit the village, I sensed that there was something he wanted to tell me, but he who was usually so blustery and opinionated was suddenly not forthcoming. He held back. I could see it in his eyes. He never wrote a letter that I received, so I never came to know what it was that he was thinking. He may have written, as he had promised, but letters traveled better on the east side of the river, thanks to Benjamin Franklin's wife who ran the postal service. It faltered here in the rugged West. After the town was burned, who knew what happened to the post.

When we moved back to the village, I finally visited the old house. I do not know what happened there, for it was stripped bare, and the heavy panels of its half doors were broken off their hinges from flapping. The land had lain fallow for all these years and was completely grown over. The sheep pasture, no longer a meadow, had altered to a scruffy wood. The great barn's aspect was gloomy and haunted. Its wide portals were barred shut and had survived. I found myself hesitating, as I had as a child, at the doors that closed over its cavernous maw. I spraddled my legs broadly beneath my skirts and unbound my grief of remembrance. I unlocked the fingers from my palms and pushed up the pins on the rusted hasps. With an effort, I slid the bar across its braces and stepped back, spreading my arms to let the doors swing wide. I did not want to enter, but feeling I must face something—although I knew not what—summoned my courage. I walked down its cathedral-like threshing aisle toward the wall where my father's hat once hung and lifted the loose boards in the flooring.

It was while inhaling the musty odors of the long-unused barn and experiencing the profound delight (and not just for the expense) of finding my mother's cast-iron oven in her secret hiding place—a hiding place no one else would seek—that I was surprised to also find the felling axe. Now as I saw the elegance of its outline on the floorboards, suddenly the smell of blood erupted in my memory. I had sniffed among my mother's petticoats and smelled that smell. It was in the autumn of the year my father had vanished, and I was but a maid of seven or eight. Crouching over the nook where it had been stashed and looking down upon the perfect edge of its head, a tumult of overwhelming doubt and misery almost knocked me over. I put my trembling hands on the floor for support. I recalled a laundry trough of water hidden in the back of a stall filled with bloody sheets. I saw my mother at the foot of my sickbed covered in blood, her braids thick with ice and her eyes wild in her face.

Now in the dark at the back of the barn, I gazed on the menace of the blade as it gleamed from the depth of its hiding place, and was reluctant to lift it. What secrets were smelted within it? The Excalibur of a Dutch farm. Finally, I reached for it and felt its weight. The truth about my family would be heavy enough, I was certain. I brought the flat of the blade into my palm and raised it to the height of the floor. I then held it heavy in my two hands and wondered. What did I really know? Nothing of my father. My brother? Never really known to me, though I lived by his side—a shadow himself—and now so receded. And my mother? What could I really fathom of the forces that drove her? I now understood, as I kneeled on these boards, that as a girl of fifteen, the age I was when I last knew her, I could hardly see beyond the five fingers of my own hand. Who was she? What had happened in the darkness of this barn?

Retrieving the oven, a vessel of nurture, and the axe, a farm tool employed for who knows what, was enough. I could not carry both, so, of course, I propped the axe in the corner of the dark barn and departed along the track with the oven. I no longer visited the old bower and forged ahead in my new life. I abandoned the innocence of a young woman and took on a knowingness more suitable to my age. I kept my dark suspicions to myself, for they were not well formed. And I did not know how I would learn anything further. I had dutifully looked to my childhood as best I could, but nothing new had emerged since the onslaught of fragments in the barn—not that I really desired it to. Childhood itself is not so very painful, but remembering it is a certain agony.

My husband stripped the goods of the old bower house further by removing the windows and even some of the flooring. We discovered that my father never held the deed to the land. It was not possible for private citizens to buy land from the Indians at that time, and I know not how he came to build a house there. It was certainly not the best land for farming, with the mickle of stones in its soil and its distance from the river.

The fate of my mother is a puzzle, as for most of my life my father's fate had been. Had she worked spinning flax in a knitting factory? The new State had been in great need of linen cloth and stockings for General Washington's army at that time, and houses had been set with wheels and looms, and flax and wool were gathered at the docks. Shillings could be earned, and although colonial paper script was worth less and less, food and shelter had been provided. Many of the new store buildings and houses, erected quickly by those fleeing the theatres of war to the south, had been built of wood, thatched, and close together. (How my mother would have hated that. She was always proud that she had a stone house with a tile roof—a proper Dutch house.) And so they would have flamed up like a hay barn, I imagine, all at once, when General Vaughan ordered his men to descend from their ship and set their torches. And all the good people in them would have turned to ashes in their beds. Had my mother been among them? Although I now know that the citizens had evacuated to Hurley, and no women were reported to have died that day, I could not help but wonder.

I thought often of her, for it was like touching a sore tooth with my tongue. Though my life was full with my own motherhood, how grieved I was not to find her again. If she were to see me, she might be pleased, and I hoped to please her. It was my agony to imagine her perished in flames, but given that there was no word of her, how could I know? Some thought she had drowned in the river, but no one knew for sure. I liked to dream that she had found a new life and a good man to love her, as I had done. My husband encouraged me in this kind of thinking and reminded me of the good in the world we hear so little about, given how long it takes to tell all the bad news.

I thought so often of my mother, and so rarely of my father, whom I remembered hardly at all, that I was stunned to hear a rumor in the village that a crazy old man, a Cheesehead, had wandered in from the mountains and was using my father's name.

I was both astounded and annoyed to hear such gossip. Who was this oddity who had sallied forward into my society; my neat little life? How dare he use my father's name! I sent my husband immediately to interview him at the tavern, where I heard he was sleeping under the outside bench and begging for cider or mead from the locals and day travelers. Hugo returned to tell me that the man had a powder musket that was a half century old and a beard that reached to the knees of his breeches, which were very much of an old style.

My husband said that the codger had detailed my mother and our life at the farm, but he could not tell whether the ancient man held forth with authenticity or not. He could hardly understand him, and Peter Vanderdonk had had to interpret. But Peter had been so excited himself that my husband could hardly make out any sense in the story. All sounded to him that it was but a dream. With Peter's help, the old man had convinced several of the old villagers that he was certainly their neighbor of yore and, indeed, my father. The younger citizens just laughed and guffawed, and then bought more rounds of lightning to augment the thunder in his tale.

But I knew it could hardly be true. And I chose to ignore it. People will indulge in silliness no matter what. Let them. What harm in it? Yet as the days rolled by, at every neighborly encounter, the water flowed to the same ditch. "Did you hear about the old man in his old clothes with the old gun, who lost his dog and twenty years of his life? Could he be your father?" Of course not, I insisted, but I gradually found myself ever more curious and angry.

So I went to the tavern myself and found him asleep on the bench, with his beard ruffling in the wind of his snore and sliding over his chest to the dust. I looked hard into his face. I myself would not know him from a horse as my own father. He just seemed ancient and strange to me. And he aired a terrible stench.

I shook him, and he awoke in a befuddled state. Looking up at me, he said with wonder, "What angel is this? Aren't you lovely?" His insouciance startled me first and just as soon annoyed me. He then went on, "My wife looks like you." And then he said my mother's name. I almost turned and ran from him, but he caught me with the words "And we have a little daughter named Judith, just seven summers old. And a son. Do you know where I can find them? I went up to the mountains and fell asleep and had an ever-strange dream. The people here, in this inn, they just laugh at me. But you look kind and reasonable, so please help me to find them. I imagine that my dinner might be ready. My wife is a good cook." As he spoke, I had to admit with much chagrin and an inner turmoil that a reminiscence blossomed. There was something about him that I knew I knew.

Heat prickled my neck and then crawled upon my cheeks from what must have been, what? Shame? Longing? Hot tears had sprung from the well of the childhood that recognized his voice. The shame of abandonment; the longing for all that had been lost. I turned away from him who was now aroused and bewildered, as he reached forward, sitting up on the bench, to grasp at my sleeve.

Overwhelmed now, I turned back upon him, and, not wishing to attract attention from any passersby, I spit a whisper through my teeth: "How dare you? You stupid beast of a man. If your wife cooks so well, then why did you forsake her? If indeed you are who you say you are, then where were you when I was laboring endlessly by her side so that we could make a table? And now you come here—with not a reasonable word to explain yourself, with your untoward sentiment, and your dreamy remembrances! What of your wife? What do you think became of her? How was she, and her name after her, dragged through the mud of your disappearance! If you were my father then, believe me, you have no entitlement to speak it to anyone, no claim upon us, for you have not been a father, as indeed you were no husband. And cannot claim to be one now. You were and are more a bedpresser! A renegade with no cause . . . no purpose! A useless, feckless dog of a man!"

My whisper had risen and grown thick in the dimming light of the day to a shout. I did not care who heard me now and howled invective at him. "Ah, do you remember the face of your wife now? And do you recognize in the scold who now takes you to task, the pride of her daughter?! We are family! Her and I. While you are nothing but an alienated dreamer who smells of dog piss." I saw the wonder in his eyes, the dawn of recognition. Oh yes, he had been here before. He had stood in awe before my mother and wondered speechlessly how to escape his pickle. In disgust, I pulled myself away and drew my sleeve from his grasp. How could I remove fast enough? I scuttled away from him and did not respond to his feeble callings after me.

As I walked rapidly through the village to my home, I shook with the tremors of my own felt violence. I thought as well of the rumors that I had heard from the village women and how I had become to believe their indictments. Again the shame of having turned from my mother and her memory flooded my heart. I was startled by the hot weeping of my eyes and the spittle on my lip, which I wiped with my sleeve. The heat of my mind cooled in the dusky distance between the tavern and my home. As I rounded the corner of the lane and saw the just-lit lanterns gleaming from the windows of the fine stone house, it suddenly occurred to me that, indeed, the appearance of this man, my true father or no, could serve its purpose—its turn on the mandrel. I must make pie from fallen apples, as my mother would have done. I would bake her name in such a pie and make the villagers eat it. I turned back into my own footsteps, with a resolve to set the circumstance to my own purpose.

So that is the how and why of taking in the old man and having a father for a little while. And what a father! That very evening, I went to fetch him and led him to my own house. He seemed to have forgotten the rancor of our previous encounter by the time I returned to the tavern. Someone had bought him mead, and it was only the promise of a good meal and a soft bed that made him wobble beside me in the lane. I invited him to our table. Not without a bath first, of course, which I made him take behind the house.

I stuffed my feelings into my tucker and introduced this strange old man to my children as their grandfather. Their excited surprise was followed, of course, by their innocent welcoming. I could feel my husband's eyes upon me as he watched with curious silence. What should I have done?

I held little affection for the old man but would use his presence to my purpose. At the same time, a good amount of trepidation welled within me about which sieve his yarn would be pushed through and what kind of mash would come out in the end. I reminded myself that we cannot control everything, nor can we divine how our lives will be told and even who will tell them. We can only live them. My husband was tolerant and mindful of filial duty, as I had married a kind and hardworking man. We were prospering and could afford to support this linsey-woolsey loggerhead, whoever he was and wherever he had been. I could not imagine, at the time, how my father's tale would mark the American literary landscape and spill forward into the next century.

We did not tell my father about our fears of how my mother might have died, for we did not like to envision it ourselves. And how were we to be sure? We ignored his questions or simply told him the truth: we did not know what had happened to her. The last time we had seen her, she had been well enough. I still prayed that she may have sailed away downriver on a sloop. Although I could hardly harbor any hope of it. One good fortune of my father's meandering home again—and the one I made the most of—was that she no longer was suspected of hacking him into pieces and cooking him up in a Dutch cauldron. How could I have doubted her? She was true. *Is* true. Leastwise he afforded me some relief in that.

The good people thought my father's tale was harmless enough. His story connected the everyday world with that other, mostly uncanny dream that unfolds just in the next wooded glade, where anything can happen. In a dream, every detail is so startlingly real, yet when you awake, you are faced with a deep disappointment that you cannot quite remember what was said and done within that other world. Who would not feel the loss of it? The old men in the village, his first audience, moved easily from one domain to the next, keeping a grasp on the reality of farming while dancing in tune and sometimes invoking the forces of that other world as a cause or explanation for what was out of their control—ghosts that offer mead, headless horsemen, banshees. Such stories must be regarded as more than fantasies. Even I could see that they lead us to something broader and more as they ease the distress of our accountability. As such, they bridge in at least a few places the gap between magic and science, law and anomaly, and, maybe, men and women. They relieve us from our responsibility and boredom.

From this point of view, while taking common pleasure in everyday life, perhaps we should also pay more attention to what the poets and storytellers, the gossips and singers— and some of our ordinary neighbors—tell us about their adventures in another world. Although it is not *our* experience, as we listen to the wondrous, the unbelievable, and the absurd, those experiences can become ours. There is a certain relief in that, which tempts us all. We love to cower in our blankets, gaze into the fire, and listen to a convincing possibility that a dream can be true.

For a while, my father was just an odd man with a very long beard in funny clothes whose tales were as wild as his whiskers. However, he soon became famous. I have to say that an unintended consequence of taking my father into our household was that it gave him a certain credibility. Cleaned up, well fed, and sometimes sober, he told his story over and over to everyone. People longed to believe it, and so they did. And soon his reputation grew and grew. Somehow he seemed authentic and reminded people of the old times. His testimonies, made for merriment, were laced with whimsy and jenever and never seemed to lack an audience.

The fight for independence was over, and it was back to the hard labor for the next meal. The people missed the excitement and all the talk of a new order. King George's transgressions were forgotten, and the blunders and justifications of a new state government were now turned over at the taverns. But need I say that politics without revolutionary fervor are tedious? As usual, we found much to complain about. The people, some of whom did not know the old life, listened to my father and laughed at him with great amusement. They challenged and mocked him and shook their heads. But you could see in the flicker of recognition underneath their toothy grins that they responded to my father's story with powerful emotion, as they did when contemplating their own dreams. Soon many of them did him the honor of repeating his tale over and over at all the taverns and before the winter fires in all the towns. Soon the version of his disappearance and return was incorporated into the almanacs of the villages up and down the river's banks. In no time, my father's story was authenticated by anyone's uncle who knew a fellow whose brother's neighbor said it was true.

My children loved their new grandfather who played a pennywhistle, knew old stories and coin tricks, and babbled endlessly about the old days. The old man was useless about the house and left a trail of detritus wherever he passed. I could not trust him to snuff his candles. If I sent him to the yard for wood, he would go readily and in good cheer, but I would then not see him for hours. When I saw him next, if I asked him where he had been, often as not he did not know, and it was clear he did not recall any initial purpose of an errand.

To divert him from the tavern, my husband once walked him to the old farmhouse. (I am not sure he could have found his way there himself.) He stumbled through the gate and to the kitchen door where the lilacs yet bloomed. "This bower," he said. "Life on this bower, I thought I had dreamt it." He wept. He broke down and sobbed in the doorway and babbled on about the sheep and a dog he once had. He called my mother's name.

After that day, my husband would often find my father at the farm. If he did not come for dinner, I would send my husband on his horse. There he would come upon my father with his hands clasped behind his head stretched out

on the ground dreaming or sometimes gazing at the doorway where she had once stood, hands on her hips, scolding,
demanding, entreating. My father would not know my
husband when he called out to him. He would mistake him
for someone from the old village, and my husband would
have to coax him home with promise of a flagon followed
by a good supper. They would walk the hour down the
track together while Hugo led the horse following behind.

My father was addled. And became more so. He told his
story over and over hundreds of times to those who would
listen and those who did not. There was perhaps some bewildered truth in it. He was a bewildered man—bewildered
by his wife, bewildered by his farm, and certainly bewildered by the new America.

He loved the attention that he received from the audi-
ences of his story, but underneath his good cheer you could
see that he was lost and that his energy was flagging. His
teeth fell out one by one, in a sequence of days, and his
cheeks collapsed against his bones. His speech became
more and more incomprehensible, and the stench from his
mouth a deterrent to society even at the tavern. And it was
a morning not long after that, that I found him cold and
sour in the bed we had provided for him.

We held a funeral at the church, and much to our surprise, people came from all over when they heard of his
death. I had never seen so many travelers brought together,
and we hardly knew any of them. Up and down the river by
sloep, in from the West in wagons. I looked for my brother
in the crowd but did not see him, so I sat in the pew and
stood by the grave with my husband and children. The

dominie eulogized my father in a way that I could hardly believe, and I was shocked to see my neighbors nodding their heads as if they agreed with him. He seemed to have forgotten that my father did not ever sit in a church pew, did not attend to his farm, and had abandoned his wife and children. He was praised as a pillar of the old life and lauded for his longevity and his great ability to narrate a tale. I could barely hide my amazement and my scoffing from my children. I was the first to throw dirt on the coffin and hear the finality of the plunk of it. I turned away quickly, but not because I was shedding tears.

It was not until after the old man had died, and the sour smell had diminished from the room in my house where he had slept (we had to burn his clothes), that my husband told me about the day he had inadvertently come upon my father and my brother together in the barn. It was a surprise to find them in company because my brother would have nothing to do with this old man who called himself our father. My father seemed impervious to the cold shoulder his own son had turned to him whenever he came upon him in the lanes of the town and followed him about the village chattering and bemoaning the loss of his wife, as my brother turned his back on him and strode away toward the sawmill.

One day when the old man with his slouched hat and unkempt beard had again been seen stumbling away from the tavern and hobbling out the track away from the village toward the clove, I had sent my handsome husband on his fine red horse after him. I was of one mind to not bother, because why should I? Once and so long lost to us, why would I need to check his whereabouts now and keep him in my sight lines? But the pull of a family is strong, even when it has not gone well. Although I could see how it is easier to trust those I had met once I had grown than my own brother or uncle or father. I had good friends and neighbors who seemed more kin to me than those connected by blood and name. Yet as soon as the old man had slept but one night in my house, I found I considered it my duty to feed him and keep guard his safety. *Soort zoekt soort.*

And yet half the time, I denied I was any relation to him. I imagined I had taken in a stranger who could not make his way in the world. It was difficult to believe that I was his progeny. My brother, perhaps, but not me. Now that my mother's reputation had recovered a bit and my father was so ridiculously famous, I wanted no more dramatics, no more mystery, no more missing persons, no more suspected murders, and no more gossip of any sort. I would sweep all the doubt and worry out the door and keep an ordered house.

So I sent my husband after him, and he, knowing that he could follow the track and find him at the farm without too much trouble, sought him there. That afternoon, he found that Big Red was a little lame, so he dismounted, walked beside his horse, tied him at the gate, and so entered the yard silently. Hearing voices and not recognizing them muffled within the barn walls, he himself did not call out but peered into the cavernous dark and saw my father, stooped and muttering. Fists clenched, a white spittle on the thin lower lip of a partially caved-in mouth, long, stringy hair which was a yellowish grey, he danced in the aisle of the barn. A moaning, anguished jig of a dance.

In the farther reaches of the barn, my husband told me, he could see another shadowy figure who was speaking in a low voice, cold and insistent, and so my husband, undiscovered at the doorway, took off his hat to listen.

He heard these words from the shadows: "You left us. Wandered off in the woods. Left us to farm. Without a word. And all this time I have thought that my mother murdered you; hacked you to pieces like she hacked that fisher. They said in the village that she had made you into sausage meat—*zult*. In this very barn."

"Now, Judith," my husband told me, "the both men spoke in Dutch, and the old Dutch of your father, so I did not understand it well. It was difficult to make out what he said in his thick and anguished words. As I am more conversed in English and French than ancient Dutch, I could barely make it out. But I think it might have gone something like this:

"'But . . . I loved her. I loved her. I fell. I fell. I fell. She was not pleased with me.'

"'Old Man, you are foolish.'

"'But Son . . .'

"'Don't call me that. You do not deserve the name of Father.'

"'It is only that I fell. As if off the steepest clove, into the very pit of a dream. And I could not climb out. I could not wake myself from my reverie.'

The younger man took a step toward his elder, his face an angry scowl, and the old man cowered.

"'I was lost. I was lost. I was lost . . . to her.'

"'And to your children.'

"'And to my children.'"

Hugo continued to describe to me the scene: "I peered around the barn door and was dismayed at what I saw. Your brother had raised a felling axe and towered high above your father. I did not wish to see your father's head split like a pumpkin, and so I roared the best of my roars, and shouted to your brother to cease and desist as I swung the doors wide. Light pierced the interior of the barn, and the moment of violence arrested itself.

"The old man turned toward me and staggered past me out into the yard. The younger man stamped his foot and loomed in the shadows but did not give chase. Now he was illuminated by the opening of the barn door, and I could see that the two men were, indeed, cut from the same cloth. They would have been the same size and shape except that your father was stooped and shrunken. And in their faces there was the same inability to reconcile their condition and situation with their tenure upon the earth.

"So fearing violence between them, especially of the son toward his father, I turned and led the old man by the elbow out toward the staked horse. He blubbered loudly and twisted to look back toward the barn as I moved him forward and untethered the large animal. We led the lame horse on the track, and the two of us at each side of the horse's nose walked the long road toward the abundance of a good dinner at your table. We left your brother in the barn, and he did not call after us. I did not listen too keenly, for the fear of hearing him weep.

"Ah, Judith," he asked me, "do you forgive him?"

"I don't know. And I am hardly sure that it matters. I miss my mother."

"Forgiveness always matters," said my wise and ever-patient husband. And I supposed that I believed him. He practiced holding me in esteem, even when I was smaller than he wished me to be. And to give me another opportunity to rise above my bitterness, he spoke again.

"The dangers of the mind are not unlike the perils of our rocky woods and the cloves of our mountains. Easy to get lost among the trees and cateracts, once you depart from the ordered tracks and the neat rows in the fields, and once you get too far away from the flow of the great river."

To put it in this way was my husband's gift, for it was to draw all humanity together across the surface of all the reaches of the earth and to make the problem of forgiveness larger than my father and myself. Each and every one of us can lose ourselves before we know it to the possibility of love. And not many of us can find our way back.

In the end there is no use in harboring a grudge against a demented and helpless old man. It could not return my mother to me. After my father's funeral, I made an especial effort to bring my brother to my table and to include him at *Kerstydt* and the *Nieuw Jaar*. Although he did not respond at Christmas, he came to us on the ice of the New

Year. I fried up *oliebollen* and told my children that "when the sun shines on New Year's Day, it will be a good apple year." I was not afraid of him, in spite of what my husband had witnessed at the barn. I know that out of the heart in shadow violent fantasies can erupt. And that we all might have them, if we have been harmed. But I decided not to fear my brother and that I would love him as best I could. I talked openly and fondly of my mother, and he joined in at times, filling in for me what I had forgotten, and together we created a history so that my children could know their path into the world.

After his death, my father's fame grew beyond the river valley and was even known in the big cities of New York and Fort Orange—now called Albany—and in all the valley towns betwixt. No one seemed to tire of it, and it was told again and again. Eventually it was taken up by certain scholars. Biscuit bakers have gone so far as to imprint my father's likeness on their New Year's cakes, and have thus given him a chance for immortality, almost equal to that of being stamped on a Waterloo medal or a Queen Anne's farthing.

I heard that my father's story was of such interest that it was even set upon the stage. That both incensed and puzzled me. For if such a store is set by twenty years of sleeping, then what of us who worked for two times ten years and tried to stay awake?

It is as my own children are growing and will soon leave me that I understand that I had much better luck in a husband than my mother did. There are many thin lines in marriages that once crossed are impossible to turn back upon. A man must be encouraged to see things and to think that he has seen them first. This is a delicate matter. My husband is a good man, and I am twice lucky that he likes to work. He thinks well of me, and we are as much of a team as the horses that pull our wagons.

My mother was not what Mr. Knickerbocker said she was, despite his reputation for scrupulous accuracy. It was not fair that his words made it to print and would soon be called history and reach so far into the future. For his words were recorded and interpolated from interviews at the local tavern long after my father had died. The stories of women are not often told in the taverns, although you might hear stories about them. Mr. Knickerbocker claimed to have studied the lives snugly shut up in the low-roofed farmhouses, but he never came to ours.

By the time he sailed upriver, there was as much English spoken as Dutch. And of the other low-roofed farmhouses he claimed to have visited—did he speak the old language? Could he hear the codes embedded in the conversation of the wives and daughters, even if he heard them speak? And would the women be speaking with their husbands and sons present, or would they be busy serving up the tea? In the evenings, with the pipes and jenever, would the women even be present? These are questions not asked by historians—nor their editors, it would seem.

To his credit, he did observe the quality of the light on the mountains, and he noted the ability of wives to interpret shapes cast by the light. But for some reason, in regards to interpretation, he thought only in terms of the weather, when everyone knows that the light's play on the mountains is an augury of all the labor lost and all that is suffered in order to make a life worthy of biography. To him, our little village must have looked quaint after the great port of Amsterdam, its sister city in the New World, the noble cities of Spain, and all his other travels. We were to him the faces of his longing for a simple and charmed life, where a good story is the measure of any summer afternoon.

So it appeared that Diedrich Knickerbocker could satisfy his editors with an ordinary tale of my father's imagination and my mother's intolerance of it, because editors do not trust their readers. They consider themselves gatekeepers of a social order, the lowest common denominator of what can be considered not true but tolerable. And they trust the perspective of historians, who gaze back in time and apply their theories, and this is the version that is set in type blocks and run through the presses.

This I do not understand. While it is true that nostalgia feeds the people and distorts their thinking, there are readers who also seek the truth amongst all the romance. Why else would they take the time and trouble to read a book? Never mind the expense. Publishers fear the fickle public and are always looking to their pocketbooks, which they seek to line by pleasing everyone. In the end they serve no one. A digestible version of the truth is put forth in a package that requires no unwrapping.

Surely even the most common reader is better than that. For it would seem to me to be better for the world and all the ordinary people in it if editors would defy what they think the public demands and would take on the role of shepherds, and herd the scolds and prophets forward, to break through sleepiness and ennui. There they would find the travails of mothers like mine.

There is nothing to fear. For children would still come forth out of our red-lined wombs, and all would move forward. Out of the sharp-tongued mouths of seemingly conventional women with pancake batter on their aprons, a howl of words would flow. And for those who would listen, the world would spin.

People hunger for the truth out of the earth's spinning, and where they can find it they feed on it. It is true these nutrients are not in every mouthful of every book. But the good people will recognize sustenance when they come upon it, and their gratitude will fill the pockets of booksellers.

It is only when truth is forsaken that bitterness and other kinds of foolishness triumph. People without food become small. The women in this village still tell tales of how my mother walked behind my father in the streets, red faced and lashing him with a serpent's tongue—how she spoke with such rough violence that it scattered the crows. Why she ended with such a reputation is a puzzle. She was of small stature and fair. Not a murderer. Not a shrew. But a reader of books and an industrious wife. She has been misconstrued. Now at least my neighbors can no longer give voice to their suspicions that she disposed of her husband in the Vly, or hacked him with farm tools and hid him in her cavernous barn. My father's brief return makes them face the fact that their own imaginations have gotten the better of them and have led them to a foolishness that does its own harm.

The yarn my feckless father spun and which was reported to Mr. Knickerbocker is a fable to another end; a nostalgia for circumstances that never were. My mother's story is yet untold, as the conditions of such a life have never been writ as history or even recorded in a common folktale. Still, her own account, spoken from her own honest heart, would have its own dreamy quality of shadows and light, evoking the dream of bone-weary work performed without bidding or thanks.

My mother would not know that her husband had not left her for another, had not fallen in the Gröt Vlys, had not been murdered by Mohicans or Mohawks, or slapped senseless by a bear. We knew that he had not suffered such a fate, and there was some relief in that. But what had happened to her? She was now our sacred mystery, our perpetual perplexity. For at last it had settled in our minds that my father had wandered into the clove of his own imagination and had been tricked by time. And the tricks of time are common enough; they occur each night in our dreaming. The difference between my father and the rest of us is that we awaken each day when the sun comes up, and we work, and he did not. In his perpetual dream, he lived in isolation, unreachable by those of us tethered to the populated world, and who, if he gave us any opportunity, might make demands of him. But in these mountains, high above the shimmering river, I suppose that such a thing could happen to any of us. Here the imagination is sometimes as wide and blinding as the radiance of sunlight and just as often as narrow and obscuring as the dank shadows cast when the sun is thwarted by the solidity of rock.

What has come before and what lives on after are often as varied as the sharp sound of a sparrow's chip at the windowsill and the long cry of the loon across a wide expanse of water. What actually happened and what the good people remember are as different as the wind and the sound of the wind. People will believe what sets easiest between their ears and within their hearts. Certainly they believe whatever they are told often enough. Three times, I think it is. What is thrice told, begets the Truth which is then known by Truth's name. Or known as a lie, but in the light of day, all agree to forgo questions they know they should ask, abandon all doubt, and call it Truth. Thus we know that sharp-tongued scolds are women without just concerns, that a man can sleep for twenty years, that revolutions are fought for the freedom of all, that the earth is round and spins like a top, that the Dutch are but Cheeseheads, that the geese that turn in flight bleating across the lonely winter sky lay eggs of gold in their spring nests, that loaves and fishes multiply, that love lasts between a man and his wife and lives between them as a memory.

Freedom

Amsterdam, 1809

Waar de dijk het laagst is, loop het eerst het water over.
"Where the dyke is low, water runs over it."

—**Dutch proverb**

NOW I KNOW that I have known all along more than all
the great men of history and philosophy could tell me
or could write for others with the broad strokes of ink on
parchment or could speak about in the great oak-paneled
halls where women sit in the last rows straining to hear.
I finger a strand of wool at my wheel, or a tress of hair
wrapped in cloth and laid at the bottom of a box. While the
memory of freedom is elusive, regret encloses me within
the prison of my own choices. I could have chosen differ-
ently then but did not. In a cranny of those dank walls, that
dungeon of remorse, I have hidden a piece of jewelry that
I had once worn around my neck and that holds a remembrance of the beloved in a small frame like a pocket watch.

I can open it in the moment when I feel that too much or not enough time has passed.

Indeed, I have one with the likeness of Judith, or of how I think of her looking now, much as I would have looked at the age when my husband disappeared and no longer walked the compass of this earth. Her visage, alas, is like a bit of him too, not in the shadow of the eyes—for hers openly shine their innocence out like a beacon—but in the fine nose and lips, which are a feminine arc of his. Then I might find myself pondering the mechanism of a firearm, forged in the coals of a metallurgist and which, under the influence of a violent intent, explodes the charge. I wonder that a heart has shut down and will not pump blood. I observe with an inquiring curiosity the sluice of a canal that holds back water to raise the level. In the morning brightness or when the light of the day is fading, and in spite of the swollen joints of my fingers, I work a mechanical device and insert and turn a key to open a door or a gate, or a book or box. The action is to fit together, or on the contrary, to be at a standstill resulting from the pressing of equal and opposing forces. Seven of them forge the future and infuse the long roll forward with all the sorrows of the past, somehow reaching beyond them. You can read such sorrows in a book—and if you are a patient reader and ply its pages more than once, it will tell them all.

Notes

Nederlands Spreekwoorden Boek, Nel Walters, R & B Lisse, The Hague, 1994 was a source for many of the Dutch proverbs.

Washington Irving adapted an old European folktale to an American setting in the romantic landscape of the Hudson Valley. The tale evokes the mystery and inevitability of time passing even in the very modern New World, regardless of whether we choose to be conscious or unconscious to many or any of its moments. Of course, it was he who first introduced and sketched the characters Nicholas Vedder, Derrick Van Bummel, Peter Vanderdonk, Judith, and Wolf the dog—I merely told their back stories. Diedrich Knickerbocker is not a historian but the fictive narrator of *The Sketch Book of Geoffrey Crayon* and *The History of New York*. The Native American creation story was told by Diedrich Knickerbocker in *The History of New York* and adapted here. Given his research methods, it is probably not Native American at all. The old man's "chance for immortality almost equal to that of the being stamped on a Waterloo medal, or a Queen Anne's farthing" is quoted from *The Sketchbook of Geoffrey Crayon.*

A *stomacher* is a triangular-shaped piece of fabric used in the front of the gown to hold the sides together. Sometimes soft, sometimes stiffened, it attaches to the bodice lining by pins and tabs, hooks and eyes, or lacing. A *tucker* is a plain or lace ruffle stitched around the neck of a gown. *Undress* in the eighteenth century referred to the everyday, utilitarian working clothes, of which a *Brunswick* is a work dress, worn over a shift. A *petticoat* was a woman's skirt-like garment worn with a gown or jacket, which were open and needed the petticoat to fill in the front.

Shakespeare's Othello speaks of the "curse of marriage" after Iago induces the green-eyed monster in him, and claims he would rather be "a toad living on the vapors of a dungeon" than share his wife (*The Tragedy of Othello, the Moor of Venice*). A toad has long been a fairy-tale icon for a potential mate, and Judith misappropriates the image to assuage her mother's jealousy, while her mother likens Mr. Van Bummel to a gape-mouthed amphibian after abandoning the idea of marrying him. The Bard also contributes "No more marriages . . ." from *Hamlet*; "All the pretty chickens . . ." from *Macbeth*; "What is honor? . . ." from *King Henry VI, Part 1*; and "What angel?" from *A Midsummer Night's Dream*. Jonathan Swift contributes "'Tis [very] warm weather" from *The Journal to Stella*.

All twenty-one verses of the Book of Obadiah are quoted almost verbatim—adapted from the King James version of the Old Testament, with the name of Esau changed to Esopus, which is the early name of the settlement at Kingston/Rondout. Obadiah and Susannah are the names of the servants in *Tristram Shandy* by Laurence Sterne, that man of infinite jest. He also contributed the concept of the "bed of justice" in which Mistress and Master Shandy lay down on Sundays to settle marital disputes, all to Master Shandy's favor.

To "cant like a Babylonian" is from Samuel Johnson. He contributed other insults as well. "The difference between the wind and the sound of the wind" is a line from a poem by Barbara Grossman.

Acknowledgments

I was sitting on my porch at the top of Platte Clove just over the Blue Mountain reading *The Sketch Book of Geoffrey Crayon*, when the roll of a summer thunderstorm posed a question to me: What was it like for a frontier farmwife to have her husband disappear without a trace on the eve of the Revolutionary War? Many helped me answer that question. First I wish to thank the historians: Russell Shorto's *An Island at the Center of the World* is an incredible book; *1776* by David McCullough, *Saratoga* by Richard Ketchum, *Almost a Miracle* by John Ferling, and *Founding Mothers* by Cokie Roberts were invaluable sources. Germaine Greer's research and commentary on Anne Hathaway, the wife of the great bard, in the context of a modern scholarship that demeaned her, was certainly an inspiration. My own talents as a historian are more in line with Diedrich Knickerbocker's, and any mistakes and misconstruction of the events and conditions of the period are my own.

The Mid-Hudson Library System loaned me source material, including a register of names of those enslaved in Ulster County. Elane Farley was ever helpful, and her love of books permeates the Haines Falls Free Library, which I will miss the musty smell of and its smallness—when it finds the money to move to its new mid-twentieth-century facility. The historical societies of Kingston, Saugerties, and Hurley subsist on the endless efforts of volunteers. Thanks to all.

I am grateful to the James Jones First Novel Fellowship for its recognition and support. Judy Hottensen and Barbara Grossman helped me wend my way toward publication, and Olivia Beens was my very first reader and offered thoughtful comments. Barbara Freedgood, David Lupato. Nadine Goodman, Jotkar Khalsa, and Susan Ribner also read faithfully and had faith. My thanks to Caryn Giananti for reading with an eye to what might have been missed, and to Roland Schimmel for checking the Dutch. Melanie Bush provided an early attentive copy edit.

My editor, Sarah Durand, welcomed me as a newcomer to the world of publishing with grace and patience. Her artful suggestions and encouragement to do justice to the landscape and history of the Catskills helped me make a better book. I cannot thank my agent, Eleanor Jackson, more for her first allegiance to the writing and for her thoughtful and supportive guidance.

My father quoted Shakespeare to me often, and when I lay down a book with splayed pages, he admonished me that I had better be cruel to animals—children, even—than to so cruelly treat a book. Thanks to my partner, who slept beside me while I wrote. And to my son, Schuyler, who for over twenty-two years has taught me much about how to live a creative life.

ACKNOWLEDGMENTS

Lastly: a salute to all those women and people of color who supported a revolution by knitting stockings and providing food and information, as well as firing cannons, without any real hope of gaining citizenship and voice, or of being known and remembered.

More Advance Praise for
Seven Locks

"Being, like all American novels, very learned, sagacious, and nothing at all to the purpose, *Seven Locks* contains divers profound theories and philosophic speculations on the conditions of the latter-day settlements of the province of Nieuw Nederlants. Along with the histories of the golden reign of Wouter Van Twiller, the chronicles of the reigns of William the Testy, Peter Stuyvesant (also known as Peter the Headstrong) and his troubles with the Amphyctionic Council, the British nation, and the decline and fall of the Dutch dynasty which I have provided in several previously published volumes, *Seven Locks* adds a dimension worth proving and which the idle reader should not overlook."

—Diedrich Knickerbocker, historian and author of *A History of New York from the Beginning of the World to the End of the Dutch Dynasty*

"The message of *Seven Locks* is to remember the Ladies!—something that my husband, in spite of the persistent petition of his much acclaimed dearest friend, declined to do."

—Abigail Adams, former First Lady of the United States of America

"The task of an author is, either to teach what is not known, or to recommend known truths by his manner of adorning them; either to let new light in upon the mind, and open new scenes to the prospect, or to vary the dress and situation of common objects, so as to give them fresh grace and more powerful attractions, to spread such flowers over the regions through which the intellect has already made its progress, as may tempt it to return, and take a second view of things hastily passed over, or negligently regarded. The novel *Seven Locks* has attempted and met each of these challenges."

—Samuel Johnson, author and journalist,
A Dictionary of the English Language,
sometimes published as *Johnson's Dictionary*

"The protagonist of *Seven Locks* should have come earlier to The Hague, where she could read and write many letters, among a civilized people. She should have brought her daughter too, and the both of them would have found the beginnings of an inclusive literature, enough to make a reading life."

—Elizabeth (Betje) Wolff-Bekker, author and activist,
Bespiegelingen over het Genoegen (Reflections on Pleasure)

"Who would have known or thought that my letter to a slave girl upon the publication of a poem, could start such a stir for Liberty among the Ladies! Thank God that we won that War, so that the novel *Seven Locks* could come forth upon the new Nation. And finally it has!"

—George Washington,
President of the United States of America

SEVEN LOCKS

CHRISTINE WADE

A Readers Club Guide

INTRODUCTION

Seven Locks begins in 1769, with the disappearance of a Dutch farmer near what's now called the Hudson River. After a spat with his wife, he heads toward the mysterious Catskill Mountains with his rifle and his dog and never returns, and she is left to run the farm while raising two small children. The father's disappearance creates fault lines in the family, as her son blames his mother for his absence and her daughter, Judith, increasingly chafes at the farmwork, preferring to spend time at school or reading on her own. Years go by without the husband's return, and when the tumult of the Revolutionary War unfolds in the Hudson River Valley, it changes life in the little Dutch village forever.

Judith's brother joins the New York militia and Judith runs away to make a life of her own, which leaves the narrator adrift and alone. When her plans for remarriage fail and her farm is devastated by an army's raid for supplies, she throws herself in the Hudson River. Rescued by two slaves, she makes her way to New York City. Estranged from her brother and his wife and her village neighbors, without children or husband or friends, she bravely boards a ship to start a new life in Amsterdam.

After the war Judith returns to the village of her childhood as a woman and a wife, where she tries to make peace with her troubled past. Suddenly her father shows up again in the village, disoriented and claiming to have been asleep for twenty years, raising old questions for Judith: Where has he been? Where is her mother now? Judith philosophically comes to her own conclusions on her own terms about what actually happened to her family, as life in the burgeoning village slides toward the nineteenth century in the newly formed American nation.

QUESTIONS AND TOPICS FOR DISCUSSION

1. The title comes from a Dutch proverb: "The future is a book with seven locks." Discuss the ways in which the proverb informs the structure and themes of the novel.

2. Judith is the only character from the family with a given name. Why do you think the author made this choice? How did the lack of names affect your ability to identify with the characters?

3. How sympathetic did you find the narrator? Were her frustrations with her life justified?

4. How does the novel's portrayal of the Revolutionary War match up with what you already knew? Did you learn anything new or surprising?

5. There are several layers of fiction and reality meshed together in *Seven Locks*. The novel treats the historian Diedrich Knickerbocker as if he were an actual person as opposed to the fictional creation of Washington Irving. (Irving actually did this himself, placing advertisements in the newspapers of the day in a pretence

of trying to locate the purportedly missing historian.)
How well did these layers mesh in *Seven Locks*? What
did they add to the foundation of the story, i.e., an
abandoned woman struggling to raise children on her
own?

6. The narrator seeks help from the local Native American
tribe in order to end an unexpected pregnancy. How did
this episode inform your opinion of her character? Discuss the ways, if any, that your opinion of her changed.

7. Over the course of the novel, Judith develops from a
child into an intelligent young woman to a world-wise
mother, with dramatic shifts in her opinions and understanding. Which view of Judith did you find the most
interesting or enjoyable?

8. How did the counterpoint between Judith's point of
view and her mother's affect your reading experience?
Were there other characters' perspectives you wish
you'd had?

9. The narrator is cast by her fellow villagers as, at best,
a scold and a nag. How much have stereotypes about
wives changed over time? Consider modern-day films,
books (such as *The Bitch in the House*), and television
shows.

10. Discuss the role of minorities and women in colonial
society, as shown by Susanna and Obadiah and by Judith

and her mother. In what ways are they valued, and in what ways dismissed? How does the narrator's quest to get identification papers in New York reveal those values?

11. Judith gradually reaches an understanding of her mother and mourns that they were never reconciled. Do you believe that she would have come to the same conclusions if they'd been reunited?

12. When Judith's father returns, she is unconvinced of his claim. Her uncertainty and gradual conviction are mirrored in other stories, such as the film *The Return of Martin Guerre* (a film version of a famous historical case of assumed identity) and the purported return of Cousin Patrick on *Downton Abbey*. Is it possible to truly know someone even though that person is much changed physically?

13. What did you believe about the husband's disappearance, before his return to the village? Judith thinks the town's acceptance of his story upon return is a sign of their nostalgia for pre-war times; do you agree? Why or why not?

14. The epilogue is a cryptic reflection from the narrator. What is she trying to tell the reader?

ENHANCE YOUR BOOK CLUB

1. *Seven Locks* is based on a famous American folktale by Washington Irving . Which one? Read the original story, contained in the collection *The Sketch-Book of Geoffrey Crayon*, and discuss the resonances and differences of the original and Wade's interpretation.

2. Judith references Abigail Adams, wife of John Adams and critic of women's limited rights of the time, especially in regard to lack of access to education. Many collections of Abigail's letters to her husband exist on these subjects. Bring Abigail's letters to a meeting and read a few together. How do Adams' words affect your understanding of the women in *Seven Locks*?